MURDER AT THE DEBUTANTE BALL

A CLEOPATRA FOX MYSTERY, BOOK 5

C.J. ARCHER

WWW.CJARCHER.COM

CHAPTER 1

LONDON, APRIL 1900

*M*y plan to blend in with the wallflowers at the Bunburys' ball failed before I'd even had the opportunity to greet our hostess. A row of elderly chaperones raised their lorgnettes as one and peered at me. They didn't try to hide their scrutiny, but they did cover their mouths with their open fans so they could gossip without having their lips read. Whatever their opinion of me, I couldn't tell. Nor did I care. I wasn't here for their entertainment. I'd only come to the ball to appease my aunt and uncle who were using the occasion to officially launch me into London society. I owed them this much after they'd taken me in with open arms.

My cousin Floyd followed my gaze. "They look like crows, ready to swoop on the unsuspecting."

His friend Jonathon, standing on my other side, leaned down to my level. His breath smelled of cigarettes and whiskey. "The only swooping they'll do will be on the supper table later."

He looked every bit the respectable gentleman tonight, dressed in a black tailcoat and crisp white shirt with his blond hair neatly combed back. But the indolent youth hadn't completely disappeared. It was still evident in the heavily hooded eyes, the sneering tilt of his lips, and over-confident manner. He'd managed to secure the first two dances with me

1

purely because he'd asked me in the presence of my aunt and uncle and they made it clear I should accept.

Lady Bunbury welcomed us with enthusiastic smiles and a warm greeting which onlookers would have believed was genuine, but our family knew was false. After learning of the Bunburys' financial difficulty during my last investigation, Lady Bunbury had pointedly not invited us to her ball, the first and most important event on the social calendar. It was only after Aunt Lilian's unspoken threat to expose the Bunburys' predicament that she'd finally extended invitations, but not before Flossy had cried herself to sleep for several nights. My cousin had been convinced her life was over.

We exchanged the obligatory pleasantries before moving on to Lord Bunbury and finally further into the ballroom itself.

Flossy stopped abruptly and clasped my hand. "Look at this room, Cleo. Isn't it heavenly?"

It was indeed marvelous. There was no sign of the Bunburys' poverty. Guests were welcomed at the Mayfair townhouse's front steps by dozens of lanterns illuminating the way, then invited up the sweeping staircase woven with garlands of leaves and white roses. More rose garlands hung above doorways and windows and filled enormous vases. Clearly the ball's theme was white, signifying innocence, a virtue the debutantes who'd recently been presented at court were expected to possess.

The *unofficial* theme for the evening was wealth. The opulence was on display everywhere, from the diamond encrusted tiaras of the debutantes to the jewels adorning the throats and ears of their mothers and chaperones. It wasn't just the wealth of the guests, but also of the Bunburys, although in their case it was all a façade. Lady Bunbury had sold her jewelry and had replicas made to look like the originals.

The Bunburys had everyone fooled. By holding the first ball of the season for many years, they'd set themselves up as the arbiters of style and ensured they remained popular. An invitation and their regard were both highly sought after. But this evening must be costing them a small fortune. It wasn't just the decorations. There were a lot of staff, too; far more than the Bunburys employed on a permanent basis. There were footmen in abundance, and there must be several more staff in the kitchen preparing the refreshments.

Flossy touched my arm and directed my attention to a girl standing with a large group. "That's Amelia Livingstone. They say she'll be debutante of the year. I can see why. She's very beautiful."

"And beauty is the chief requirement," I muttered.

"You're so cynical, Cleo. It's just as important to be amenable, accomplished in the gentle arts, and well-bred. Oh, and thin." She sucked in her stomach. "If Lady Bunbury does crown her as debutante of the season, she'll be engaged to be married before August."

"It looks like the eligible bachelors are already circling."

Miss Livingstone was surrounded by people, not just young men, but their mothers, too. She smiled sweetly at something one of the gentlemen was saying. Indeed, she'd been smiling the same way ever since I'd laid eyes on her. It never wavered. Not even when the others laughed at a joke. She continued to smile inanely. Either she wasn't listening, or she had a different sense of humor to the others. Or none at all.

Flossy took my arm. "Come on, Cleo, let's mingle."

"I'll stand over there, out of the way."

Jonathon put out his hand to me. "You will not. You promised me two dances."

The musical ensemble struck up a slow tune and I inwardly groaned. I'd prefer something jaunty if I had to spend a few minutes alone with Jonathon. The less intimate the better.

I allowed him to lead me onto the dance floor. He was a good dancer, thankfully, as I was a poor one. He would have had lessons, whereas I'd been taught by my grandparents in their parlor. I had to concentrate, and that meant I didn't notice him watching me until I finally looked up.

He smiled. "You scrub up well, Cleo." The cheerful tone didn't match the intensity in his eyes.

"Thank you. So do you."

"It's nice to see you out of black and gray."

3

I'd set aside my mourning clothes which I'd been wearing since my grandmother's death six months ago. To some, I'd shed the dark colors too soon, but younger women were often encouraged to come out of mourning earlier than their elders. My off-the-shoulder evening gown of white satin and ecru lace, woven with coral velvet ribbon through the bodice at the waist with velvet nasturtiums sewn onto the skirt in a cascade was the most elegant thing I'd ever worn, not to mention the most expensive. Another four ballgowns hung in my wardrobe back at the Mayfair Hotel, as well as new evening dresses and daytime outfits, all made by the best seamstresses in London. My uncle paid for them. I could never repay him, but I would dance with a few gentlemen of his choosing as a mark of my appreciation, beginning with Jonathon.

I didn't dislike Floyd's friend. He could be charming and amusing. But he was a little too full of himself, not to mention a wastrel. I didn't want to encourage him. Once our two dances concluded, I made a show of rejoining my cousins, both of whom had danced the last dance with attractive partners. All three men immediately fell into conversation about a long-distance rally to Edinburgh and back, staged by the Automobile Club of Great Britain.

Flossy gossiped about the other girls with Floyd's dance partner. None of it was unkind, but I didn't know many of the people they spoke about, so I tuned out. I spotted Miss Hessing standing by the wall, a little apart from the group that included her mother. She had also tuned out of their conversation, and her gaze wandered the room. The wealthy American heiress was a guest at the Mayfair Hotel with her mother. She was here looking for an English husband who could rescue her from her horrid parent. Shy Miss Hessing was completely overwhelmed by her exuberant mother. I quite often asked her to join me for a game of cards when I spotted them in the foyer or at afternoon tea with Mrs. Hessing's friends. She was very grateful for any respite.

I excused myself and headed her way, ready to rescue her again. But it wasn't her mother she needed rescuing from. Three gentlemen walked past. One of them said something to his friends and they all laughed. Miss Hessing's face fell and her eyes filled with tears. She dipped her head to hide them.

"Is everything all right?" I asked.

She sniffed and offered me a smile. "Oh, Miss Fox. I am glad to see you. I'm quite all right now that you're here."

I wanted to ask her what the men had said but decided against it. Perhaps it was better if she ignored them. Unfortunately, the three men returned moments later. One of them neighed as he passed.

Miss Hessing lowered her head again. "I hate these things."

I squeezed her hand. "I loathe them too."

"But you're so popular with the men."

"Two dances with my cousin's friend don't count."

"It's better than nothing." She sighed. "I don't know why we come."

"Because you're invited?"

She smiled. "I suppose so."

"You should smile more often. It lights up your eyes."

She blushed. "You're too kind."

I nodded at the retreating backs of the men. "Ignore them. I plan to."

"What if one of them asks you to dance?"

"I'll tell him I don't dance with moronic boys. I prefer men with at least half a brain."

She giggled. "I wish I had your confidence."

Mrs. Hessing suddenly and loudly burst out laughing. "Mother," Miss Hessing hissed. "Everyone's looking at us."

A cluster of women that included Lady Bunbury peered down their noses at Mrs. Hessing. Then something caught Lady Bunbury's attention and she hurried off in the direction of a lady and gentleman studying one of the many paintings dotted around the room. She sported a look of terror as she forged a path towards them. The pair didn't see her approach. They were too intent on the painting.

Mrs. Hessing covered her mouth with her fan and leaned towards her daughter. "You have nothing to be ashamed of, child. You're better off than most in this room, including our hostess. I've just heard the most interesting rumor about the Bunburys. Believe me, if they had a son your age, his mother would be throwing him at you." Mrs. Hessing turned to her friends, leaving her daughter blinking at her back.

"Nobody will throw their sons in my direction," Miss Hessing said to me. "They all want that girl over there."

I followed her gaze to Amelia Livingstone, dancing with a man shorter than her. He stepped on her toe and apologized. She gave a small wince, but her smile remained. Her partner looked besotted with her, and grateful to be in her sphere.

Jonathon joined us and bowed to Miss Hessing. "Good evening. We haven't met."

Miss Hessing didn't correct him. She performed a little curtsy and blushed.

"You met Miss Hessing at the hotel," I told him.

"Ah. I do apologize. Dreadful memory for faces." He nodded at Amelia Livingstone being led off from the dance floor by her partner. "I saw you watching her. I just heard the most scandalous thing about her. Do you want to hear it? It will make you feel better."

"Better about what?" I asked.

"Your situation in comparison to hers." He leaned in. "I heard something that throws shade over her virtue."

"Don't, Jonathon. I'm not interested in nasty gossip."

He held up his hands in surrender. "Very well, but if you change your mind, let me know. It really is scandalous." He chuckled to himself.

He wasn't the only one who'd heard salacious gossip about Miss Livingstone. Going by the way a few of the young men looked at her with sly smiles, rumors about her were circulating fast. The extent to which her virtue was muddied wasn't clear, however. For most girls, a mere kiss wasn't a cause for scandal, but for a society girl, it would be the end of her good name. Her reputation would be ruined, and she'd be ostracized by the Lady Bunburys of the world. It would be the social death of her.

If these people knew I'd kissed Harry Armitage mere weeks ago, I'd be the one subjected to their whispers and stares. While being ostracized by them didn't bother me, it would affect my family. It wasn't just Flossy who would suffer, but my aunt and uncle too. They found their guests among these people. If they suddenly stopped being invited to balls and dinners, they would lose touch with the society leaders who sent their friends to stay at the Mayfair and spoke favorably about the hotel to their social circle.

I was suddenly glad I hadn't heard from Harry since the kiss. Clearly he'd decided to pretend it never happened. That was the best thing for me to do too.

If only it hadn't felt so wonderful, it might be easier to ignore it. But the more I tried not to think about him, and the way he'd responded to the kiss, the more I did think about it.

Miss Livingstone appeared to be doing her best to ignore the gossips. She continued to smile sweetly at those around her, as if she were slightly removed from them. It wasn't until Lady Bunbury approached that she came to life. She straightened and lifted her chin. She gave Lady Bunbury a small curtsy as she passed, as if she were the queen.

Lady Bunbury failed to notice. She was glaring at her husband, as if willing him to look at her. The gentleman and lady she'd spoken to at the painting had dispersed. The lady was nowhere to be seen, but I caught sight of the man through the door on the landing outside the ballroom. He was a handsome fellow, perhaps early thirties, with an air of confidence about him as he strode towards a tall potted palm. A rather pretty maid stood there, her face lifting when she spotted the gentleman. They spoke and he handed her something before they parted. She limped off along the corridor while he returned to the ballroom where he fell into conversation with a group of young ladies who fluttered their eyelashes at him, hanging on his every word.

"Who is that?" I asked Jonathon, still standing beside me.

"Ambrose McDonald." He made a sound of disgust in his throat. "Don't set your heart on him, Cleo. He's a cad." He nodded at another gentleman, standing alone. He was Ambrose McDonald's opposite in every way. Short, overweight, with protruding front teeth and spotty skin. "Poor Cuthbert Calthorne. He can't win tonight. He continues to get snubbed by every girl he asks to dance. Can't blame them. He has the biggest feet. Imagine getting trod on by those hooves!"

Cuthbert Calthorne suddenly looked our way as if he sensed we were talking about him. He self-consciously looked away but then turned back to us. Or, rather, he turned to look at me. With a determined tug on his cuffs, he headed my way.

Jonathon swore under his breath.

Mr. Calthorne greeted him amiably and bowed to Miss Hessing and me. "Introduce me to your delightful friends, Hartly."

Jonathon obliged then added, "Miss Fox has just agreed to dance with me."

Mr. Calthorne's smile slipped.

"I didn't," I pointed out.

Jonathon asked to see my dance card. I obliged with a frown. He perused it then wrote down his name with the attached pencil. "If my name is there, you have to dance with me. Calthorne, you'll need to find another partner."

There was an available partner right beside me, but Mr. Calthorne merely bowed and made his excuses. He walked off.

Miss Hessing went very still. The snub was cruel indeed, and I knew she would feel it keenly. I wanted to tell her to ignore Mr. Calthorne, that he was not worthy of her, but I knew she would consider them empty words, even though I meant every one. Mr. Calthorne *was* beneath her.

"There you are!" Floyd joined us, breaking up the tension with his easy manner. "I've been looking for you everywhere."

At first I thought he was talking to Jonathon, but he bowed to Miss Hessing. "If you're not otherwise engaged, will you do me the honor of dancing with me?"

She stared at him, her eyes huge and clear. "M—me?"

"If you don't mind me stepping on your toes, that is. I'm a terrible dancer."

"Oh. I'd be happy to dance with you, Mr. Bainbridge."

He grinned. "Excellent." He took her hand and led her onto the dance floor. "Don't say I didn't warn you, though. Your pretty shoes will be scuffed by the end."

She blinked up at him as if he'd just rescued her from drowning. In a way, he had.

"He's a good man," Jonathon said. "It's no wonder all the wallflowers love him. He should be careful, though. If he dances too many times with them, the better prospects will grow tired of waiting." He held out his hand to me. "Shall we?"

I opened my dance card and struck a line through his name. "I'm afraid you're not on my card, Jonathon. It's probably just as well. If the other gentlemen see me dancing three times with you, they'll grow tired of waiting." I turned and walked off. I didn't care what affect my comment had on him. I was quite sure his ego could cope with it.

I couldn't find Flossy, so I stood near the door and observed. My first society ball was proving to be a little disappointing. The young men were either immature or dull, the girls desperate for attention, and their parents grasping. Everyone was out to impress in one way or another. Most of them directed their efforts towards Lady Bunbury. She was very popular with the girls and their mothers, all hoping to win her favor. She was the consummate hostess, however, giving them equal attention.

A lady passing me delighted in telling her companion about the daughter of a peer who'd been caught kissing a fellow behind a tree at a flower show.

"Lady Bunbury won't choose her now," the companion said with a wicked gleam in her eyes.

"Speaking of Lady Bunbury, she looked very cross earlier. Do you know why?"

They continued on and I settled back against the wall, growing more and more bored by the minute. I was beginning to wish I'd danced with Jonathon after all when an acquaintance of Floyd's approached and asked me to dance. I readily accepted.

I didn't stop dancing until supper was announced. All the guests headed through to the room where it was being served, only to find we had to queue for food. I joined Flossy at the back.

"Thank goodness for this interlude," she said. "I'm starving and my feet are sore. They've been stood on so many times, I can't feel my toes. And look at my shoes! They're filthy." Her delicate pink silk shoes were black at the toes. One of the poor hotel maids would have a devil of a time cleaning them tomorrow.

"Perhaps you should vet your dance partners more carefully," I teased.

"We can't all have our pick of men."

I frowned. "Are you saying that I do? I'll have you know I was quite alone until one of Floyd's friends rescued me. I'm sure Floyd put him up to it."

"You were alone for five minutes, and I can assure you Floyd did not put him up to it." We shuffled forward in the queue. "Speaking of Floyd's friends, what did you say to Jonathon? I saw him leaving in a huff."

"He was being unkind."

"Not to you, I'm sure. He likes you."

"No," I said quietly. "Not to me."

We finally arrived at the first table and Flossy breathed a sigh of satisfaction at the array of roasted fowl, trifle, cakes, iced sherbet, bonbons and ices. "I'm glad you're not interested in Jonathon. As much as I want you to marry someone rich and titled, he's not deserving of you. Three years ago, he called me fat. I've never forgiven him."

"Then he has just gone down even further in my estimation."

Flossy eyed Miss Livingstone as she perused the delights on the table, only to select a single wafer before stepping away. She wasn't the only girl to ignore the food. Most chose just one item or none at all.

Flossy sighed again, this time more heavily. She put down her plate. "I'm not hungry."

I picked up her plate and handed it back to her. "You just said you're starving. As am I. I think we should divide and conquer. You go down the left side of the table and I'll take the right."

We gathered a selection and met again at the end of the room. We joined Aunt Lilian, standing in the corner with her back to everyone. She was stuffing a croquet of pheasant fried in pastry into her mouth as if she hadn't eaten all week. Embarrassed to be caught, she placed her fingers to her lips as she chewed. Her fingers trembled.

Flossy gave her mother a disappointed look. "You've taken a second dose of your tonic tonight, haven't you?"

Aunt Lilian swallowed her mouthful. "I needed it to get

through the evening. If I hadn't, my head would be pounding and I'd be falling asleep in a chair. This way I can enjoy myself." She picked up another croquet from her plate. "Don't glare at me, Flossy. You don't know how I feel. Now, go. Leave me alone and mingle. Both of you. Oh wait, Ruth is about to make her announcements. This will be interesting. My money's on Miss Livingstone taking a sweep of all three categories." Her words tumbled out on top of each other, making her a little difficult to understand amid the noise of the crowded room. When she saw us both still studying her, she pinched each of us on the arm and nodded at Lady Bunbury, waiting for the guests to quieten.

As a hush descended, some of the debutantes pushed towards her, still vying for her attention even now. Miss Livingstone stood nearby, her serene smile in place, her pert chin thrust forward, confident in her position as the favorite. Beside her stood an older man, beaming. Flossy informed me he was Sir Ian Livingstone, her father.

Lady Bunbury gave a short speech, thanking her guests, then launched into her so-called awards. As Aunt Lilian predicted, Amelia Livingstone won the title of the most beautiful debutante, the most graceful, and the most accomplished. She accepted the three posies of flowers—white, of course—with a little curtsy for the hostess. Her father preened like a peacock.

Miss Livingstone's rivals congratulated her and told her she was a worthy winner. Their smiles slipped off when then they turned away, and more than one muttered something under her breath.

With supper over, Lady Bunbury stood by the door to farewell the elderly guests who were ready for their beds, while the musical ensemble resumed their places in the ballroom. The younger guests were eager to enjoy themselves now that the contest had ended.

Except that it hadn't. The scramble to secure the most desirable dance partners created a frenzy of activity. Gentlemen jostled one another and ladies scribbled names on their cards. Miss Livingstone was popular, but other girls were too. Flossy sported a broad smile so her card must have filled. My own didn't fill up at quite the same rapid pace, but

C.J. ARCHER

I had enough partners to keep boredom at bay for a little longer.

The ensemble struck up a lively tune and we were about to head onto the dance floor with our partners when a piercing scream ripped from the depths of the house.

The music stopped. The guests froze.

Being near the door, I was among the first to exit the ballroom and race downstairs in the direction of the scream. I found a lady trembling by the door to the library. She pointed a shaking finger into the room.

I peered in and saw the body of a man lying on the floor, legs akimbo. I couldn't see his face, but it was obvious from all the blood matting his hair and staining the carpet that he was dead.

CHAPTER 2

*T*he library was soon overrun with guests and staff, but thankfully someone with an authoritative voice ordered them all out and asked for the police to be fetched. I had mere moments to study the scene before my presence was noticed and I was asked to leave too.

I was surprised to see the victim was a guest I recognized. Ambrose McDonald was the handsome gentleman who'd studied a painting in the ballroom, alongside a lady, and had given a maid something in the corridor. Jonathon called him a cad. Now he was dead, his sightless eyes staring straight ahead until one of the other guests closed them.

A large silver candlestick smeared with blood lay on the carpet nearby. A matching one stood on the mantelpiece. I picked it up to gauge its weight before returning it. Steeling myself for a gruesome sight, I once again looked down at the body. Going by his position, the victim had been facing away from the door and the murderer when he was struck. Either he'd turned away from the murderer, or he'd never seen them enter the library in the first place. There were no signs of a struggle on his body, clothing or around the room. All was in order.

The only odd thing about the room was a large blank space on the wall. Something was missing, either a painting or mirror. It was possible it had nothing to do with the murder, however.

13

With only a few gentlemen remaining in the library, I was conspicuous. Lord Bunbury gripped my elbow and steered me towards the door. "Come along, Miss. This is no place for a lady." He clearly didn't remember meeting me at the beginning of the night. But I knew him. He was much older than his wife with a balding head and boney fingers that dug into me. "Find your mother and go home. The ball is at an end."

"It most certainly is not." Lady Bunbury swooped down on her husband as I walked away. They exchanged words in harsh whispers before she clicked her tongue and strode off.

She told the hovering butler that the evening was over and to see that coats were ready to collect and carriages brought around.

"The guests can't leave yet," I said. "The police will want to speak to everyone."

Lady Bunbury's nostrils flared then she picked up her skirts and all but stomped up the stairs. She reminded me of a child unhappy with her parent's directive.

Lord Bunbury ignored me and closed the door to the library. At least the scene would be preserved for the police, but it seemed as though the guests would be allowed to leave.

Some had remained near the library, watching on with macabre fascination, while the rest had returned to the ballroom upstairs. The butler disappeared through a door and there were no other servants about. I wanted to observe the guests and staff in the immediate aftermath of the tragedy, but my uncle put a stop to me returning to the ballroom.

"There you are, Cleo!" He descended the staircase ahead of my aunt and cousins. "We've been looking for you. What are you still doing down here?"

Uncle Ronald would not approve of my sleuthing, so I hadn't told him about the previous cases I'd solved. Although I hated lying to him, if I wanted to continue, I had to.

"I was looking for you," I said. "I thought you were down here."

"We returned upstairs along with everyone else." His curt tone left me in no doubt he suspected I was lying. "Floyd, fetch our coats."

"We can't leave yet," I said. "The police will want to speak to us, and the other guests."

Even as I said it, guests came downstairs in a steady stream.

Uncle Ronald indicated I should walk alongside him. "Your aunt feels unwell. The...events have upset her. She needs to lie down."

It wasn't the murder that had her looking peaky, it was the effects of the tonic wearing off. But he wanted to pretend all was well with my aunt, so I went along with it.

Lady Bunbury rejoined us in the entrance hall to send off her guests. Her husband was nowhere in sight. It was not the usual place to farewell one's guests after a ball, but the night had not ended in the usual way. We each thanked her for her hospitality, and she smiled in response. There was no mention of the dead body in the library, the murderer amongst us, or any other unpleasantness.

It was quite possibly the most bizarre situation I'd found myself in. There was not a single genuine word exchanged in our final minutes at the Bunburys' townhouse.

Our journey home should have been filled with chatter about the ball, but instead, we were silent. I was bursting to talk to someone about the murder but didn't dare bring it up in front of my uncle.

I didn't have the opportunity to discuss it until the following morning when my maid, Harmony, joined me for breakfast. I'd slept poorly. Ambrose McDonald's sightless gaze haunted me when I closed my eyes, and a thousand questions gnawed at me. Harmony had barely closed the door when I blurted it all out.

"There was a murder at the ball. The victim was Ambrose McDonald, a guest. Handsome fellow, charming, bit of a cad, apparently. I saw him give a maid something before he was murdered. Lady Bunbury also spotted him talking to someone. She looked angry, or worried. Lady Bunbury, that is—not the other woman. He was hit over the head with a candlestick in the library. Then Lord Bunbury sent everyone home before the police arrived, although Lady Bunbury seemed keen to continue with the ball."

Harmony had looked more and more shocked with every detail. When I finished, she finally lowered herself onto the sofa, still staring at me. "I cannot believe that woman wanted to continue dancing while there was a dead body in her library! We shouldn't be surprised, I suppose. We know how much appearances matter to her."

"Indeed." Now that Harmony had digested the facts, I posed the theories and questions that had kept me awake. "What was Ambrose McDonald doing in the library? Was he lured there? Was it a pre-arranged assignation? Did he know his killer? It could have been a man or a woman. The candlestick was large, but not unwieldy, and he wasn't tall. With his back turned, he wouldn't have seen it coming. And what did he give the maid earlier? Why did Lady Bunbury make a beeline for him and the woman? And does the murder have anything to do with the empty space on the library wall?"

"And why did Lord Bunbury insist everyone leave before the police had the opportunity to speak to them?" she added.

"You think that's important?"

"He ought to know better." She picked up the pot of coffee only to pause before pouring. "Perhaps he was protecting one of the guests, giving them time to think up a story."

"Or organize a false alibi."

She poured the coffee and handed the cup to me. "When it comes to the Bunburys, false seems to be a word that comes up a lot."

It did indeed.

It was good to discuss the possibilities with Harmony. She had a sharp mind. Discussing clues with her often helped me see them in a different way. There was another person who had proved useful in the past, but I'd vowed to stay away from Harry Armitage.

Besides, the investigation wasn't mine to take on. For one thing, there was no client and therefore no fee. For another, the police had it in hand.

Or so I thought.

They did not come to the hotel to interview us, nor any of our guests who'd also happened to attend the Bunburys' ball. The murder was on everyone's lips, however, from the staff to the guests staying in our best suites on the fourth floor. Even Mr. Chapman, the hotel steward, deigned to speak to me to find out more. Usually he ignored me or narrowed his gaze when I passed him to enter the dining room. He'd disliked me ever since my arrival in the hotel, and I wasn't quite sure why. I suspected it was because he was a snob and disliked having to treat me as though I were a lady when he considered me no better than himself.

"Is it true the victim was Ambrose McDonald?" he asked when he accosted me in the foyer.

"Yes. Do you know him?"

"Of course not."

"But you've heard of him?"

"No." He made a scoffing sound then walked off. I watched him go with a frown.

The foyer was busy with guests checking in and others lingering before going out for the day. My uncle was there, playing the amiable host, something he liked to do from time to time. He wanted to reassure guests that the new restaurant would be finished soon and that the noisy construction work wouldn't continue all day. It was louder in the foyer, as the builders had knocked through the wall at the end where the senior staff offices had been. The two senior staff who lived-in had moved into the nearby residence hall with the rest of the staff and their former quarters now acted as temporary offices. I'd overheard both Mr. Chapman and Mrs. Short grumbling about the arrangement.

Uncle Ronald beckoned me to join him then introduced me to the Indian maharajah who was staying for the week. We politely chatted about the opera he would be attending that evening and the Great Spring Flower Show currently being held at Temple Gardens. The conversation was very pleasant, but I just wanted to talk about the murder. The maharajah hadn't attended the ball.

Nor had the other newly checked-in guests my uncle asked me to meet. There were several international guests who spoke in a myriad of interesting accents, but there were many English ones too. Some had just returned from months abroad in the warmer climes of the south of France, Monte Carlo and Biarritz and were merely staying a few days in London before traveling on to their country homes. The health spas flourished in those places, apparently. Some guests would stay for a while in the Mayfair Hotel, perhaps even for the duration of the London social season. Considering the cost of one of our rooms for a single night, it always amazed me how so many could afford such lengthy stays. It was no wonder my uncle wanted to welcome them personally to the hotel and talk to them about the extraordinary dining experience awaiting them if they were still here in a few weeks' time.

"Thank you, Cleo," he said to me after we finished welcoming a Dutch diamond magnate and his wife who'd just arrived from Nice. "We had some important guests arriving today and it was imperative that members of the family be seen. People stay here because we are one of the few independent luxury hotels left in London. We may not be as large as others, but that means we can offer a more personalized service." He puffed out his chest and smiled at a passing couple. "Our family's reputation is our greatest asset."

Hearing that, it wasn't a great leap to assume that he'd invited me to live here because the extra addition to the family appealed to the guests. Put simply, it made him look good.

But I'd had quiet words with both Uncle Ronald and Aunt Lilian, and I knew they'd asked me to live with them because they wanted me here. My uncle might be single-minded sometimes, when it came to the hotel, but I was his wife's sister's daughter, and that meant I belonged with them. He meant well. If only he and I agreed on what was best for me.

"Why didn't you ask Flossy and Floyd to greet the guests with you?" I asked. I knew my aunt would be in bed with a headache after the ball, but my cousins were available.

"Flossy hasn't quite got the knack like you. She lacks your maturity. It will come, I'm sure, but she's not suited to this yet. And Floyd..." He heaved a sigh. "Peter informed me Floyd has already gone out."

It was early for Floyd to be up and about after a late night. I was quite sure he'd left again immediately after saying goodnight to everyone outside his room. He'd even winked at me when he said it.

"Cleo, do you know anything about Floyd's actress?" Uncle Ronald asked.

"His what?"

"The actress he is…getting about with."

"No. I don't know anything about an actress. Why?"

He waved off the question. "Never mind."

I knew Floyd kept a mistress, and it wouldn't surprise me if she was a performer. My uncle's concern was new, however. Usually he turned a blind eye to Floyd's wilder escapades. Floyd thought that meant he didn't care, but I was convinced Uncle Ronald was merely waiting for Floyd to mature, as he was with Flossy.

I spotted Mrs. Hessing emerging from the lift with her daughter in tow. They stopped to talk to a group of ladies chatting loudly about the murder. I excused myself and joined them, telling my uncle I wanted to speak to Miss Hessing. While that was true, I also wanted to listen in. Several of the group had been at the ball. Perhaps one of them had seen something.

My hunch was proved right when I arrived in time to hear one of the ladies say, "He was a terrible flirt, apparently."

They all nodded their heads knowingly.

"Lady Bunbury told me he couldn't be trusted," said another.

"Around the girls?" asked one.

"She meant his word couldn't be believed."

I was keen to hear more, but Miss Hessing drew me aside. "Are you lunching with your cousins today, Miss Fox?"

"No." My response was a little brusque, but I was trying to listen in to the gossip about Ambrose McDonald.

Miss Hessing didn't seem to notice. "Perhaps I'll see you all at dinner tonight. Your cousins will be dining in, I assume?"

"I don't know. Flossy probably will, but one never knows with Floyd."

"Oh." She shuffled her feet and shifted her bag from one hand to the other. "Pity."

She seemed to have developed a *tendre* for Floyd after the ball. Knowing Floyd, it would not be reciprocated. He'd rescued her by asking her to dance, but it had been done out of kindness, not any depth of feeling on his part. If she pursued him, she was going to get her heart broken. I couldn't think what to say to put her off him. Anything would sound too cumbersome, and this was a situation that required delicacy.

Before I could attempt to deter her from Floyd, Mrs. Hessing moved away from her friends. "Come along, Clare."

Miss Hessing flashed me a smile before hurrying after her mother.

I watched them go with a sinking feeling. I didn't like to interfere in the private lives of others, but I may have to in this case. I didn't want her hopes to be raised.

Mr. Hobart approached with purposeful, unhurried steps. He was clearly heading for me, but he paused on his way to nod at one guest or exchange a few words with another. My uncle liked to think the Bainbridge family was the reason the guests returned every year, but I suspected the manager had more to do with it. He remembered everyone; not just the more important guests but even those who only stayed a single night. He knew the names of their family members, and even that of the lady's maid or valet if the guests brought them. He kept notes on every little detail, from which room they preferred to the flowers they liked filling their vases, or the ailment they'd suffered from on their last visit. He studied the notes before each guest arrived and made sure to welcome as many in person as he could. He made himself available. Nothing was too much trouble. Whatever a guest wanted, the guest received, and always with a smile. Many would have been exhausted keeping up the charming façade, but that was the thing—it was no façade for Mr. Hobart. He was as agreeable in private as he was at work.

"Miss Fox, I'm so glad I caught you. My brother telephoned. He would like to see you." He looked around to make sure no one was close enough to hear. "Meet him at Harry's office in thirty minutes."

"Harry's office? Why not interview me here?"

"He's not interviewing you about last night. Apparently an arrest has already been made."

"Oh. Then why does he need to speak to me at all?"

Mr. Hobart was called away by Peter, who needed assistance with a guest's request. I watched him go, not quite sure what to think. My heart had done a little flip in my chest at the prospect of seeing Harry again, but then it plunged. For one thing, seeing Harry was a bad idea. For another, I was disappointed that the murderer had been caught.

It was silly to feel disappointment. I ought to be pleased that he or she no longer posed a threat. But I'd been keen to piece the puzzle together myself. If nothing else, it would have given me something to do.

I returned to the fourth floor to fetch my coat, hat and gloves, only to be stopped by Flossy, emerging from her room.

"You're heading out, Cleo? Where are you going?"

"Uh, the museum."

She narrowed her gaze. "You're investigating the murder, aren't you?"

She knew me too well. "Apparently there has been an arrest, so my services aren't required."

"So you really are going to the museum?" She sighed. "Well, enjoy yourself. Perhaps later, we can discuss what to wear to the next ball. It's only four days away."

"Of course. It's never too early to prepare for a ball."

"Quite true."

Thirty minutes later, I drew in a deep breath and went to push open the door to the office of Armitage and Associates. I stopped myself at the last moment. Barging in had been all well and good when I was trying to be Harry's friend. It was too familiar for someone who was trying to keep her distance.

I knocked.

He opened the door.

We stared at one another for barely a second, but it felt longer. In that moment, the memory of the kiss we'd shared in St James's Park came flooding back. I may have instigated it, but he'd responded with enthusiasm.

Until he hadn't. He'd broken it off and walked away. We'd not seen one another since.

He stepped aside to allow me through. "Good morning, Miss Fox."

I eyed him as I passed. "We agreed on first names, Harry."

Detective Inspector Hobart greeted me and pulled out a chair for me to sit. "You're looking well, Miss Fox. Isn't she looking well, Harry?"

"She always does." Harry sat opposite and pushed a

steaming cup of coffee from Roma Café closer to me. "For you. *Cleo.*"

I smiled sweetly at him over the rim of the cup. "That's better. We don't want things to go backwards. Let's just pick up where we left off, shall we?"

Harry hesitated then nodded. "I think that's for the best."

Good. It was resolved. We were friends again and the kiss could be relegated to the past, a mistake never to be repeated. Harry and I were on the same page.

His father, however, was not even reading the same book. He glanced between us. "Is something the matter?"

"Everything's fine," Harry assured him with one of his charming smiles.

"Good. It would have been awkward, otherwise."

"Why?" I asked.

"Harry, have you heard about the murder at the Bunburys' ball last night?"

Harry sat forward. "No. It wasn't in this morning's papers."

"They managed to keep it suppressed for the time being, but tonight's editions will probably report it. A guest was murdered. Hit over the head with a candlestick in the library. Miss Fox was there."

Harry's brows rose. "You asked her here to interview her?"

"No. None of the guests will be interviewed, so my superiors have stipulated. They say it's not necessary as a footman has been arrested and charged."

"You don't think he did it, do you?"

D.I. Hobart shifted his weight in the chair. He wasn't a large man, but he was in his sixties and looking ahead to retirement. Sometimes, he seemed tired, as if the burden of his work became too much. He was always thorough, however. He would never make an arrest unless he was certain of guilt.

But I agreed with Harry. Something wasn't right.

Not that D.I. Hobart admitted it outright. "Due process has not been followed," was all he said. "I would like to have more time to investigate properly. Guests should have been interviewed, background checks made. None of that happened."

On our last investigation, Lady Bunbury discovered I was helping the police, something which very few people had known. D.I. Hobart alluded to the fact that her husband knew his superiors at Scotland Yard and my involvement may have been revealed at that level. Perhaps Lord Bunbury had exerted his influence again and made sure an arrest was made in order to avoid dragging out the investigation. He wouldn't want his guests to suffer the indignity of being interrogated by the police.

Or perhaps he was protecting the killer.

"Are you asking *us* to investigate?" Harry asked.

His father nodded. "Quietly, of course. No one must know."

"They'll find out if we discover the killer wasn't the footman."

"If you have enough evidence of another's guilt, my superiors will have to release the footman and arrest the real killer. Your case must be watertight, however." He shifted his weight again. "Unfortunately, Scotland Yard won't pay your fee. But there is one party with an interest in this case who might pay you for solving it."

"Not the Bunburys, surely," I said.

"No, not the Bunburys. To understand who, I must start at the beginning. Three weeks ago, on the night of March thirtieth, a painting was stolen from a house on Grosvenor Square."

"So the empty space on the Bunburys' library wall *was* relevant," I said.

Harry put up a finger to stop me. "You saw the crime scene?"

"And the body and murder weapon." I winced. "It was awful."

His gaze softened. "I'm sure."

"You're right, Miss Fox," D.I. Hobart said. "A painting was stolen from their library. Lord Bunbury noticed it and informed me upon my arrival. I immediately thought of the earlier theft. I organized a search and one of my men discovered the Bunburys' missing painting with the footman's things. Lord Bunbury confirmed it was the one that usually hung in the library."

"Was it found in the footman's room?" Harry asked.

"He wasn't one of the live-in staff. He was hired on a temporary basis for the ball." D.I. Hobart removed his notebook from his inside jacket pocket. "The catering firm, Searcys, organize the extra staff." He returned the notebook to his pocket. "The painting was found in a cupboard with the footman's coat wrapped around it."

"You think someone else took down the painting and wrapped it up in his coat to frame him," Harry said.

"No. The footman confessed. He claims he took it. But he also claims he was about to put it back, but then the murder happened and he couldn't do it without being seen."

"Maybe he did murder the victim," Harry said. "Perhaps he was in the process of putting the painting back, the victim saw him, so the footman killed him to stop him raising the alarm."

"Then why didn't the footman put the painting back *after* he killed Mr. McDonald?" I said.

Harry rubbed his jaw. "Good point."

"Did the footman say why he was going to put the painting back?"

D.I. Hobart nodded. "He claims it's a fake."

Harry and I exchanged glances. He must have remembered the Bunburys' financial problems from our last investigation.

"According to the footman, it wasn't well executed," D.I. Hobart went on. "The artist of the original is considered a master. It's unlikely a casual observer would realize, but a close study revealed the poor quality. The footman claims to be an artist in his spare time, and once he gave it a thorough inspection, he realized it wasn't done by the original artist and decided to put it back."

"An independent assessment will verify his claim," I said.

D.I. Hobart shook his head. "There will be no independent verification and the Bunburys' will vow it is an original if the matter is ever raised by the defense in court. The prosecution will say the footman is lying and that he never intended to return the painting. Since he admits stealing it, there is a very real chance the jury will find him guilty of the murder too. Guilty of one crime, guilty of another—so many believe."

The Bunburys didn't want a thorough investigation because they didn't want the public to know their paintings were fakes, just like they didn't want word to get out about their replica jewels. By denying the footman's story, they could maintain the façade of wealth.

But rumors of their financial troubles were already circulating last night. It might be too late to contain them.

"Do you think the footman stole the other painting three weeks ago?" Harry asked.

"I'm not entirely sure," his father said. "When I asked him where he was that night, he said he was with a friend but refused to give the name of that friend."

We all knew what that really meant. He was with a lover whose reputation would be compromised if it was known she was with a man.

"It seems too coincidental that the thefts happened independently of one another," D.I. Hobart went on. "But I can't prove they're linked. I also can't prove that the thefts are linked to the murder. They may not be. The upshot is, the footman may indeed be guilty of both thefts *and* the murder. I simply don't know yet. I want to be absolutely certain we have the right man, but there are too many unanswered questions for my liking. I don't want to close this case yet, but I'm not allowed to continue with it. Hence why I want you two to investigate. You're proving to be very capable private detectives."

It was high praise indeed coming from a man with his experience.

I was about to tell them what I knew about the victim when Harry said, "I'll take the case, but I don't think it's wise to involve Cleo. Her family is too close to the Bunburys and many of the guests who were there last night. It would put her in an awkward position."

I bristled. "Nonsense. It puts me in the perfect position to observe them. This is the perfect case for me and glaring at me won't change that, Harry. Your father agrees or why would he have asked me?"

Harry continued to glare. I continued to glare back.

D.I. Hobart withdrew his notepad again and wrote down two addresses. He pointed to the first. "The footman's name is Reggie Smith and this is his address. He lives in a boarding house. It might be worth questioning the other residents. The second is the Grosvenor Square address where the painting was stolen from three weeks ago. You should speak to the owner. I didn't work on that investigation, but I can speak to the detective involved, if necessary." He pushed himself to his feet. "I'll help in any way I can, but my hands are mostly tied now. Keep me informed." He plucked his hat off the stand near the door and settled it on his head. "And try to set aside whatever has come between you and work together on this. There may be a murderer on the loose. Petty squabbles aren't important."

"We're not squabbling," I muttered at the same time Harry said, "It's not petty."

Despite our protests, D.I. Hobart was right. We were acting like children and it had to stop. There were two ways to ease the tension—confront the issue and get it out into the open, or ignore it. Based on his silence, Harry had chosen the latter. I wasn't sure it was the wisest choice, but I was willing to go along with it if it worked.

I just wanted things to return to normal.

CHAPTER 3

The silent treatment wasn't the best way to restore harmony between us. Of that I was certain. So I did the opposite. I talked about the case without pause. By the time we reached the footman's flat, Harry knew all the gossip I'd heard at the ball and afterwards. He also knew everyone's movements on that night, as far as I could remember them. He was most interested in the sighting of Ambrose McDonald studying the painting, who he studied it with, and why Lady Bunbury was so keen to speak to them.

"The most likely answer is that she didn't want them staring at it too long," I said. "She was worried they'd discover it was fake—like so many other things in their house, including the library painting."

Harry shook his head sadly. "I don't understand why the Bunburys are so determined to maintain a façade of wealth. If they sold the London townhouse, they could still live a very comfortable life on their country estate."

"Unless they're heavily mortgaged."

"Even more reason to sell up here and live within their means instead of hosting lavish parties. Maintaining the façade sounds exhausting to me."

"To me too, but we've never had what they have. We can't know what it's like to lose it. Their identities are so tightly entwined with their wealth that it's impossible for them to imagine what their lives would be like if they were as ordinary as us."

His lips tilted in that familiar way that I liked so much. I was very glad to see it return. It meant the tension had finally eased between us. "We're far from ordinary, Cleo."

I smiled, as much from relief that he was being friendly as from the sentiment itself.

Harry's knock on the boarding house door was answered by a matronly woman wearing an apron dusted with flour. She introduced herself as the landlady and housekeeper, in charge of five bedrooms in the old house, all of which were currently let to lodgers. The smells of baking wafted from the service area at the back and, despite the house's state of disrepair, it was filled with homely furnishings. If I were a single man in London, I'd want to live under her roof. I suspected this pink-cheeked woman took better care of her lodgers than their own mothers.

Her smile turned sad when we introduced ourselves and told her our reason for calling. "The police came this morning and searched Mr. Smith's room," she said. "I cannot believe he is a murderer. I simply can't fathom it. Such a nice man. He has always been kind to me, greeting me of a morning and sometimes even helping me tidy up after supper. I can't fault his manners. He was a bit of a rascal, mind, in a roguish way."

"It must have been a shock when the police arrived and informed you," I said gently.

She withdrew a handkerchief from her pocket and dabbed her eyes. "It was. I'm convinced there has been a mistake. Is that why you're here? To do the work the police failed to do?"

"We want to tie up some loose ends."

"What kind of loose ends?"

"Did the police tell you he stole a painting from the place where he worked last night?" Harry asked.

Her eyes widened. "Oh! No, they didn't."

"Are you surprised?"

She twisted the handkerchief around one of her fingers. "He never stole from me."

It wasn't an answer to Harry's question, but her avoidance

28

was telling. "He was something of an artist himself, wasn't he?"

She indicated an oil painting on the parlor wall, hanging in pride of place above the mantelpiece. It showed the house we now sat in from the street. "I'm not an expert, but I liked his work."

"Did he paint in his room?" I asked.

"Oh no. That's not allowed. He went to his friend's studio. Sometimes he'd be so lost in his work that he'd miss curfew and have to stay overnight."

"Was he there on March thirtieth or did he come home that night?"

"What has that got to do with the murder?"

I merely smiled benignly, waiting for her to respond.

"I can't recall that specific night, but he did spend several nights at his friend's studio around that time."

"A male friend?"

"Oh yes. Mr. Smith referred to him as 'he' or 'him.' Besides, he'd never compromise a woman by staying overnight. He was a good man." She pursed her lips, indignant that I would suggest such a thing.

"Do you know the friend's name?"

"I don't, but Mr. Smith visited him regularly until a week or so ago."

"Why did he stop going?"

She shrugged. "I suppose they had a falling out. It's such a shame. He could do with a friend now."

"May we see his room?" Harry asked.

She hesitated before rising. "I don't see why not. The police haven't said no one can enter."

She led us up the stairs and unlocked a door using one of the keys hanging at her waist. The door to the next room along the corridor opened a crack and a man peered out.

"Good afternoon," I said. "May we have a word?"

He closed the door then a moment later, opened it wider and stepped out. He was a small man who blinked a lot. I couldn't tell if it was a sign of nerves or simply a tic he always had. "Are you with the police?"

"We're assisting with the investigation," I said. "You know about Mr. Smith's arrest?"

He nodded.

"Do you know the name of his friend, the one whose studio he painted in?"

The lodger's gaze darted to the landlady and back to me. "How is that relevant?"

"It may not be, but we'd like to speak to him nevertheless."

The lodger twisted his ink splattered fingers around each other. "I don't know him, sorry."

"Does the name Ambrose McDonald mean anything to either of you?"

They both shook their heads.

Harry had been studying Reggie Smith's room from the doorway, but now he turned to the lodger. "Did he tell you where he was going before he went out of an evening? Or where he'd been the night before?"

"Sometimes."

"What about the night of the thirtieth of March. Was he here? Or did he go out and stay overnight with his friend, perhaps?"

The lodger's lips pinched. "I ask again, how is that relevant?"

Harry merely smiled and disappeared into the room.

"I have a pie in the oven," the landlady said and bustled off towards the stairs.

Instead of following Harry, I approached the lodger. "One more thing, Mr...?"

"Underwood."

"Mr. Underwood, I gather from your reactions that there was something going on between Mr. Smith and his friend with the studio."

Mr. Underwood retreated backwards to his room. "I don't know what you're implying. Good day."

I went after him and put a hand up to stop him closing the door in my face. "We're trying to save Mr. Smith's life. If he's found guilty of murder, he will hang."

Mr. Underwood swallowed heavily. "What do you want to know?"

"Mr. Smith and the man with the studio were lovers,

weren't they? That's why he sometimes spent the night there."

He gave a slight nod. "I think you might be correct."

"Do you know why they fell out?"

"No." After a moment's hesitation, he added, "About nine or ten days ago, I saw Mr. Smith come home one afternoon. He was very upset. I tried comforting him, but he didn't want company. He never told me what happened, but after that, he stopped going out unless he had to work."

"And the night of March thirtieth?"

"I am sorry, but I truly don't remember if he was in or out. Is that when the murder occurred? The police told us nothing."

I decided it couldn't hurt to give him some specifics. Some of it would be released in the newspapers later today anyway. "A fellow by the name of Ambrose McDonald was murdered last night at the place where Mr. Smith worked. Mr. Smith stole a painting, and the theory is that he was caught in the act by the victim and killed him to keep him quiet."

He blinked rapidly back at me for a long time, taking it all in. "And on the thirtieth of March?" he asked in a thin voice.

"There was another art theft. We're trying to establish a link between the two thefts, or lack thereof."

"I see. I'm afraid I can't help you."

"Thank you, Mr. Underwood. If you remember anything at all, please don't hesitate to contact us. My associate has business cards. Wait a moment and I'll fetch one." I hurried into Mr. Smith's room. "A card please, Harry."

He fished one out of his inside jacket pocket then continued his search under the mattress.

I returned to Mr. Underwood, glad to see he hadn't disappeared. Indeed, he accepted the card readily and with a curious expression.

"I have thought of something, as it happens." He withdrew a silver card case from his pocket and added Harry's card on top of one with a blue dove printed in the center. "The thing is, before he fell out with his...friend, Mr. Smith didn't work. He didn't need to. He painted all day. Although he was good, I don't think he sold very many. Certainly not enough to live on. After he and his friend fell out, he found employment as a footman with a catering firm."

So Reggie Smith's lover was most likely also his patron. When their relationship ended, so did the financial support. It would have been a terrible double blow.

"Thank you, Mr. Underwood. You've been a great help."

"I hope so."

"One more thing. Do you think him capable of theft?"

He went to close the door but paused. "I couldn't say."

Couldn't or wouldn't? "What about murder?"

He simply shook his head, but I wasn't sure if that meant he didn't know or didn't think him capable.

I returned to help Harry search Mr. Smith's room. We found nothing of interest. No stolen artworks, no private correspondence, no photographs of a man who could be a lover. As we searched, I told Harry what Mr. Underwood had told me.

"That explains why Reggie Smith didn't give the name of his alibi on March thirtieth when my father interviewed him. He wanted to protect his lover."

I agreed. If his lover was a wealthy man, the scandal would probably make the newspapers. It could destroy him. Love between men was not only scandalous, it was illegal. "It means he *did* have an alibi for the night of the first theft."

Harry didn't want to accept that as fact until we knew for certain. "Speaking of lovers, what if McDonald's murder has nothing to do with the art heist and everything to do with his relationships? You say he was a known cad. Perhaps he bedded the wrong woman and a jealous husband took revenge."

"It does sound like a recipe for jealousy to me." We exited the room and he closed the door behind us. "And jealousy is a powerful motive."

We both looked to the next door along the corridor through which Mr. Underwood had disappeared.

* * *

THE SECOND ADDRESS on our list from D.I. Hobart was for an impressive house on Grosvenor Square in Mayfair, not far from the Bunburys' townhouse. I started up the steps, but Harry stopped me.

"I'll go alone," he said. "The owners might recognize you."

I angled my hat lower over my forehead. "I doubt it."

"That won't fool anyone."

"We'll see, shall we?"

The butler answered the door and left us standing in the entrance hall while he checked to see if Lord and Lady Quorne were home for callers. He returned a moment later and led us to the drawing room where a middle-aged lady dressed in cream lace with a hairstyle so voluminous and blonde that it had to be a wig, sat on a sofa upholstered in buttercup yellow. The walls were painted in the same shade, making the room feel like a meadow in summer. She stroked a ginger cat curled up on her lap.

I recognized her immediately. She'd been a guest at the ball. At one time, she'd spoken to my aunt and uncle. I touched the brim of my hat and dipped my head. Hopefully she thought I was doing it in deference and not to hide my face.

Harry introduced me as his associate without naming me. I melted into the background and let him take the stage. It didn't matter. She'd barely glanced at me from the moment he smiled his charming smile.

"We're helping the police to investigate the murder of Ambrose McDonald," Harry said as he sat on the chair nearest her. "He died at the Bunburys' Ball last night."

"Yes, I was there."

"You were?" His tone suggested that if he had eyes in the back of his head, he would be glaring at me.

Lady Quorne's fingers stilled in the cat's fur. It raised its head in protest and she resumed patting it. "I wondered when the police would question me. I've been waiting all day."

Harry didn't inform her that the police thought they had their man. He must think she'd be more co-operative this way. He was probably right. "Did you see anything?"

"I don't think so. I was in the ballroom when I heard the scream. We all were. Poor Mr. McDonald."

"How well did you know him?"

"Only in passing. Ruth—Lady Bunbury—only invited him to make up numbers. There's always a shortage of eligible men at these things so one can't be too particular."

"You don't think he should have been invited?"

"I wouldn't go so far as to say that. He was charming and handsome. The young girls liked him. But that's also the problem. He was a dreadful flirt and he took the attention away from some of the more worthy gentlemen."

"Worthy?" Harry echoed.

"From better families. No one knows much about Mr. McDonald. He could be a blacksmith's son who inherited a little money from a distant relative. That's the thing. No one knows and so one ought not to entrust one's daughter or niece to his company. It would be quite a to-do if he trapped her into marriage. But with such a charming manner, it's impossible to keep the silly girls away. Isn't that right, Foxy?"

"Foxy?" I blurted out. It was a nickname I'd been given in school.

Lady Quorne looked up from Foxy the cat and studied me properly for the first time. "Don't I know you?"

I lowered my head further and shook it.

"My apologies," Harry said. "She has a habit of repeating what people say in a very loud voice. It makes it almost impossible for her to be out in public. I thought in the privacy of a home, it won't be so embarrassing."

I was going to throttle him when we got out of here.

Lady Quorne bestowed a smile on Harry. "It's very good of you to take her out. She's fortunate to have a friend like you."

"Thank you. It can be difficult, but I manage." How did he keep a straight face? "Since you were at the ball last night, did you hear that a painting was taken from the wall of the library some time before the murder?"

Lady Quorne's fingers stilled in Foxy's fur. She glanced at the wall behind Harry. "Good lord. No, I didn't."

Harry followed her gaze to a picture of a stream with willows dipping into the water and a stone bridge crossing it. "Is that the painting that was stolen from you? It's been found?"

"No. It's a replacement. The stolen one was of Paris in the evening. Is there a connection between the Bunburys' stolen painting and mine? Was the same thief responsible?" She gasped. "Did the thief murder Mr. McDonald?"

"That's what we're trying to discover."

"I do hope this is the breakthrough the police need to retrieve our Grandjean." She sighed. "My husband and I had lost hope of it ever being found. I didn't think the police had a suspect, but now...well, this is marvelous news. Perhaps it won't be long before it's recovered."

"Our focus is on solving the murder."

Her eyes had begun to dance brightly, but now they dimmed. "Of course, but there might be a link between the thefts and the murder. In fact, there must be. It's too great a coincidence."

"It's possible, which is why we want to find a connection between your painting and the Bunburys'."

"They are great art lovers. They have some fine pieces." If she knew or suspected their paintings were fakes, she hid it well.

"Tell us how yours came to be stolen."

She frowned. "I've already told the detective in charge of the investigation."

"If you would be so kind as to repeat it for us. We just want to make sure there have been no misunderstandings."

She accepted his explanation with a nod. "Someone entered in the night and took it off the wall."

"How did they get into the house?"

"No one knows. There were no signs of forced entry, so the police said. They think one of the staff left a latch off the hook, but the housekeeper and butler deny it."

"You had a ball here just days before the theft."

"It was a party, not a ball."

"Did you do the catering yourself or hire a firm?"

"I used Searcys. They do much of the cooking and provide the extra staff." She gasped. "You don't think one of their employees did it, do you?"

"It's too early to say. Do you have a guest list?"

"Good thinking, Mr. Armitage. One of my friends may

have noticed a staff member acting suspiciously." She stood and handed the cat to Harry.

Foxy looked annoyed at being disturbed until he stroked her head and back, then Foxy started kneading his thighs with her claws. After a moment, she closed her eyes and settled down, curling into a ball as he continued to pat.

Lady Quorne closed the drawer of the escritoire and waved a piece of paper in triumph. She handed it to Harry. "Foxy likes you."

"She dug her claws into me."

"That's just her way of showing affection. You must be special. She's friendly enough to most people but will only settle with a few."

Foxy purred loudly in agreement then protested with a low growl when Harry returned the cat to her owner. Lady Quorne rang for the butler.

"One more thing," Harry said. "Where can we find Searcys, the catering firm?"

Lady Quorne didn't know so asked her butler. "Their office is above a teashop on the corner of Oxford and Holles Streets, sir," he intoned.

Once safely outside and on the pavement, I raised the brim of my hat to reveal my entire face. "I told you I wouldn't be recognized."

"You seem to forget that she did."

"But she couldn't place me. As far as she's concerned, I'm a maid she once hired for a party."

"It was a close call. If we have to see her again, you shouldn't come."

I chose not to remind him that it wasn't his decision to make. "I won't do anything to jeopardize my situation, Harry. You have my word."

He merely grunted, neither agreeing nor disagreeing. "See if you recognize any names on Lady Quorne's guest list." He handed me the paper with the names. There were two per line and twelve lines in total.

"I recognize six couples. They were also at the ball last night. I don't know the others." I tucked the list into my bag. "I'll see what I can find out about all of them when I return to the hotel."

"We should go to Searcys now." He pulled out his watch by its chain and checked the time. "Do you have to be somewhere this afternoon?"

"My presence isn't required until this evening. There's a dinner I'm being dragged to with my family. Flossy is probably already getting ready now, but I only need a few minutes." The sun hadn't sunk behind the buildings yet. We should catch someone in the Searcys office before they went home for the day. I suddenly had a thought. "Wouldn't it be fortuitous if Searcys is the caterer for tonight's dinner?"

He stopped and rounded on me. "Do not investigate. Don't question anyone, whether they be guests or staff. It's too much of a risk with your uncle present."

"I agree, and I wasn't going to. I will merely observe and listen to gossip."

According to the staff member on duty in the office, Searcys wasn't the caterer for the dinner party I was attending that night. They'd been hired for other events, however, and she was run off her feet taking telephone calls from her clients with last minute demands. When she realized we weren't potential clients, she asked us to return tomorrow morning when it was quieter.

Harry and I parted company on Oxford Street after agreeing to meet at his office in the morning.

I returned home but paused to speak to Frank at the door. He was patrolling the pavement outside the hotel, as he liked to do when he wasn't greeting guests. He spared a glare for the decorators leaving the construction site next door, tin lunch boxes in hand.

"You can't possibly be annoyed with them," I said as the foreman locked up. "Papering walls makes very little noise."

Frank's features folded along well-worn lines. "They talk too much, and sing. I can hear one of them every time the door opens. Sings all day, he does. Sounds like a howling dog."

I'd heard the man singing and thought he was quite good. His co-workers obviously didn't mind. Frank was the sort of person who found fault in anything. He'd once complained the sky was the wrong shade of blue. It hurt his eyes.

37

I showed him the names on Lady Quorne's guest list. "Do you know any of these people? Have any stayed here?"

He shook his head. "None look familiar. Are you investigating the murder of that gentleman from last night's ball?"

"Yes, but keep it between us."

"If I help, will I get paid?"

"No one is getting paid. Not even me."

He screwed up his nose. "Then why are you investigating?"

"I have nothing better to do."

He scrunched his face even more.

Before he could rattle off a list of things that were more interesting to him than investigating, I added, "If my family ask, tell them I was at a museum today."

"I don't like lying to Sir Ronald or Lady Bainbridge."

"Very well. Tell them you don't know where I went."

"Right you are, Miss Fox."

Inside, Peter told me Harmony was waiting in the staff parlor. He glanced around then leaned closer. "Miss Bainbridge said you were at a museum today, but we wondered if you'd been investigating the murder."

"I have. In fact, perhaps you can help." I showed him the list. "Do you recognize any of these names?"

He pointed to a couple, lower down. "They came to the New Year's Eve ball one year."

"What are they like? Is there any gossip about them?"

"I just know the name. Sorry. Ask Mr. Hobart. You should catch him now before he leaves for the day."

I headed to the senior staff offices, passing the post desk where Terence was sorting newspapers into piles. They must be the evening editions, just arrived. Mr. Chapman stood to one side, reading an article on the front page of *The Evening News*. I picked up another copy. "Footman arrested for murder at society ball," the headline read. I skimmed the article, but it contained nothing I didn't already know, and returned it to Terence.

I found Mr. Hobart locking the top drawer of his desk as he prepared to leave for the evening. He looked up at my entry and smiled.

"There you are, Miss Fox. How did your meeting go with my brother and Harry?"

"Very well, thank you. D.I. Hobart wants us to investigate the murder. He's worried due process wasn't followed and the wrong fellow was arrested."

"Does he think Lord Bunbury is exerting some influence over the situation to avoid scandal, as he did last time?"

"He does. Mr. Hobart, do you know any of these people?" I handed him the list. "They were guests at Lady Quorne's dinner only a few days before her painting was stolen."

He scanned the list. "You think one of them may have been involved in both art thefts?"

"It's a possibility. The arrested footman admitted to stealing the Bunburys' painting, but your brother is quite sure he has an alibi for the night the Quornes' Grandjean was taken, although he's being rather secretive about who he was with."

"Perhaps someone encouraged him to take the Bunburys' painting last night. The same someone who'd already stolen the Quornes' picture."

It was something I'd considered too. Mr. Smith may not have decided to steal the Bunburys' painting on his own. He could have been encouraged by another, someone who made sure to have a watertight alibi for themselves for the night of the second theft. If so, then that meant they also had an alibi for the murder. And if they had an alibi for the murder, we were back at square one.

CHAPTER 4

"$\mathscr{I}$ recognize some of these names, but only in passing." Mr. Hobart pointed at the same couple that Peter drew to my attention. "These two have been to our ball. And this lady has taken afternoon tea with your aunt." He handed the list back to me. "I know nothing about them, however."

"No gossip?"

"Sadly, no. Your aunt would be the one to ask, but it's probably not wise to involve her."

I smiled and thanked him. Asking for my aunt's help might not be the worst thing to do. She'd helped me before and not told my uncle. On the other hand, I didn't want to put her in a position where she had to lie to him.

I wouldn't ask her unless absolutely necessary.

I found Harmony alone in the staff parlor. It was a little late for the maids to be enjoying a cup of tea. They would have finished cleaning rooms hours ago. Some would soon be arranging the hair or tightening corset laces of those guests who hadn't brought their own lady's maids. Harmony was usually sought after with her expert hairdressing skills, but Flossy often insisted she attend to her first.

She peered over the top of the newspaper she'd been reading then turned it around to show me. "They arrested someone for the murder. Pity."

"Why a pity?"

"Because it means you can't take the case."

I smiled.

She lowered the newspaper to her lap and tilted her head to the side. "Why do you look like the cat that got the cream?"

"Because D.I. Hobart is worried the wrong man has been arrested. His superiors refuse to entertain the possibility he's innocent, so he asked Harry and me to investigate."

Her brow plunged into a frown. "Oh."

"I thought you'd be happy that I've got another investigation to keep me occupied."

"Why would I be pleased when you won't get paid because there's no client? And it means you're working with Mr. Armitage again. You vowed never to see him."

"It's all right. We're both pretending the kiss never happened."

"You *kissed* him?"

I bit my lip. I'd forgotten I hadn't told her. I'd replayed it so many times in my head that sometimes it felt like I must have blurted it out. "It happened after the last investigation. We were walking through the park and I couldn't stop wondering what it would be like to kiss him. Next thing I knew, I did."

"*You* kissed *him*?"

"Yes."

"Cleo! What got into you?"

"You do remember how handsome he is." It was a joke, but Harmony was in no mood for laughing.

She narrowed her gaze. "You can't kiss every man you think is handsome. And you should never have kissed that one. It was a bad idea."

"I know."

"No matter what your feelings for him, you have to suppress them. Your family would never accept him, and I know you don't want to walk away from them now that you've found them."

"Harmony, that's not why it was a bad idea. If Harry and I wanted to be together, I wouldn't let my family's opinion sway me."

She arched both her brows in a challenge.

"I wouldn't!"

41

"Then what's stopping you?"

"I've made it clear that I don't intend to marry. Everyone here knows it, and Harry does too. It wasn't fair of me to encourage him, for want of a better word. If he'd allowed the kiss to continue, it would mean he intended to...take things further. And then what? Keep me as a mistress while he looked for a wife? No. He's not the sort. The only thing he could do in the circumstances was end the kiss, which he did."

"It was the right thing to do," Harmony said thoughtfully. "Or perhaps he simply didn't like the kiss. Or didn't like kissing *you*."

"You are dreadful for one's self-confidence, do you know that? Anyway, I can report that he kissed me back with enthusiasm, if only for a moment. He enjoyed it, as did I. Very much."

Her gaze was still censorial, but it softened a little. "It's going to make working with him on this investigation difficult."

"We've managed so far. We both ignored the elephant in the room and by the end of the day, the elephant was no bigger than a cat." A ginger one by the name of Foxy with a loud purr and more than a passing tolerance for men who paid her attention.

"Ignoring tension is something we English do well," Harmony added with a wry smile.

The door opened and Victor sauntered in, a pack slung over one shoulder. He was dressed in regular clothes, not his chef's whites, and he didn't have his knife belt slung around his middle. "Afternoon, Miss Fox. Harmony."

"Good afternoon, Victor," I said. "Have you just arrived for the dinner shift?"

He shook his head. "I was working the lunch and afternoon shift today. I'm heading home." He adjusted his pack. "I thought I'd come in here and see if anyone wanted to walk back with me." His gaze settled on Harmony.

They both lived in the nearby residence hall. Lately, Harmony often waited up with me in my room then left when she knew the chefs finished their evening shifts. She pretended it was just coincidence, but I suspected she did it so she could walk with Victor. He liked her, and I was quite sure she liked him. Indeed, the more times she waited up, the more certain I became.

But now she shook her head. "I have to do Miss Bainbridge's hair soon."

Victor glanced at the clock on the shelf. It had just gone five. Harmony would have finished work hours ago, and yet she had stayed at the hotel. It wasn't a great stretch to assume she'd stayed for him, and yet now she claimed she couldn't go home.

He shifted his pack again. "Very well."

He left the parlor, just as Goliath and several waiters entered, so I didn't get the opportunity to ask her if she'd decided walking with Victor was a bad idea for the same reason I'd decided kissing Harry couldn't happen again. She'd vowed never to marry too.

She glanced at the clock then asked Goliath to pour her another cup of tea while he made a cup for himself. I asked her to come and help me with my hair after she'd finished with Flossy.

I went in search of my cousin and found her rummaging through the false hair curls, buns, rolls and rats in her dressing table drawer while her bath filled with water.

"How was the museum today?" she asked without looking up.

Now that I knew I was certain I was investigating the murder, I saw no reason not to come clean. She wouldn't tell her parents. "Actually, I'm helping D.I. Hobart to find Mr. McDonald's murderer."

She gasped. "I knew it! How thrilling. But haven't they caught someone?"

"He wants to be completely sure."

"I see. That's commendable of him. You wouldn't want to send the wrong man to the gallows."

"In fact, I'm hoping you can help me." I handed her the list of names and explained the connection between Lady Quorne's dinner party, the theft of her painting, and the murder. "Which ones of these were also at the Bunburys' ball?"

She perused the list. "Almost all. These two and this couple were the only ones not at the ball."

"Do you know any of them personally?"

"Not particularly well. Mother will. They're around her age." She handed the list back to me. "If you ask her now, be aware she was in rather a foul mood when I left her. She hadn't taken her tonic and her head was aching." She sighed and turned to stare at her reflection in the mirror. "She can't go on like this, Cleo. She just can't."

I squeezed her shoulder. "We need to find her another doctor."

She sighed again but said nothing. She knew getting her mother to see another doctor would be almost impossible. Aunt Lilian liked her current doctor because he gave her tonic whenever she asked for it. He didn't warn her to use it sparingly, as we did. He was happy to sell her more and more. And poor Aunt Lilian needed more of it to keep the headaches at bay.

I left Flossy's suite and returned to my own. I decided not to call on my aunt. It wasn't just because of what Flossy said. I'd already decided I couldn't place Aunt Lilian in a position where she had to lie to my uncle. I would have to think of a subtler way to find out about Lady Quorne's guests.

I ran myself a bath then soaked in it, memorizing the names on the list until the water grew cold. Harmony arrived and helped me dress in an evening gown of off-white *crepe de chine* with black *fleur de lis* embroidered across the bodice and small bows at the elbows. After arranging my hair, she made me stand and twirl.

"Lovely," she declared. "It's a shame you don't want to be kissed."

That was the thing. I did want to be kissed. It was marriage I wanted to avoid.

* * *

"I'M SO excited for you to meet the Newcombes, Cleo," Aunt Lilian said. She sat opposite Flossy and me in the carriage, looking small and frail beside her robust husband. Her busy fingers twisted the fringing of her shawl until the silk threads became knotted. "Mrs. Newcombe is a dear, and she has the most charming daughters. They're too young to join us tonight, of course, but her son will be there." She bestowed a mischievous smile on me then Flossy. She had him in mind for one of us, but it wasn't clear which one.

"I met them at the ball," I said. "They seemed very nice."

"Oh yes! So you did. You even danced with their boy, too. Silly me, I forgot." She touched her temple. "I wonder if you also met some of the other guests who'll be there tonight."

Partly to divert her away from matchmaking, and partly because her chattiness meant it was a good time to obtain information from her, I tried to subtly find out more about the guests who'd attended both the Quornes' dinner and the ball. If I could narrow the list down to ones who might be having financial difficulties, or were suspected of being light-fingered, it would give us some strong suspects for the art heists.

I began at the top, with the hosts themselves. "Speaking of the ball, I heard something interesting about the Quornes last night, but I can't remember what it was. Do you know what it could be, Aunt?"

Her eyes widened and she leaned forward to tap my knee. "I do, as it happens."

Uncle Ronald drew his double chins in and peered down his nose at me. "I didn't think you like to gossip, Cleo."

"Leave her be, Ronald," his wife chided. "She's just making conversation to pass the time. You remember the Quornes, don't you, dear? Lord Quorne was almost forty when he met his future wife. She was only eighteen at the time."

Flossy pulled a face. "Don't you dare marry me to a forty-year-old. He must be thirty at the absolute worst."

"Their age difference isn't the interesting part. Lord Quorne met her when he was traveling up north, but no one knows where precisely they met, or how. Her family are complete unknowns." She leaned forward even further and lowered her voice. "She could be the daughter of the village blacksmith. We simply don't know. When he returned to society with her, they were already wed. He simply intro-

ARCHER

duced her as his wife, with no mention of who her father was. Their first child was born a mere seven months later."

"Lilian," Uncle Ronald scolded.

"The girls are old enough to know how babies are made, dear." She turned back to Flossy and me, her eyes huge in the dim light of the swaying carriage lantern. "We were all dreadfully curious about her, but no one dared ask. Did you ever speak to Lord Quorne about her, Ronald?"

"He's a quiet, serious man, not prone to conversation."

Aunt Lilian settled back into the seat. "I'd forgotten all about it until now. Who brought it up, Cleo?"

"I can't recall." The intrigue surrounding Lady Quorne was a good start. I filed the information away and tried picturing the list in my head. "Speaking of gossip, what do you know about the Begg-Forsythes?"

"Nothing really. Why? What have you heard?"

"Perhaps it wasn't them. The Campbells?"

She shook her head.

I rattled off a few more names until I thought it best to stop. My uncle was frowning at me, his expression somewhere between disappointment and confusion.

We'd slowed down anyway, and finally came to a stop. A footman opened the carriage door for us and assisted my aunt down the step to the pavement.

He helped Flossy next. "Why did Floyd not have to come tonight?" she asked.

"I told you," Aunt Lilian said. "The Newcombe girls aren't old enough."

Flossy rolled her eyes.

I was pleased to be seated next to a middle-aged gentleman who liked to gossip. By the end of the evening, I'd asked him about every guest who'd been at both the ball and the Quornes' dinner. While he had some interesting pieces of information, none of it was relevant. Like the suspicions surrounding Lady Quorne's background, none of the gossip pointed to a thieving past or financial woes.

I also inspected the ladies' jewelry as subtly as I could, but their gemstones looked genuine to me. After the ladies withdrew, leaving the men to their port in the dining room, I took a turn about the drawing room to admire the paintings

46

hanging on the wall. One in particular had caught my eye earlier and I now had the opportunity to take a closer look. It was by Grandjean, the same artist of the painting stolen from the Quornes.

"You have an interest in art, Miss Fox?" I hadn't noticed the hostess, Mrs. Newcombe, come up behind me. She was a handsome woman in her forties, plump and short, with dimples in her cheeks. She nodded at the painting. "It's Paris in the autumn. Aren't the colors vibrant?"

The Quornes' painting had been of Paris, too. I wished I were an expert and could tell whether this one was genuine or not. After learning that Reggie Smith wanted to put back the Bunburys' painting because it was a fake, I'd wondered how important that fact was to the case. The murder could be about the two thefts, or it could be about the Bunburys' being a forgery.

"I can see why you love it so much," I said. "Did you get it over there?"

"It's from Lady Treloar's gallery." She spoke as if I knew her.

"Where is her gallery?"

"My apologies, I forgot you haven't lived in London long. It's on Regent Street. Everyone knows it. She has a good eye."

"And she's a lady?"

She nodded. "The widow of Lord Treloar. He left her with nothing, the poor thing, but she has done very well for herself. The gallery is a triumph."

While ladies working in trade was frowned upon, some women had managed to rise above the stigma and carve out good reputations for themselves. I knew of a fashion designer who'd divorced her philandering husband and opened her first shop to stave off poverty, and a publisher who'd inherited her father's company and refused to hand over the reins to a man. Owning an art gallery was a respectable business for a lady.

"Perhaps you saw her at the Bunburys' ball last night," Mrs. Newcombe said. "My age, striking features."

An art expert who'd been left with nothing after her husband died and was also at the ball. Now I was even more intrigued by Lady Treloar. It would be worth paying her a visit tomorrow.

I couldn't wait to tell Harry.

* * *

HARMONY INFORMED me the following morning over breakfast that Mr. Hobart wished to see me before I left the hotel. "He didn't say what it was about, but he looked worried. Maybe he heard about the kiss."

I stabbed a sausage with my fork. "I doubt that would worry him."

I spent the next little while passing on all the gossip I'd learned the previous night. We agreed that most of it wasn't relevant to the case, although Harmony did point out that Lady Quorne could have been an art thief before she met her husband. "I'm serious," she said when I laughed. "We know nothing about her."

We parted ways outside my room after breakfast, and I went in search of Mr. Hobart. I found him farewelling guests in the foyer after they checked out. Goliath and the other porters pushed trolleys laden with luggage across the tiles and through the front door, held open by Frank. Peter greeted me as he passed, a clipboard in one hand and pencil in the other. All looked in order. Mr. Hobart seemed to be his usual cheerful self.

His smile vanished upon seeing me, however. I stood at the post desk and read the newspapers until he was free.

"I'm worried about Mr. Bainbridge," he said when he joined me.

My first reaction was one of relief. Nobody had died or been injured. But Mr. Hobart wouldn't be worried about Floyd under ordinary circumstances. Something must be wrong.

"The night porter told me this morning that Mr. Bainbridge has been coming home just before dawn several times in the last few weeks, and not in a very good state."

"Floyd often comes home late, and he's often drunk. I've seen it myself."

"Yes, but Philip says it's different lately. Mr. Bainbridge is usually cheerful. Drunk, but happy. But these last few weeks, he seemed troubled. And early this morning…" He glanced around to check that we weren't overheard. "Early this morning, he came in crying."

That certainly didn't sound like Floyd. "Is Philip certain? Floyd's eyes may have been watering from the cold air."

"It was a relatively mild night." He watched me closely. "I'm sorry to burden you with this, Miss Fox, but I didn't know who else to turn to. Lady Bainbridge is too fragile to help her son if he's in difficulty, and I didn't want to inform Sir Ronald yet. His reaction might make it worse."

I could well imagine my uncle growing angry with Floyd for his late nights and gambling. Knowing him, he might bully Floyd and tell him that a real man never cries. A response like that from his father could push Floyd away when he needed help the most.

"You were right to tell me, Mr. Hobart. Thank you."

His body heaved with his sigh. "If there's anything I can do, anything at all, please don't hesitate to ask."

I clasped his forearm and offered him the kindest smile I could muster. "I won't speak to Floyd yet. I'll let him sleep a while and talk to him this afternoon."

"I think that's wise."

Floyd occupied my mind all the way to Harry's office. So much so that I forgot my intention never to enter without knocking first, and I barged right in. He looked up from the desk where he sat, pen in hand.

"Are you all right?" he asked. "You look troubled."

"It's nothing. Just Floyd being Floyd."

He nodded knowingly. "Late nights, coming home drunk and smelling like he'd gone for a swim in the Thames?"

I couldn't help smiling. "You know him well."

"The night porter would regularly wake me up to help Floyd to his room." Harry used to have his own private chamber on the ground floor, and with the night porter being unable to leave the foyer once the other staff went home, it made sense to ask for Harry's assistance. With Harry gone and Peter, the new assistant manager, living off-site, Floyd now had to make his own way to his rooms. Jonathon sometimes helped, but he wasn't always with him.

"Try not to worry," Harry said. "I'm sure he'll sort himself out."

"I hope you're right." I withdrew Lady Quorne's guest list from my bag. "Now, let's begin with the hosts."

He tended to agree with Harmony and me that the gossip I'd learned couldn't help with our investigation. None of it seemed relevant. "We'll keep to our original plan and return to the caterer's office this morning."

"I want to call at an art gallery on Regent Street first." I told him about Lady Treloar as he put on his jacket. "She sold a Grandjean to my dinner hosts, so it's possible she sold the Quornes theirs, too."

"Then stole it back a year later?"

It didn't make sense to me either, but I still wanted to speak to her.

Harry slapped his hat on his head and opened the door for me. "She wasn't at the Quornes' dinner."

"No, but if she sold them the painting, the dinner is irrelevant. She already knew where the painting hung and quite possibly how to get inside."

He indicated I should leave the office ahead of him. "Lead the way."

Regent Street was close by. We walked in silence, which allowed my mind to wander back to Floyd. I'd always dismissed his late-night escapades as harmless fun. For privileged gentlemen, drunken rousing was part of growing up, a phase they went through before settling down.

But it was clearly no longer fun for Floyd. Something had happened. The more I thought about it, the more worried I became.

Harry noticed. "Floyd?"

I nodded. "I think he's in over his head this time."

"If you want to talk to me, I can assure you it won't go any further."

"I know I can trust you."

His gaze connected with mine for a fleeting moment, but it was enough to send a jolt through me. He didn't just look at me. He *saw* me.

I cleared my throat. "Floyd came home just before dawn in an emotional state."

Harry's lips flattened. "I see why you're worried. I can speak to him if you think it will help."

"Thank you, but I'll try first."

The art gallery was an open, brightly lit space in a prominent position on Regent Street. A woman welcomed us with a smile and a sweeping gesture, then asked us to kindly wait while she finished with a customer. Lady Treloar was middle aged with high cheekbones and wide-set gray eyes. Dressed in forest green with a white lace panel down the front of her gown, and pearls at her throat and ears, she was the epitome of style and elegance, as well as wealth.

But the thing I found most intriguing about her was the familiarity. I recognized her from the ball. I'd seen her studying the painting in the ballroom alongside Ambrose McDonald.

What had the gallery owner and the victim been talking about?

CHAPTER 5

A sofa positioned near the front of the gallery was an inviting place for customers to wait. Neither Harry nor I sat, however. Without exchanging a word, we both decided to peruse the artwork.

Electric light bulbs hanging from the ceiling illuminated the paintings and their gilt frames, so that even on a dull day the brushstrokes could be admired. Lady Treloar was deep in conversation with her customer, explaining the provenance of a large landscape with a country manor in the background. It had been sold by the estate's executors along with several other pieces to pay the deceased former owner's debts. Lady Treloar spoke with a hint of sorrow in her voice, sympathizing with the impoverished heir. The customer despaired over the state of the nation and its disappearing gentry, but the glint in her eye as she studied the painting revealed her true feelings. Another's loss was her gain.

I didn't find any paintings by Grandjean, but I recognized the names of a few well-known artists. An archway from the main part of the gallery led through to a smaller room. It was a little darker and the frames weren't as ornate. I wasn't going to go in, but Harry indicated I should.

"See what's through there," he whispered, nodding at a closed door opposite. "I'll make sure no one comes near."

I glanced past him to where Lady Treloar was still in deep conversation with her customer. I told Harry that I'd seen her talking to the victim before his death, then hurried to the door and slipped into the room beyond. It was a staff room, barely larger than a cupboard. Unlike the gallery, it was messy and poorly lit with just a single bulb throwing out very little light. A kettle resting on a copper stand over a portable stove was positioned at one end of a narrow bench. Beside it was a cobalt blue and gold china teacup and saucer, and beside that were strewn art books and catalogues for auction houses. At the far end of the rectangular room was a commode with a chamber pot inside. Two unframed paintings leaned against the wall. The floorboards were scuffed and scratched, and the entire room needed a coat of paint.

This was Lady Treloar's private room, not an office. She didn't use this to write up orders. There was a Queen Anne style desk in the gallery for that. She probably kept her bag in here. I found it quickly among the mess, since there were so few places to look, and rummaged through it. Aside from a few subtle cosmetics, I found nothing of interest and returned it to where I'd found it, beneath the bench.

I opened the door, peered out and, seeing him alone, rejoined Harry near the archway. I shook my head.

Lady Treloar farewelled her customer then turned her smile onto us. "I do apologize, but I hope the wait has been worth your while. Have you seen anything you like?"

Harry handed her a business card then introduced himself. As he'd done the previous day with Lady Quorne, he introduced me as his associate without naming me, no doubt trying to protect my identity. Going by the slight pursing of Lady Treloar's lips, she thought it ill-mannered of him. She was a woman in business, and a successful one at that. I suspected she appreciated other women who did not allow men to speak for them. She also didn't seem to recognize me, so I thought it safe to give her my name.

I put out my hand and introduced myself. She smiled and shook it heartily.

She held up Harry's card. "Does this have something to do with the murder of poor Mr. McDonald?"

Harry nodded. "We're working with the police to tie up loose ends."

"I was wondering when I would be questioned, but then I

read about the footman's arrest, so I thought it might not happen. Yet here you are..."

"Did you know Mr. McDonald?"

"A little. We were acquaintances rather than friends."

Harry indicated the gallery and paintings with a sweeping gesture. "You're clearly an expert."

"You flatter me, Mr. Armitage. I am somewhat knowledgeable but no expert."

"Have Lord and Lady Bunbury ever been customers of yours?"

She blinked, the question clearly taking her by surprise. "No. I believe their artworks are old family pieces inherited by Lord Bunbury."

"What about Lord and Lady Quorne?"

"I sold them a Grandjean last year. In fact, I learned at the Bunburys' ball that it was stolen quite recently. It must have been quite a shock for them. Lady Quorne loved that painting."

"You hadn't heard about the theft before the ball?" I asked. "I imagine it would have been common knowledge among their acquaintances and the art world."

"I've been abroad. I spent the last four weeks enjoying the sunshine in Biarritz, and only just arrived back in London the day before the Bunburys' ball."

"You would have had the opportunity to study the Bunburys' paintings on the night of the ball," I said. "What did you think of them?"

She shifted her glance to Harry then back to me. "That's an odd question."

"Was there anything...unexpected about them?"

She touched a frame of one of the paintings on the wall to straighten it, although it looked perfectly straight to me. "I don't understand the question."

"Were any of them fakes?"

She stilled. "I don't see how that's connected to the murder."

"It may not be," Harry said. "We just want to get a broad picture, and we've been reliably informed that the artworks in their townhouse are not originals."

Harry's light manner and encouraging smile seemed to

relax her. "This cannot go further than this room, and if it does, I will deny the information came from me. You're right. All the paintings that I saw are copies. I knew they owned some pieces by the masters and was keen to see them, but I knew instantly they weren't the originals."

"Did Mr. McDonald know they were fakes?" I asked.

She bristled. "I can't say what another person knows, Miss Fox."

"You were seen talking to him at the ball. What were you talking about?"

"A painting. He wanted to know what I thought about it. I told him it was an intriguing piece and left it at that. I'm not going to blurt out that it was a copy. It would be cruel to the Bunburys."

"But you suspect he knew?"

She hesitated before saying, "I think he had an inkling and was after confirmation."

"What did Lady Bunbury say when she joined you?"

Her brows arched. "You do have an observant source, Miss Fox. Lady Bunbury joined us for conversation as befitting a hostess. We exchanged nothing of interest."

"But?" I prompted.

"But I think she was worried that I would say something about the painting to Mr. McDonald. It would be devastating for her if I told the biggest gossip in the room that the painting was a copy."

"What do you mean 'the biggest gossip?'" Harry asked.

"Precisely that. Mr. McDonald had a reputation. I don't know how he learns things, but he always seems to know about scandalous goings-on."

Perhaps he was killed to stop him spreading gossip. The Bunburys' financial situation, for example.

"I'm glad the police have arrested the killer." Lady Treloar folded her arms and hugged herself. "I feel safer knowing he's not gaining entry to people's homes through his work for Searcys."

"You believe he did it?" Harry asked.

"Well, yes. Don't you?"

"Why do you think that?"

"You mean aside from the fact he was arrested for the

crime? For one thing, he knew Mr. McDonald. I saw them acknowledge one another as the footman passed him. They didn't exchange words, but they exchanged knowing looks. Indeed, it was an angry glare on the footman's part."

So they *did* know one another. Since Reggie Smith's neighbor, Mr. Underwood, had alluded to Mr. Smith having a relationship with his male patron, perhaps the patron and lover was Ambrose McDonald.

"Did Mr. McDonald have a paramour?" I asked.

"It's likely, and probably more than one. It's even possible his lover was a man. I've heard rumors…"

I feigned surprise, but I was not at all shocked. The only emotion I felt was triumph. We'd connected the victim to Reggie Smith. We still needed more, however.

"Was Mr. McDonald a painter?" I asked.

"He dabbled, so he told me. In my line of work, one never knows if they tell me that so I will ask to see their work or if they genuinely mean they're a hobbyist. It's possible in Mr. McDonald's case that he was trying to make a living from it. He didn't work, as far as I am aware, so I don't know where his money came from. Perhaps he inherited it."

"Did he have a studio at home?" I asked.

"I don't know. As I said, I didn't know him particularly well."

It would be easy enough to find out from D.I. Hobart.

We thanked her and Harry asked her to contact him if she thought of anything else.

Outside, I couldn't wait to discuss what we'd learned, and I blurted out the thing topmost on my mind. "I think Ambrose McDonald and Reggie Smith were lovers. I'll wager he has a studio where Reggie Smith painted each day until they had a falling out. He quite possibly painted the Bunbury fakes there. Or Ambrose McDonald did."

Harry wasn't so sure. "You believe everything Lady Treloar said?"

"Don't you?"

He shrugged. "She could be trying to throw shade over Reggie Smith to deflect us from looking too closely at her connection with Ambrose McDonald. Perhaps *she* was his latest lover."

He had a point. It wasn't like me to take every claim at face value. But this time, her words had a ring of truth. The more I thought about it, the more I was sure Mr. Smith and Mr. McDonald were lovers.

"I can't see her stealing the paintings," I said. "For one thing, she was in Biarritz when the Grandjean was stolen from the Quornes, and for another, why would she be the one coercing Reggie Smith into taking the Bunburys' painting when she could tell they were copies? I don't doubt that she's an art expert. She would know a fake from a real one."

Harry conceded my point. "If we agree that she's telling the truth, it would seem McDonald was trying to find out from her whether the paintings were indeed fakes, which means he didn't paint them himself or know who did."

"And when Lady Bunbury saw them together, she panicked. Knowing what a gossip he is, she separated them as soon as possible."

"But if she was too late, she might have killed McDonald to stop him spreading the gossip that night."

It was an excellent theory. In our last investigation, I'd not been convinced that Lady Bunbury was a murderer, and it turned out that she wasn't guilty. This time, however, I'd learned that she and Lord Bunbury were in more financial difficulty than we realized. They'd sold all their valuable paintings and jewels, and gone to great lengths to hide that fact by having copies made.

How much further were they prepared to go?

* * *

A DIFFERENT WOMAN was on duty in the Searcys office this morning. She reminded me of a school mistress with her clipped tone and haughty briskness that invited no idle conversation. I knew one thing for certain within moments of meeting her. She would not succumb to Harry's charms.

We introduced ourselves and gave her the usual spiel that we were helping the police tie up loose ends. She didn't take our word for it, however, so Harry told her to telephone his father at Scotland Yard.

After a brief call, she hung up and clasped her hands on the desk in front of her. "How may I help you?"

"May we see a list of all the staff who worked the night of the Bunburys' ball?"

She opened the drawer of the filing cabinet behind her. She found the relevant file and handed us a list. On it were the names and addresses of all the temporary staff that had worked that night. There were twelve.

"Have Searcys employed these people before?" Harry asked.

"Most have done several events for us, but four are new." She asked for the list back then marked four names. "These ones started in the last month."

"Did any of them also work at Lord and Lady Quorne's dinner on March thirtieth?"

She looked through her filing cabinet and pulled out another file. She compared the lists side by side then shook her head. "No. Lady Quorne only hired three staff from us. None worked at the Bunburys' ball."

Harry indicated the list of twelve. "May we borrow this?"

"No, you may not." She pushed a notepad, pen and ink pot towards him. "Copy it down."

As Harry wrote, I thought of one other thing to ask. "There was a maid who worked the night of the Bunburys' ball. Taller than me, reddish brown hair, walks with a limp." I indicated the list. "Can you tell me which one she is, please?"

"Was something wrong with her work? Was she idle?"

"No."

She looked as though she wanted to interrogate me further, but thought better of it. She pointed to one of the names with an asterisk beside it.

"Jane Eyre? Is this serious?"

"Do I look like the type of person who makes silly jokes?"

I swallowed my retort and shook my head.

"That is the name the girl gave me. Perhaps her mother was a flibbertigibbet who liked to read novels."

I opened my mouth to retort that reading novels didn't mean a woman was silly, but I caught sight of Harry out of the corner of his eye, warring with a smile. That was precisely what he expected me to do. I wouldn't give him the satisfaction of being proved correct.

We took our copied list and headed down the stairs.

"That brought back memories of the school where my mother worked," he said as he pushed open the door that led outside. "The headmistress was a dragon. I was terrified of her. She's the reason I stayed in most afternoons after school and read books."

It was good to hear Harry make light of his past. Usually he either didn't want to talk about it or he grew melancholy when he remembered his birth mother. She'd raised him on her own while working in a school for girls, where they'd also both lived. She'd died when he was eleven, leaving him truly alone.

I indicated the teashop with its frilly white tablecloths and yellow roses in vases on each table. "Shall we discuss our next moves over tea and cake?"

"No."

"Is this place too feminine for your masculine pride?"

"It's too close to the shops your cousin and the Mayfair Hotel guests frequent. It's the sort of place they'd stop at for refreshments on a day out. It's not far to my office from here. We'll have coffee at Roma Café instead."

I used to insist that I didn't care about being seen with him, but not anymore. It was easier to agree with him since he was too stubborn to back down. Besides, I preferred the atmosphere of Luigi's café. There was nothing pompous about it. He also served the best coffee in London. The smell of it was inviting enough, but Luigi's hearty greeting made me feel like an old friend.

"*Bella*! Come in, come in. I haven't seen you for a long time. Is Harry not treating you well?"

I laughed. "I've been busy."

"Too busy to see me? Ah, Miss Fox, you break my heart." He shook a dishcloth at Harry. "You should treat her like a lady, or she won't come back."

"Is that so?" Harry said darkly.

"A lady like Miss Fox deserves the best coffee every day." Luigi tapped his chest. "That's why I'm never lonely."

The two elderly regulars who inhabited the stools at the

counter like a pair of statues suddenly came to life. They spoke in loud Italian with exaggerated gestures to Luigi and Luigi responded in the same language and a shrug of his shoulders. From the few words I could make out, I suspected he'd broken the heart of a woman they knew.

Somehow Harry managed to order two coffees amid the exchange. We sat at the table near the window while Luigi made them without interrupting his argument with the two customers.

Harry and I divided the list between us according to locations, and after finishing our coffees we separated. Before we parted, Harry helped me devise the best route for greatest efficiency. He knew all the rail and omnibus routes, and suggested I begin with the furthest address and make my way back to Soho and Mayfair. My list had to include Jane Eyre since I could identify her, but I wasn't hopeful of finding her.

My hunch was proved correct. She'd given a false address to go with her false name. The elderly man who answered my knock had heard of the literary character but not the maid with the limp.

I did have some success, however. One of the Searcys footmen claimed a gentleman had given him a note to pass on to Mr. McDonald, which he had duly done. That had been a mere thirty minutes or so before the scream that alerted us to the murder.

"What did the note say?" I asked.

"I didn't read it."

That was hard to believe. "Be honest with me. You won't get into trouble."

"It said to meet him in the library immediately."

This was the breakthrough we needed. "Who was the gentleman?"

"He signed the note 'Livingstone.'"

Mr. Livingstone was the father of Amelia Livingstone, the girl declared debutante of the season after sweeping all three of Lady Bunbury's awards. Why did he want to meet Ambrose McDonald?

"One more question," I said to the footman. "Did you notice anything about your colleague, Mr. Smith, that night?"

"The one who got arrested for the murder?" He shrugged. "Like what?"

"Did you see him with the victim?"

"No."

I asked the same question to the rest of the staff on my list. With the murder on the front pages of all the newspapers, they were all keen to tell me what they knew, but it amounted to nothing. No one could confirm Lady Treloar's claim that Mr. Smith and Mr. McDonald knew each other.

Harry had more success than me with that question, however. When we met at his office in the afternoon, he told me one of the maids he'd spoken to had seen them having a discussion outside the ballroom. "She didn't say it was heated, but it didn't look friendly either."

"So Lady Treloar was right about the angry look Reggie Smith gave Ambrose McDonald."

Harry picked up one of the newspapers he'd had delivered that morning and indicated the sketch of Mr. Smith. "It's not looking good for him."

"I wouldn't necessarily say that," I said.

"You found Jane Eyre?"

"No. The maid gave a false address. But I learned something that throws up another suspect. One of the footmen passed a note from Mr. Livingstone to Mr. McDonald, asking McDonald to meet him in the library. That was only thirty minutes before the body was discovered."

"Livingstone... The name doesn't sound familiar."

"It's unlikely he has stayed at the hotel. He's wealthy. His daughter, Amelia, was the most popular debutante at the ball."

Harry sat back and crossed his arms over his chest. "I wonder what they spoke about."

"It could have been nothing," I said slyly. "Or it could be something to do with gossip. Stopping it, to be precise."

Harry suddenly sat forward, a spark brightening his eyes. "McDonald was a notorious gossip. If he discovered something scandalous about Livingstone, Livingstone may have killed him to silence him."

Something about this turn of events was beginning to seem familiar. It took me a moment to remember something

Jonathon had told me on the night of the ball. "The gossip might not be about Livingstone, but about his daughter, Amelia. Apparently she's involved in some sort of scandal, but I don't know what. I didn't ask."

"You won't make a very good detective if you don't like to hear gossip, Cleo."

"I'll be sure to listen next time, just on the off-chance it relates to a murder." I rose. "We need to speak with him and find out why he met with Mr. McDonald. I'll call at the hotel and ask if your uncle knows where we can find him."

"Then you'll pass the information on to me and I'll call on Livingstone alone."

I went to open the door, but Harry put his hand to it, keeping it closed. I tried not to think about how much I liked the nearness of him, and how my insides somersaulted when he lowered his head to meet my gaze. It wasn't easy to remain focused.

"It's too dangerous for you to speak to him," he said. "If he recognizes you—"

"He won't. We weren't introduced at the ball."

"Even so, we've tempted fate too many times already."

I grinned.

He frowned. "Why are you smiling at me like that?"

"I didn't think you were a believer in fate."

He frowned harder. "Stop changing the subject."

"Either you move aside or we stay in here forever, because I'm going to call on Mr. Livingstone with you whether you like it or not. We can pretend I am your unnamed associate, if you like, but I *am* going with you."

He expelled a measured breath. "I don't know why I thought I'd win. Self-preservation isn't one of your strong suits." He opened the door for me.

* * *

HARRY WAITED on the other side of Piccadilly from the hotel but joined me when I signaled to him. "Frank says my uncle has gone out and won't be back until later tonight. No one will tell him you were here."

Frank held the door open for us, his gaze watchful but not

censorial. Goliath and Peter greeted Harry with easy smiles, although both called him Mr. Armitage. Old habits were hard to break, and they weren't on a familiar basis with him. If Harry came here more often, they would change, but he had avoided the hotel unless absolutely necessary.

We found Mr. Hobart in his office, but he didn't know where the Livingstones lived. He knew almost nothing about the family since Mr. Livingstone wasn't one of the gentlemen in my uncle's circle and there was no Mrs. Livingstone to partake of the hotel's afternoon tea.

"I believe the daughter may have been here once last year, with a family friend, but I haven't got any notes on her. Miss Bainbridge will know more about her, I'm sure. Lady Bainbridge, too, although she's taken to her bed today."

"Is Flossy in her room?" I asked.

"You should catch her there before she comes down for afternoon tea. She's meeting a friend today."

"Perfect."

Harry refused to come with me, however.

"She won't tell her father you were here," I assured him.

"It's not that. Not entirely, anyway. She'll be more inclined to talk freely if it's just you."

He had a point. I left him in his uncle's office and headed up the stairs to the fourth floor. Flossy was preparing for afternoon tea. She asked me to join her as I'd met her friend before, but I declined.

"I'm a little busy investigating the murder."

"Still?" She turned her head from side to side to study her reflection for different angles. Her curls bounced around her ears. "You mustn't let it take up too much of your time or someone will notice you're never around."

"I'll be careful. But Flossy, you can't tell anyone about this. I shouldn't be involving you at all, but I need your help."

"I won't tell a soul." She drew a little cross over her heart. "What do you need to know?"

"Where does Amelia Livingstone live?"

"Why do you want to talk to Amelia?" She gasped. "Is she a suspect?"

"Her father may have witnessed something on the night of the ball. He's the one we need to speak to."

She rose and headed through to the sitting room. Her suite was identical to mine with a separate bedroom off the sitting room where a desk faced the window. Behind it was a small table for dining, a sofa and two armchairs, all upholstered in soft feminine shades. She opened the desk drawer and pulled out an address book. She flipped the pages then pointed to an entry for Amelia Livingstone. She lived in Knightsbridge.

"What do you know about Amelia and her father?" I asked as she copied the address onto a piece of paper. "Are there other children?"

"Just Amelia. Her mother died when she was a baby and her father never remarried. He's devoted to her." She handed me the paper. "So much so that he's blinded to her faults."

"According to Lady Bunbury, she doesn't have any."

She wrinkled her nose. "That's because Lady Bunbury is corrupt. Her awards are often given out to her family members or daughters of friends. Perhaps Mr. Livingstone is a close friend to Lord Bunbury. I don't deny that Amelia has a lot of the qualities Lady Bunbury looks for, but she has faults too."

"Such as?"

"For one thing, she's vain. She believes it when someone tells her she's the most beautiful girl in the room, or the most accomplished. She thinks the rest of us are beneath her. She looks down on everyone, even the daughters of peers. She also likes to get her own way. She told everyone she'd win all three of Lady Bunbury's awards and look what happened! I think her father has given in to her on everything over the years and that's made her selfish. Very few girls my age like her, although our mothers think she's perfect."

"Have you heard any rumors that question her virtue?"

"Such as?"

I shrugged.

"No, nothing. Why?" She clasped my forearm. "What do you know, Cleo? Tell me or I'll simply die for wondering."

"Then get your affairs in order because I can't tell you. I don't know. Jonathon heard something about her at the Bunburys' ball, but I wouldn't let him tell me."

She clicked her tongue and rolled her eyes. "And you call yourself a detective."

I laughed. She and Harry were not usually so alike in their thinking.

She indicated the piece of paper with the address. "Go and ask Jonathon now. He's with Floyd in Floyd's suite."

Instead of returning to her bedroom to finish getting ready, she followed me to Floyd's room. When he opened the door upon my knock, I was glad to see he looked well. There were no signs of a late night spent drinking, but his smile wasn't as bright as usual, and worry pinched the corners of his eyes.

I asked to see Jonathon. Floyd's mouth opened. "Really? Well, well."

Flossy squeezed past him and thumped his arm for good measure. "We're here to gossip, not flirt. Cleo isn't interested in Jonathon. Sorry, Jonathon," she added as she entered the sitting room where he sat sprawled on the sofa. "But Cleo thinks of you like another cousin."

"Lucky me," he drawled.

She pushed his feet off the sofa and sat just as he stood to greet me. "What was the gossip you heard about Amelia Livingstone?" she said.

Jonathon and Floyd exchanged glances.

"Just tell us," Flossy growled. "Honestly, why hide it now?"

Floyd thrust his chin at Jonathon, a universal masculine gesture that indicated he should speak.

I sat and Jonathon resumed his seat too. "There was a rumor circulating amongst the men at the ball that Amelia Livingstone had..." He cleared his throat. "That she was not...what everyone thought her to be." He fidgeted with his tie and avoided our gazes.

"Not what?" Flossy prompted. "What are you talking about?"

Jonathon's face turned red. Floyd dug his hand through his hair and looked away.

I decided to let them off the hook. "He means she was not a virgin."

Flossy's lips formed a perfect O. "But...how do you know?"

65

Jonathon put up his hands. "It was just a rumor. It may not be true."

"Who did you hear it from?" I asked.

"Lenny DeVille. He claims he heard it straight from the horse's mouth."

Flossy gasped. "Amelia spread the rumor herself?"

"No, idiot," Floyd muttered. "The fellow did." He exchanged another, darker, glance with Jonathon.

"Who was it?" I asked, although I suspected I already knew.

Flossy grabbed her brother's hand and shook it violently. "Tell us!"

"It was the man who was murdered. Ambrose McDonald."

CHAPTER 6

*E*ven though I expected it, it was still shocking to hear that a debutante barely out of the school room had been involved with an older gentleman. A gentleman who most likely was also involved with Reggie Smith, the man accused of murdering him.

Our list of motives was growing, as was our list of suspects. If McDonald had been with Amelia Livingstone, as well as Mr. Smith, one of them may have learned about the other and killed out of jealousy. Or Amelia's father could have killed him to keep him quiet. Her reputation, and therefore her value on the marriage market, depended on her remaining a virgin.

If Mr. Livingstone was the murderer, he'd failed to stop the rumor. It was already circulating on the night of the ball amongst the gentlemen. In that case, perhaps *revenge* for gossiping was the motive for the murder.

"Is that why you called him a cad?" I asked Jonathon.

"He's notorious," Jonathon said. "Everyone knows he's had a string of lovers, one after the other."

"Often at the same time," Floyd added.

Flossy's eyes widened and her face turned pink.

"His lovers weren't always women, were they?" I asked.

Both Jonathon and Floyd shook their heads. Flossy's blush deepened.

I rose, as did Jonathon. I thought he was simply being gentlemanly and not sitting while a woman in the room stood, but he followed me to the door, as did Floyd.

"Why do you want to know all this, Cleo?" Floyd asked.

"No reason."

He stood in front of the door. "You're investigating the murder, aren't you?"

Jonathon snorted a laugh, but when no one joined in, he pulled a face. "Why would you do that?"

I remained silent. Both men looked at me with disappointment.

Floyd dragged his hand through his hair. "If my father finds out—"

"He won't, because you won't tell him," I said.

Flossy joined us and poked her finger into her brother's chest. "Don't you dare say a word to him."

"I won't, but…why, Cleo? I understand why you wanted to solve the dressmaker's murder. You found the body and the culprit was on the loose. But this time, the police have someone in custody. There's no point to you digging about further."

"Detective Inspector Hobart has confided to us that he's not convinced the man they have is the murderer."

"'Us?'" Floyd frowned as he connected the dots. He knew D.I. Hobart was Harry's father, and that Harry had become a private detective. It was a short leap from there to the correct conclusion. "You're working with Armitage, aren't you? Bloody hell, Cleo. You know Father loathes him."

I bristled. "This doesn't concern you, Floyd. Please step aside."

"It does concern me. You're my cousin." He moved out of the way, however, and opened the door for me. "Just be careful. That's all I ask."

The concern in his voice dampened my temper. I clasped his arm. "I will be. And Harry is very capable in a situation."

"I know. That's why I'm not more concerned for your safety."

We exchanged small smiles, an understanding passing between us. He would keep silent unless he absolutely had to intervene.

Jonathon couldn't understand that, however. "You're just going to let her do it?"

"I can't stop her," Floyd said. "If I forbid her, she'll do it anyway. I'd rather know what she's up to than be shut out altogether."

Jonathon shook his head, disappointed. "What if someone finds out?"

"My father isn't observant enough. He's too caught up in his own affairs here to notice what one of us is doing." It was spoken with a healthy dose of bitterness.

I squeezed his arm in sympathy.

Jonathon barreled on. "I don't mean Sir Ronald. What if someone else finds out? Her reputation will be ruined."

I huffed out a humorless laugh. "It's not as though investigating is on par with Amelia's relationship with Mr. McDonald."

"Isn't it? For God's sake, Cleo! Have a care for your good name!" For someone who wasn't my relative, he was getting quite worked up about it.

"I fail to see how my business has anything to do with you, Jonathon."

His gaze leveled with mine. The anger in it quickly faded, replaced with a warmth that I'd hoped never to see. "Do you?"

Flossy's jaw dropped. Floyd looked down at the floor, pretending he hadn't heard.

I thought that was the wisest course of action at this juncture. I walked away and headed for the stairs.

Jonathon followed. He fell into step beside me. "Of course, you should do what you want."

"I will."

"I only wanted to point out that it's beneath you, Cleo."

"That's a matter of opinion."

"Yes! Everyone's opinion! The niece of Sir Ronald Bainbridge can't go about with a strange man poking her nose into other people's business."

I picked up my pace, determined to leave him behind. Unfortunately, he kept up. "Harry isn't a strange man, and if you don't think justice is a noble cause, then I have nothing to say to you, Jonathon. Clearly you and I have different ethics as well as opinions."

"You're twisting my words."

I bit my tongue to stop myself saying more.

"Cleo, I don't want to argue with you. In case you haven't realized, I care about you."

"Don't, Jonathon. Don't say anything more."

His pace slowed. I thought I'd finally got through to him and he'd leave me alone, but he caught up to me again between the first and ground floors. "Are you doing this because of that Armitage fellow? I know all the girls like him, but he's beneath you too, if I may be so blunt."

I stopped and rounded on him. There was only so much I could ignore. "What I do has nothing to do with him, or with any man. I investigate because I want to. And if you want to be blunt then I will be blunt, too. Harry is one of the finest men I know. He's not beneath anyone. Now, please stop following me if you value our acquaintance."

I must have finally got through to him because he let me go. I was still seething, however, when I collected Harry from Mr. Hobart's office. He was there alone.

He eyed me as though I were a steaming volcano on the verge of eruption. "Did you learn something about Amelia Livingstone that upset you?"

"I learned that Floyd keeps poor company." I showed him the piece of paper with the Livingstones' address written in Flossy's childlike handwriting. "I also learned that Amelia and McDonald were lovers."

He stared at me. I'd genuinely shocked him. "That would be enormously damaging if it got out."

"It did get out. The men were talking about it on the night of the ball. I think McDonald himself is the source of the rumor."

Harry shook his head. "There's a name for men like him but I won't repeat it in front of you."

"Cad?"

"Much worse." He tucked the piece of paper into his pocket. "If you still insist on coming with me to question Livingstone, we'd better go now."

It was nice not to be lectured. Like Floyd, he knew he couldn't tell me what to do, that ordering me about would only damage our friendship. I'd meant what I said to Jonathon—Harry really was one of the best men I knew.

"Thank you, Harry."

He'd been about to open the door, but now paused. His gaze connected with mine. "What for?"

"For being good company." I tore my gaze away from his before its warmth melted my resolve not to kiss him again.

* * *

I WAS QUITE sure Mr. Livingstone took no notice of me at the ball, but I lowered my hat brim and my head just in case. I'd been concerned that Amelia might be present, but she was either out or in her room. If the rumor about her and Ambrose McDonald was circulating, then she might be laying low until it all blew over.

If it ever did. Nasty rumors had a habit of leaving stains.

Mr. Livingstone wasn't a very remarkable man. If he hadn't been so exuberant with his applause when his daughter won Lady Bunbury's awards, I wouldn't have noticed him that night at all. Everything about him was average, from his height to his looks. He greeted us with bland indifference in his study, as if he were doing us a favor by granting us an audience.

But from the way he leaned forward when Harry introduced himself as a private detective, I suspected he was worried. That worry only deepened when Harry asked him why he'd wanted to meet Ambrose McDonald in the library thirty minutes before the body was discovered.

Mr. Livingstone clearly hadn't expected to be asked that. He made all sorts of noises through his mouth and nose in protest before he finally got the words out. "I didn't!"

"The servant who delivered the note to Mr. McDonald has come forward and identified you," Harry said.

"He's mistaken! He mistook me for someone else!" He surged to his feet and strode to the door. He opened it and shouted for the butler.

"Denying it only makes you appear guilty."

"I don't care how it looks. You are not the police. You are no one, and I don't have to speak to you. Get out!"

"We know you wanted to meet him to stop him spreading rumors about your daughter."

Mr. Livingstone's jowls trembled with indignation. "How dare you!"

"But you were too late. He'd already started spreading the gossip."

Mr. Livingstone blinked in surprise. He'd expected Harry to say something else. Were we wrong? Was Mr. Livingstone not too late? Had he expected us to accuse him of the murder because he was, in fact, the murderer and he thought we knew it?

The butler arrived along with a footman. "See that these two are escorted from the premises," Mr. Livingstone snapped.

We turned to go.

"Wait! What did you say your names are?"

"Harry Armitage." Harry held out a card, but Mr. Livingstone refused to take it. Harry left it on the bookshelf next to the door.

"And your companion?"

"My associate."

Mr. Livingstone narrowed his gaze at me. "Do I know you?"

I lowered my head further and shook it. Harry ushered me out of the office ahead of him.

Outside, on the pavement, we quickly walked away.

When we reached the corner, I glanced over my shoulder to see the butler finally closing the door. He'd watched to make sure we didn't double back and descend to the basement service area to speak to the servants. "I know you want to say 'I told you so', so go ahead and get it out of the way. You told me he'd recognize me."

Harry shortened his strides to match mine. "I'd never say that."

"But you're thinking it."

"But I'd never say it."

We fell into silence as we headed back to his office, both of us lost in thought. It was a companionable silence, the sort that good friends who were comfortable with one another fell into. Neither of us felt compelled to fill it. It was a relief to know that our relationship was back to where it had been before the kiss.

I hoped it would remain that way now.

We decided to part before we reached his office. "Shall we meet tomorrow morning?" I asked.

"Of course."

"I'll bring the coffee."

"Best bring some ideas with you, too, because I haven't got a clue where to turn next."

Neither had I. Hopefully one of us would have some inspiration overnight, or we'd be twiddling our thumbs tomorrow.

* * *

I'D INSTRUCTED Philip the night porter to ask Floyd to wake me when he returned to the hotel after a night out, no matter what the time. Even so, I muttered curses under my breath as I padded across the floor in bare feet to open the door on my cousin's knock. He leaned against the doorframe. Or, rather, the doorframe propped him up. For a moment I thought he was asleep on his feet, but then I noticed his eyes were open a crack.

I yawned and signaled him to enter.

He stumbled inside, bumping me as he passed. "Is this about Jonathon?"

"No."

"I know he can be a bit of a prick sometimes, but he means well. He just doesn't see the world like you."

I followed him into the sitting room, turning on the light as I went. Floyd flung his arm over his eyes then stumbled into the sofa. I directed him to sit down and was about to sit next to him when he lay down instead, taking up the entire length of the sofa.

"He's a snob and a bore," I said.

"That's not his fault. He has had everything given to him

73

on a silver platter his entire life. It's no wonder he's insufferable most of the time."

"It's not an excuse." I almost pointed out that he'd had
everything given to him too and he wasn't insufferable. Floyd
would disagree with me. He claimed his father withheld
more than he gave. The thing was, Floyd received more than
most. He just couldn't see it because he never got the one
thing he truly wanted—his father's respect.

"Do I need to have a word with him and tell him you're
not interested?" he asked.

"I already have."

He opened his eyes only to wince and close them again.
"He'll be hurt. Believe it or not, he does have feelings."

"He'll bounce back when he realizes how incompatible we
are. In time, he'll thank me for not encouraging him. He's
more suited to a girl with a similar background to his own.
Someone born to this." I indicated the beautiful room
around us.

But Floyd wasn't listening. He pinched the bridge of his
nose, his mouth set in a grim line. He sighed heavily.

I perched on the edge of the sofa beside him. "Floyd,
what's wrong?"

"I'm tired."

"I know it's more than that. Something's upset you. Philip
said you came home in a bit of a state last night."

"Bloody Philip. He shouldn't have."

"He was worried about you. You should be thankful you
have people here who care about you."

His chin wobbled and he pressed his fingers into his
eyelids. I gave him a moment to compose himself then gently
prompted him. "I've done something that I regret," he finally
admitted.

"Have you killed someone?"

"No! Bloody hell, Cleo."

"At least I got you looking at me. So you haven't killed
anyone. Let's see... Have you slept with someone you
shouldn't have?"

That produced a faint smile. "Probably, but that's a reason
to be happy, not...this."

"Have you stolen something?"

"No."

"Slighted someone's good name?"

"Definitely not."

"Lost a fortune?"

He made a whimpering sound.

"Try not to worry. I know it's hard to do, but you must cut your losses and not attempt to win it all back. You can begin again, but you *must* stop gambling. I'll help you break the habit, if you like."

He shook his head over and over. "It's not that. It's not simply that I lost a fortune. It's that I lost a fortune I don't have to someone with a reputation for breaking the knees of people who owe him."

"I see. And you're rather attached to your knees."

"This isn't a joke, Cleo. He's a very dangerous man."

"Tell me what I can do."

He sighed. "Nothing. I made my bed, now I must lie in it."

"I admire you for taking responsibility for your predicament." I was sincere. Not many young men born into privilege would admit their failings. "But don't be stubborn and push away help when it's offered to you."

"Thank you, but you can't help me. No one can. Anyway, I've found a way to pay him back. I have a meeting lined up with a financier who'll loan me what I need."

"At what interest? How long will you have to pay the financier back? And what will happen if you don't?"

He frowned. "How do you know about interest and loan terms?"

"I know all sorts of things because I read. You ought to try it some time. It might give you an idea for how to extricate yourself from your predicament without getting bogged down in another one."

He closed his eyes and groaned. "Your lectures are worse than Jonathon's. At least he softens the blow with brandy."

Jonathon and I agreed on something, for once.

I knew I wouldn't get back to sleep now. It was five-thirty, and while there was always someone on duty in the kitchen to take orders for room service, it was too early for my breakfast. Besides, I liked to have it with Harmony, and she usually came between seven and eight. I ordered a pot of tea instead.

I didn't ask for an extra cup. If Floyd felt like some, he'd have to use mine.

It turned out not to matter. He'd fallen asleep by the time I turned away from the speaking tube, and was snoring softly with his mouth open.

He wasn't awake by the time Harmony arrived at seven-thirty with our breakfast tray. I asked her to return later.

She tried to peer past me. "Have you got a man in there?"

"Just Floyd. He needed to talk when he came home." I took the tray from her. "Why did you jump to the conclusion that I had a gentleman friend in here?"

She shrugged. "Well, you say you're not getting married…"

"That doesn't mean I want to be someone's mistress."

"Why not? Seems like a good solution to me."

I opened my mouth to disagree then shut it again. I couldn't think of a winning argument.

I carried the tray into the sitting room and set it down on the table. I poured coffee from the pot into one of the two cups and sipped gratefully. I certainly needed strong coffee today after my early start.

Floyd stirred on the sofa. A moment later, he yawned and opened his eyes. "That's good of you to order breakfast for me."

"It's not for you."

"Who is it for?"

Too late, I realized my error. I couldn't tell him I ate breakfast every morning with one of the maids. For one thing, he might suggest docking her wages to pay for it. At the very worst, he could order me to stop our ritual. While he wasn't as miserly as his father, he wouldn't like one of the maids to take advantage. At his core, he was still the hotel owner's son.

"Me," I said. "I like a big breakfast."

"With two cups?"

"They sent one extra in error."

"And the two plates and two sets of cutlery?"

I scrambled to think of something to explain it, but my mind went blank.

"Whoever it's for, just make sure he's gone before my father sees."

"He? Floyd!"

He snatched a piece of toast off the plate and chewed around his smug smile. "I can't help it if I jumped to the first conclusion to enter my head. You said you're not intending to marry, so…"

The rotten sod. He'd overheard Harmony and decided to tease me. At least he'd proved me wrong and was joking about it, not threatening to dismiss her. I wanted to be sure, however.

"You won't tell your father, will you? Or Mrs. Short? Harmony's a hard worker and much liked among the other staff."

"It's all right, Cleo, I won't get her into trouble. But if I know one thing, it's to be careful who you choose as friends. Don't let her take advantage of your good nature."

Considering his friend was Jonathon, I didn't think Floyd was well qualified to give out advice about friendship. On the other hand, Jonathon had told me some time ago that he was worried about Floyd, so as a friend, perhaps he was worthy.

I let Floyd think his advice was noted then watched him leave. A moment later, there was another knock on my door and Harmony entered without waiting for me. She left her housemaid's cart in the corridor and carried a jar labeled furniture polish in one hand and a cloth in the other. She smelled faintly of vinegar and lemon juice.

"Did he eat my breakfast?" she asked as she set the jar and cloth on the desk and sat at the table with me.

I passed her a cup of coffee. "Only a piece of toast."

"You look tired."

"Floyd woke me at five-thirty."

"As early as that? You must be exhausted, poor thing. However will you cope?"

I eyed her over my coffee cup. "There's no need to make your point with sarcasm. Unlike you, I go to bed late. Now, eat up while I tell you everything Harry and I learned yesterday."

By the time I finished, she'd eaten a sausage and boiled egg and was eyeing off the bacon. She seemed more interested in the food than the case, and her long pause had me wondering if she'd even been listening. After selecting a rasher, she nibbled it thoughtfully.

"Well?" I prompted.

"The bacon's crispy today."

"I meant about the investigation. Do you have any thoughts?"

"I think society is cruel to girls who just want to have a little fun before they settle down. Why are men encouraged to have mistresses before they marry but women are considered ruined if they so much as kiss a boy?"

"A fair point, but do you have any comments that aren't about the society we live in?"

"Not particularly. It does seem as though gossip is the motive for the murder, either to stop it before it spreads, or in revenge for gossip already in circulation." She finished the bacon and wiped her fingers on the napkin. "So what's next?"

"That's the problem. We don't know. We've questioned all the staff and some of the key guests who were there that night. Unfortunately we can't speak to the arrested man, Reggie Smith, but we have spoken to those who knew him, including his neighbor, co-workers and landlady." I shrugged. "We've reached the end of all our leads and need another."

We finished our coffees in silence as we pondered that dilemma. I still hadn't thought of anything by the time I gathered the empty plates and cups, but Harmony had a curious look on her face. From past experience, I knew it meant she'd thought of something.

"Don't keep me in suspense," I told her. "What have you come up with?"

"It's time to look at this from another angle. You say you've questioned everyone you can and investigated suspects. But have you investigated the victim?"

"What do you mean?"

"Look at his life and background, that sort of thing. Go to his home and see if you can find personal correspondence or something that may incriminate someone. The key to solving this may be with Ambrose McDonald, not the suspects and witnesses."

I assumed the police had already been through his home, but that didn't mean it wasn't worth doing again. They weren't looking for clues that pointed at someone other than Reggie Smith, but we were. "I like the way you think. Thank you, Harmony."

She took the tray from me. "Glad to be of service. Now open that jar and help me polish the furniture. I'm behind schedule."

* * *

I DEPOSITED a cup of coffee from Luigi's café on Harry's desk and took my seat opposite him with the other cup. "I have a plan for our next step," I announced.

"Before you say anything, I have something to tell you." He sipped his coffee. The pause caused my nerves to stretch as I waited for him to go on. "I spoke to my father about McDonald's flat. Apparently it's large and has a studio attached."

"Then it's likely we were right. Reggie Smith visited Mr. McDonald and painted in his studio. According to Mr. Underwood, Reggie's neighbor, it also means the men were lovers. Perhaps they were together on the night of the first art theft, giving Reggie an alibi." I shrugged. "The point is, we now have a motive for murder—jealousy. If Reggie discovered his lover was with Amelia Livingstone, he could have confronted Ambrose McDonald on the night of the ball in the library and killed him."

"It's not looking good for Smith," Harry agreed. "I told my father everything we learned last night over dinner. He's keen to press on to find definitive evidence, but he concedes that Scotland Yard may indeed have their man."

"If he wants us to find evidence, can he give us the key to Mr. McDonald's flat? We should look over it ourselves."

"I asked him the same thing and he said he can't. It's too much of a risk for him. He can't be seen going against his superiors' orders and continuing with the investigation." The hint of his rueful smile intrigued me.

I put my cup down and leaned forward. "But you're thinking about getting inside anyway, aren't you?"

His smile grew. "Are you up for a little illegal activity?"

"I can't think of anything better to do today."

"Then finish your coffee and let's go."

* * *

AMBROSE MCDONALD'S flat was housed in the handsome red-brick Park Mansions, located in Kensington. The exclusive address hinted at the luxury inside, but I was still surprised to see a porter as well as a lift. We waited for the porter to be occupied with a resident before slipping past him and taking the stairs. We didn't want either the porter or lift operator to be witnesses to our presence.

The carpeted corridor softened our footsteps as we hurried to the fourth door on the fifth floor. I kept watch as Harry went to work with his lock picks. He had the door open in moments and we snuck inside.

I released a relieved breath as I closed the door, then followed Harry across the marble floor to the sitting room.

The flat was spacious with high ceilings, a sitting room that took up more space than my entire suite at the hotel, and a grand bathroom with all the modern conveniences. A brass speaking tube in the wall of the sitting room must be connected to a service area in the basement. The furniture was stylishly modern and well made. A chandelier hung from a ceiling rose in the sitting room, its crystal drops glinting despite the low light. Dead flowers in a vase on the central table marred the otherwise elegant room. Mr. McDonald had good taste. Expensive, too.

Ambrose McDonald wasn't short of money.

"I found the studio," Harry said from the doorway to one of the rooms off the hallway.

He searched through it while I entered the study. It was more masculine than the other rooms, with the mahogany bookshelves and desk. I switched on the electric lamp and searched through the contents on top of the desk then looked through the drawers. I pulled out a book of accounts and sat to inspect it.

Mr. McDonald kept thorough records, noting down his income and expenditures in neat columns. The problem was, the income sources were a jumble of letters that didn't make words. They might refer to paintings he'd sold. The amounts were in plain numerals, however, so it was easy for me to see that he had a steady income and was very well off.

I took the book into the main bedroom where I found Harry looking through the bedside table drawers. "Found anything?"

"He liked books on Ancient Rome." He indicated the weighty tome titled THE LIFE AND CAREER OF JULIUS CAESAR on the table. "There are photographs in the sitting room of an elderly couple, probably his parents who died a few years ago, my father told me. I haven't found any correspondence of a personal nature."

"What about in the studio?"

"Just a few paintings, one of them unfinished. There are portraits of a man I assume is McDonald. I never saw him, but the subject looks like his picture in the newspapers." He nodded at the ledger I held. "What did you find?"

I sat on the bed and showed him. "It's his income and expenses. What do you think these entries mean?"

He studied them for a few moments, then shook his head. "It could be a code representing a person or a service he rendered."

"A painting he sold?"

"It's possible. We need the key to break the code."

We split up again and I searched the study for a reference to the code's key. Finding nothing, I tried the sitting room, but again, found nothing. He had some fine things on display, several of them artefacts that appeared to have been dug up from archaeological sites. He certainly liked his Ancient Roman objects. Aside from incomplete pottery pieces, there were tiles and coins, clay tablets and even some jewelry. Some would have cost a fortune, but from the look of the amounts in the account book, he could afford them.

I sat on one of the armchairs and listened to Harry quietly moving about in another room. If I were Ambrose McDonald, where would I keep my code's key? Did I even need one? Perhaps I kept it in my head. Perhaps the letters referred to the initials of something. They couldn't be the initials of *someone*. There were too many. The interesting thing about them was that they were repeated. There were four unique ones, but each of those four appeared several times, at regular intervals and with the same amounts listed next to them. There was only one reason for a pattern like that.

I closed the book with a thud and leapt up. I found Harry looking under the mattress in a spare bedroom. "They're names of people he's blackmailing," I said. "People are paying him to keep quiet."

$\mathcal{I}$ pointed out the four unique entries in the ledger, each one repeated on a monthly basis. "There are four people, all paying differing amounts on different days."

Harry peered over my shoulder. His chest brushed my back, but if our close proximity affected him as much as it did me, he showed no sign. He was entirely preoccupied with the book. "If those codes refer to names, it won't be too difficult to crack it. We already know he might be blackmailing the Bunburys."

"But not the Livingstones," I added. "Mr. Livingstone refused to pay, and that's why Amelia's secret got out—her father refused to pay the blackmail Mr. McDonald demanded for his silence." I pointed to the letter E in each of the codes. It appeared twice in several entries. "E is the most commonly used letter in the English language."

Harry shook his head. "But not necessarily in codes."

"Could it represent the letter B? B for Bunbury?" I counted on my fingers as I spelled the name in my head. "It appears in the right spot and there are seven letters in those entries and seven in Bunbury."

Harry clicked his fingers then strode out of the room. I followed and joined him at the dressing table in the main bedroom. He picked up the book on Caesar and flipped to the index then found the page he wanted. He tapped his finger on a table with two columns, each listing the letters of the alphabet. In the left-hand column, the letters were ordered from A to Z. In the right-hand column, the alphabet started at D and ended at C, but was otherwise in order.

"I thought so," he said. "It's the Caesar Cipher."

"The what?"

"It's the code Julius Caesar developed while on military campaign. If his plans fell into enemy hands, they couldn't be deciphered without knowing the cipher. It's very simple. All you do is shift the alphabet along by a particular number of places, like in this table. The number of shifted places is called the key. Caesar usually used three, as it does here as well as in McDonald's ledger. So the letter A is now represented by the letter D, B is represented by E, C is represented by F and so on until the letter Z is represented by C. All one needs to know to break it is what numerical key is used."

We moved to the study and used the table in the Caesar book to decipher Mr. McDonald's code. We were right. The Bunburys were listed a few times, as were the Quornes. But we'd been wrong about the Livingstones. Their name was in the ledger, although there was no payment against it for over a month. The fourth name took me by complete surprise. Indeed, I deciphered it a second time to be sure.

"I don't believe it," I said. "Could it be him? Could it be Mr. Chapman, the Mayfair's steward?" The deciphered entry just read "Chapman" with no first name, no place of work, or other identifying information.

Harry rubbed a hand across his jaw. "I suppose... If McDonald knew something scandalous about him, Chapman wouldn't want Sir Ronald to hear about it. Your uncle isn't the most understanding or forgiving man when it comes to his employees' indiscretions."

"Indeed. But Mr. Chapman's not wealthy like the others. Was it worth blackmailing him?"

Harry pointed to the amounts next to the name. "He was paying considerably less. McDonald adjusted the amount accordingly." He frowned. "I can't believe I'm going to say this, but Chapman is now a suspect for the murder."

"No. He couldn't have done it. He was just leaving the hotel for the night when we arrived home after the ball. He'd been in the dining room all evening." It was something of a relief to exclude him. The last thing I wanted to do was suspect one of the staff, even if I didn't like him much.

Even so, we ought to question him about his relationship with McDonald. But if I questioned him, he would tell my uncle in retaliation. Harry, on the other hand, could speak to him in his capacity of private detective.

"You have to interrogate him," I said.

Harry shook his head. "Neither of us will. Not until we know for certain we have the right Chapman. The name isn't uncommon."

"Very well. We'll leave him until it becomes absolutely necessary to confront him. In the meantime, I'll ask Harmony and some of the staff to watch him."

"He'll get suspicious."

"They can be very discreet."

"I don't think it's a good idea. If he was being black-mailed, he clearly had something to hide. What if it's some-thing that could ruin his professional relationship with the staff? He's their manager and deserves their respect."

I hadn't expected him to object so strongly, but perhaps I should have. Like Mr. Chapman, he'd been in a position of authority in the hotel. He expected the staff to treat him as a manager deserved. If something damaged that respect, he would lose his authority.

It was why Harry couldn't remain in the hotel after my uncle fired him. Harry thought he'd lose the respect of the staff when they learned why he'd been dismissed. He was wrong, but it was how he felt and far be it from me to tell him how he ought to feel.

I set aside Chapman and concentrated on the other three names. "His reason for blackmailing the Bunburys and Livingstones is obvious," I said. "But I wonder if he was blackmailing the Quornes because their stolen painting was also a fake, or because there's something in Lady Quorne's background she's trying to hide."

"Let's find out." He indicated the book. "Bring that with you."

"You want to steal evidence?"

"Borrow, not steal."

He seemed thoughtful as we headed for the door, but it

was me who asked him to wait while I checked one more thing before we left. I hadn't seen the paintings, and something had occurred to me. Was Reggie Smith good enough to have painted the fake Grandjean? While I was no art critic, I should be able to tell if he was an amateur or not.

I entered the room used as a studio and stopped in front of a large painting on an easel. It was almost complete, except for the hands and feet. Whoever did it, must have trouble with those parts of the body. From what I knew of the male nude, the rest looked...lifelike. The artist had also captured Mr. McDonald's confident air and Mona Lisa smirk to perfection.

"Learn anything?" Harry's voice was quiet, but it still made me jump.

"No! I mean, yes." I cleared my throat and dared to sneak a peek at him out of the corner of my eye. He sported a roguish half-smile.

I turned away to study the two other portraits of Mr. McDonald leaning against the wall, both completed. One was signed R. Smith, the other was unsigned. I indicated the signed one. "This and the unfinished one on the easel are done by the same person."

Harry turned to study the unfinished painting. "How do you know? The unfinished one is unsigned."

"You can tell by how thickly the paint has been layered on both, as well as the hands and feet. They're poorly rendered in the completed piece and left until the end in the unfinished one. Mr. Smith clearly struggles with them."

Harry indicated the third painting, the other finished one leaning against the wall. "Who is that by?"

"It's also unsigned, but it's different to the other two. For one thing, the artist knows how to do hands and feet."

Neither of us knew what any of it meant, except it was confirmation that Reggie Smith used this studio and liked painting nudes of Mr. McDonald.

We left the flat and I thought we would take the stairs down to the ground floor foyer where we'd have to hide until the porter's back was turned. But Harry had other ideas. He thought it was time to reveal ourselves and get answers about our victim from those who would have seen visitors coming and going.

He started by questioning the lift operator as we slowly descended, but the fellow remained tight lipped. He was a good employee, loyal to the residents who perhaps tipped him well to keep their secrets.

After we exited the lift and before we reached the porter, I suggested to Harry that we ought to use an incentive too. Telling the staff we worked for the police was getting us nowhere.

He handed the porter some money after we introduced ourselves. "What can you tell us about the people who visited Ambrose McDonald on the fifth floor?"

The porter tucked the coins into his jacket pocket and glanced around. "I can tell you a lot of folks came and went from Mr. McDonald's flat."

"Do you know why they visited him?"

"Considering most didn't want to be seen, I reckon they were his intimate friends. But I saw them." He tapped the side of his nose. "I see everything."

"Can you describe those who came regularly?"

"Let's see. There was a man who visited a lot up until a week or so ago. Slim, handsome fellow, young, brown hair..."

It could have been Reggie Smith, but the description was too vague to be certain.

"There were other men, too. One in particular hated it when I greeted him. He always tried to hide his face. He was also slim, but shorter than the other fellow. Brown hair, nice clothes. I reckon he was a toff on account of the way he spoke, like he was better than me." He shrugged. "The women were the same. All hoity-toity, the lot of 'em."

"Old or young?" I asked.

"Older than Mr. McDonald. I remember one who used to come regularly. She was rude to me. I complained to Mr. McDonald once, and he said not to feel inferior. All her jewels were fakes, and she and her husband were struggling to pay their bills. It surprised me that she was married. It was the first I heard that Mr. McDonald's female companions had husbands. Maybe the men had wives, too." He shrugged.

That had to be Lady Bunbury. Had she come to pay the

blackmail money, or were they intimate friends, as the porter suggested? "You say she was a regular visitor," I said. "How regular?"

"She came at least once a week for a while, but she stopped coming about three or four months ago."

"What about a young lady?" Harry asked.

"There was only one. She came during the day, holding Mr. McDonald's hand and giggling. Real pretty, she was. Fine figure, too, and dressed real nice. He never brought girls that young here, so I thought it odd. Maybe he was ready to settle down, I thought. But if he was considering marriage, he wouldn't have brought her back here without a chaperone. Not a girl of quality like her."

Indeed he wouldn't. I was quite sure the girl in question was Amelia Livingstone. She must have snuck away from her chaperone and met up with Mr. McDonald before he brought her here. It sounded as though she was a willing participant in the dalliance. As Harmony had said, Amelia was probably just having some fun.

The consequences of her actions hadn't occurred to her at the time. She knew them now. She must have been devastated when he started spreading the rumor about her losing her virginity, conveniently leaving his own name out of it. Not only had she had her heart broken, but she'd been betrayed by a man she trusted.

Harry handed the porter a business card. "If you think of something else, let me know."

The porter flicked the card with his finger. "I'll pass this on to the coachman. He ferries the residents around, and often drove Mr. McDonald about. He's not here now, but I reckon he'll have something to add." He jangled the coins in his pocket.

Harry nodded in understanding. "We'll make it worth his time if his information is good."

Our next steps were now clear. We had to take a closer look at the main suspects again, although instead of Mr. Livingstone, I wanted to speak to Amelia. I also didn't think we'd get answers from Lord or Lady Bunbury, but their servants might be amenable if we paid them. And we also needed to learn about Lady Quorne's past to know whether she was being blackmailed about that or about her painting being a fake, too.

I expected Harry to be thinking the same as me, but as we exited the building into the sunshine, he suggested we visit Reggie Smith's boarding house again.

"If we're going to be asking witnesses to describe who they saw with McDonald, we need to show them a photograph of our suspects. The only one we can easily obtain is Smith's. There was one in his room."

* * *

THE LANDLADY of the boarding house greeted us like old friends and escorted us up to Reggie Smith's room. The door to Mr. Underwood's room opened a crack before closing again. I thought he wouldn't bother to come out, but he emerged a moment later, buttoning up his waistcoat with ink-stained hands. He wore no jacket and his hair hadn't been combed. Perhaps he'd just got out of bed. It would seem he didn't work, or if he did, not during the day. He'd been here both days we'd visited.

"Everything all right?" he asked.

"Yes," I said as the landlady unlocked the door.

Harry ducked inside, but I remained to talk to Mr. Underwood.

"Any word on how Mr. Smith's case is progressing?" he asked. "Do the police have enough evidence to release him?"

"Not yet."

"Are you getting closer?"

"I'm afraid I can't tell you."

"Of course." He sighed. "I do hope the real killer is found soon and he can return home."

"Aye," the landlady said as she relocked the door after Harry emerged. "I can't hold his room for him forever."

* * *

HOW DOES one ask a married lady whether she had an affair with a man who was murdered in her house? Lady Bunbury would slam the door in our faces if we confronted her. The

C.J. ARCHER

servants would also refuse to talk, unless we paid them, and both Harry and I were short on funds. With no one paying us for our time, we would never recoup our losses.

We considered attempting to get the servants to trust us enough to talk, but that level of trust couldn't be gained in one afternoon. Two of the servants already knew us, anyway. We'd met Lord Bunbury's valet and one of the maids during our last investigation. We'd also learned that the Bunburys kept very few servants. Financial constraints had meant they'd let most go.

I proposed we sneak inside via the back door when both Lord and Lady Bunbury were out and search her rooms. The house was large enough that we should be able to avoid being seen by the handful of servants. To my surprise, Harry agreed.

"If we're caught, we'll come clean about the investigation," he said.

"And risk them telling Lord Bunbury who will then inform his contacts at Scotland Yard? If you're recognized, your father will be dismissed on the spot. I'll go in alone."

"No."

"It's easier for me."

He rounded on me and grasped my arms, turning me to face him. "Don't try telling me that you're too unremarkable to be remembered. We've been through this and you forced me to say that you're the most memorable woman of my acquaintance. Do I have to say it again?"

I wasn't going to let his earnestness dissuade me. I tilted my head to the side to regard him. "Do cease with the flattery, Harry. It doesn't work on me."

His fingers sprang apart, releasing me. He straightened, swallowed.

I tried not to smile at the bewildered look on his face. "Besides, that's not what I was going to say. I meant I'm smaller and can more easily find a place to hide if I hear someone approach."

That heated gaze swept my length, lingered a moment on my chest, then returned to my face. He arched a brow. "I'd like to see you try to slide under a bed wearing that."

A corset and new day dress weren't the most ideal clothes

90

for sleuthing, but I didn't want to go home and change. I'd wager Harry would take on the role of sleuth in my stead, and that wasn't ideal.

He eyed the townhouse on the opposite side of the street and sighed. "Very well, I'll allow it."

"I wasn't asking for your permission."

"But I'll be inside, too. I'll gather the servants together to keep them out of your way and ask some general questions about the ball and the murder. I'll tell them I'm working for the police, tying up loose ends to ensure Reggie Smith's conviction. As long as they think I'm going along with the status quo rather than looking for evidence that exonerates Smith, they won't see a need to tell Lord Bunbury. Mr. Holbeck should remember me from last time."

"The young maid certainly will," I said wryly.

He chose to ignore me, as he often did when I mentioned his looks. He was rather sensitive about being handsome. That didn't stop him from using it to his advantage from time to time. "Now all we have to do is find out if Lord and Lady Bunbury are home and wait for them both to leave."

Patience wasn't one of my virtues, so I paid a boy kicking a stick along the pavement a penny to find out whether Lord and Lady Bunbury were in. He made inquiries at the basement door and returned a moment later.

"His lordship has gone out and her ladyship is leaving shortly," he said.

"How did you get the servants to tell you that?" Harry asked.

"I told them I was sent by their neighbor who wanted to speak to them about the noise."

"What noise?"

"Well, I don't know, do I? I'm just the messenger." He picked up his stick and walked off.

Harry chuckled. "Either we've just been given a lesson in interrogation techniques, or we're going to regret sending a boy to do an adult's task."

Ten minutes later, the Bunbury coach rounded the corner and stopped outside their house. The butler held the front door open for Lady Bunbury then he hurried past her to reach the coach first and held its door open.

"Shouldn't a footman do that?" I asked. "They still have one."

"They may have let him go, too."

The coach drove off and the butler returned to the house. I headed behind the row of townhouses to the mews. I found the rear door to the Bunburys' and, with a fortifying breath, opened it. As we suspected, it wasn't locked. Servants came and went between the house and the mews, so it wouldn't be locked until nighttime.

I slipped inside and listened. Harry's deep voice came from within. He'd managed to get through the front door, but had he gathered all the servants? There weren't many, but if just one was roaming the house, I could be discovered.

I had to trust him.

I tip-toed up the service stairs and emerged onto the fourth floor where I assumed the main bedrooms were located. I found Lord Bunbury's first. After giving it a cursory search, I headed down the corridor and entered the next bedroom. It was Lady Bunbury's with a dressing room attached.

I quickly searched all of the most obvious places, including the dressing table and writing desk, but didn't expect to find evidence of an affair with another man. Lady Bunbury wasn't a fool. She wouldn't leave correspondence or photographs lying around for her servants to find. There'd been no signs that she shared her husband's bed, and no sign of masculine things in her rooms, so I assumed their marital relations were non-existent. That didn't mean he would accept her affair, but it might mean she wasn't too concerned if he discovered she was with Mr. McDonald. The servants were another matter. They gossiped.

There were no loose floorboards or tiles around the fire-place. Nothing was stored under the bed except a few dusty cobwebs that the overworked maid had left. I checked inside coat pockets and empty boots, and between the folded clothes on the cupboard shelves, even though Lady Bunbury's maid would most likely see something hidden there. I checked the pillows and ran my hand along the mattress, both above and under it, looking for split seams or lumps. Finding nothing, I remade the bed to the maid's standard, which was as good as Harmony's bedmaking skills.

I stood in the middle of the room and blew out a frustrated breath. Where would I hide something I didn't want the servants to find? They touched almost everything. They didn't lift heavy furniture, but I couldn't imagine Lady Bunbury choosing a hiding place beneath something she couldn't easily move.

Then it struck me. A single painting hung on the wall. It showed a lake bathed in moonlight, the shadows on its banks looming like creatures from a nightmare. It wasn't something I'd want hanging near my bed as I tried to sleep. On closer inspection, it wasn't particularly well done. The strokes were lazy, the colors too dark. It was probably a copy of an original.

It was neither large nor heavy and I easily took it off the wall. I turned it around and my heart leapt. Tucked into the frame at the back were three letters.

I removed them and quickly read each one. I could have kissed the painting when I finished. It was just the evidence we'd hoped to find. All of the letters were from Mr. McDonald. Addressed to "My dearest Ruth", they were signed, "Your loving Ambrose". They were filled with tender words of love and sprinkled with references to their trysts. They were brief but sensual. Luckily, I was alone and could blush in private.

The final letter was dated three months earlier—a mere two days before the first payment from the Bunburys' as recorded in Ambrose McDonald's coded blackmail register.

I was about to return the letters to the painting when I noticed something else common to all of them. They were crumpled. Although I'd found them folded in half, they all showed signs of having been scrunched up then flattened out. Had Lady Bunbury thrown them away after he blackmailed her, only to have second thoughts?

I returned the painting to the wall. How ironic that she'd hidden the private love letters from the man who'd known her paintings were fakes behind one of those fake paintings.

The door handle rattled as it turned.

My heart scudded to a halt. Someone was coming.

CHAPTER 8

$\mathcal{I}$ acted without thinking and flattened myself to the floor, sliding under the bed. My corset made the action uncomfortable and awkward. The walrus I'd once seen lumbering about on land in its enclosure at the zoo had more grace. If Harry had been here, he would have laughed. The dust and cobwebs under the bed added to my discomfort. I tried not to breathe too deeply.

A woman wearing sensible black shoes entered the room. She went through to the dressing room and emerged a few moments later. She left the bedroom, closing the door behind her. I waited a few minutes, listening, but the house fell quiet.

I dragged myself out from under the bed by my forearms and dusted myself off as best as I could before slipping out of the room. I tip-toed along the corridor and down the stairs to the service area. Harry was still speaking, but I couldn't hear what he said.

I exited the house via the mews and waited for him on Upper Brooke Street, a few doors down from the Bunburys' townhouse. He joined me five minutes later.

"I see you managed to hide," he said with a nod at my dusty skirt. "Sorry I couldn't keep Lady Bunbury's maid away. Her mistress returned and requested a shawl."

"It's all right. I found something, as it happens."

"I can tell by the look on your face. Don't keep me in suspense any longer."

I told him about the letters behind the painting. "I don't think it's a coincidence that his last letter was sent two days before the blackmail started. The question is, did he genuinely care for her when he wrote those letters? Did he only blackmail her after *she* ended their relationship?"

"Without knowing her final response to him, we can't be sure, but I doubt there was any deep regard on his part. According to multiple sources, he had other lovers. My guess is, he was reeling her in with the letters then decided to end it when he had enough evidence to blackmail her."

"Evidence in the form of her letters to him," I added. But it didn't quite make sense. "Where are those letters? We looked through his flat and found nothing. If he needed them to blackmail her, he would have kept them."

"Perhaps he hid them. One thing I'm sure is, the feelings were one-sided. He didn't care for her. He was using her."

It gave her a compelling motive for murder.

"There's something else," Harry said. "When I showed the servants the photograph of Reggie Smith, the butler said he'd seen him give Lady Bunbury a menacing look. She never spoke to him. She had no need to interact with the temporary staff from Searcys that night. But from the look he gave her, there was genuine loathing from Smith towards her."

"He was jealous. He must have known about her relationship with Ambrose McDonald."

Harry agreed. "Is that what prompted him to take their painting off the library wall? It seems an unlikely thing to do, but..." He shrugged. "Also, the young parlor maid knows something, I'm sure of it. I asked some general questions about the ball and McDonald in particular, and she seemed nervous."

"Perhaps you made her nervous."

"I wasn't threatening. I was overly nice."

"That's what I mean. Your niceness coupled with your good looks turned her into a nervous girl. She was probably captivated by you."

It was meant to tease, but Harry suddenly stopped. He turned on me, his gaze fierce. He opened his mouth to speak, then shook his head and walked off, his strides purposeful.

I picked up my skirts and raced after him. "Did I say something to upset you?"

"It's difficult to put into words without…crossing a line I don't want to cross."

The line must be the one I'd also set for myself—the kiss couldn't happen again. We had to avoid repeating whatever had led up to it. The problem was, there were a multitude of things that had led up to it, some of them tangible, others not.

If I was prepared to cross that line again, I would mention his many other virtues to reassure him it wasn't just his good looks that attracted me. But I wasn't prepared to cross that line again.

Nor was he.

He lengthened his strides even more.

"Harry, slow down. I've already had to dive under a bed today. I don't want to run a race too."

His place slowed. "Dive?" He looked at me sideways, one brow arched and a small smile on his face. I was relieved to see it. "I wish I'd been there."

"It was the most elegant dive. It put the swimmers in the Hippodrome's aquatic show to shame."

He laughed softly. "Come on. Let's see what we can learn about Lady Quorne's secret past."

* * *

THE QUORNES HAD MORE servants than the Bunburys, so sneaking in and searching bedrooms was too much of a risk. We also decided not to question them about Lady Quorne's past. If they were loyal, they might report us to their mistress or master. We didn't want them knowing they were suspects yet.

Harry had an idea, however, and he suggested he approach the service door alone.

"Why can't I come?"

"You're not dressed appropriately." He left before I could ask what he meant.

I didn't have to wait long for his return and an explanation.

"I'll tell you on the way," he said, indicating we should walk.

"Where are we going?"

"The Mayfair." He told me that he'd spoken to the butler. "I pretended to be the butler for a duchess who wished to remain anonymous. She'd tasked me with approaching Lady Quorne's lady's maid about taking up a new position with her. She'd admired the maid's hairstyling. I told the butler I wasn't comfortable poaching another household's staff without first finding out about the relationship between mistress and lady's maid. If they'd worked together a long time, I didn't want to put a wedge between them."

"Very diplomatic. What did he say?"

"He said the maid had been with Lady Quorne from the start of her marriage and that they were very close."

"If they've been together that long, she might know her mistress's background. But she won't say anything to us. She'll be too loyal."

Harry gave me a smug look. "I was about to leave when the butler called me back. He put on a display of reluctance, but I got the impression he saw me as his opportunity to get rid of the lady's maid."

Some wealthy households had conflicts between servants, particularly when it came to the hierarchy. A lady's maid had the ear of the mistress, giving her enormous power. As the most senior servant, the butler might resent that power.

"He told me Lady Quorne's maid has a fondness for drinking at the Fox and Hound when her mistress is out of an evening." He pointed down a narrow street opposite. "Apparently Lady Quorne is out tonight."

"Let me guess. We're going to buy the maid a few drinks to loosen her tongue. No, wait—*you* are going to buy her drinks." I stopped myself from saying that he'd have better luck than me at charming answers out of a middle-aged woman. I didn't want him to get cross with me again.

"I was going to suggest we both question her. You can be the duchess's current maid, helping to find a replacement before you leave service altogether and take a position as a shop assistant. Are you free tonight?"

"Oh. Uh, yes. So why are you escorting me back to the hotel?"

"Because Lady Quorne won't be going out for hours, and you need to change into something plainer." He eyed my dusty skirt. "And cleaner."

He had a point. I would put on one of the old dresses that I'd brought to London from Cambridge. They were the sort of thing a sensible lady's maid would wear.

"The butler told me in passing that most of the staff had been there a while," he said. "But the only one who'd worked for the Quornes longer than the lady's maid was the coachman. We should speak to him too. He might know where his master met his wife."

Although few masters confided in their coachmen, they tended to know all sorts of interesting things about their employers simply because they drove them everywhere. It was entirely possible he knew where Lord Quorne had met his future wife.

"If it's all right with you," he went on, "I'll speak to the coachman on my own after we finish with the lady's maid."

"He may be out most of the night, driving his employers back and forth. I have a better idea. One where we don't have to wait for him."

"I don't understand how we can avoid it."

"*We* don't have to wait for him. Someone else can."

* * *

WE AGREED on a time for Harry to meet me outside the hotel, then I waved him off. Before entering, I told Frank I wanted to speak to him and the others in the staff parlor, if he was available.

He asked the other doorman to take charge then followed me inside. We sent Goliath to find Victor and Harmony and I informed Peter I wanted to see him too. It was mid-afternoon, when a slight lull gave the staff time to enjoy a few minutes in the parlor with a cup of tea before they either stopped for the day or became busy again. Most new guests had checked in, and ladies had not yet arrived for afternoon tea. We wouldn't have long to ourselves, however.

Harmony was already in the parlor, reading a book. She set it aside and made tea while we waited for Goliath and Victor. I wasn't sure if Victor's shift would allow him to join us, but he did, dressed in chef's whites with his knife belt slung around his waist like a cowboy's gun holster. He nodded a greeting to all of us, including Harmony. His fingers brushed hers as she handed him the cup and saucer.

She glanced at me and, seeing that I'd noticed, snatched her hand back.

Victor smiled to himself as he sipped his tea.

"I need help tonight," I began. "Lord and Lady Quorne's coachman may have some information about his mistress's past, but I'm tied up elsewhere and can't question him."

"Where are you going?" Harmony asked. "I'm not scheduled to do your hair."

"Harry Armitage and I are going to question another suspect at a pub."

She gave me a disapproving look. I wasn't sure if it was because of Harry or the pub.

Peter cleared his throat. "If I can be so bold as to say something, Miss Fox?"

"Go ahead."

"You shouldn't be seen at a pub with a man, even if it's just Mr. Armitage. It's not right."

I sighed. "You too, Peter?"

He put up his hands in surrender. "I apologize if I overstepped."

"So you should," Frank snapped. "Who are you to say what Miss Fox can and can't do? She doesn't have to answer to you."

Peter's nostrils flared. "You disagree with me?"

Frank lifted his teacup to his lips. "That's not the point. The point is, you're management now. You shouldn't even be in here. You should be having tea with Mr. Hobart in his office."

"I'm still one of you. Nothing's changed."

Frank grunted and looked as though he'd protest again, but Goliath kicked his ankle. Frank winced.

"Don't bicker in front of Miss Fox." Goliath turned to me. "I'll speak to the coachman. Tell me where to find him and what you need to know. You can rely on me to be subtle."

Frank snorted. "You're as subtle as a giraffe wearing heeled boots."

"I'll go too," Victor said.

"I'm afraid I can't," Peter said. "It's my grandparents' wedding anniversary tonight. Fifty years they've been married. Can you imagine it?"

"A life sentence," Frank muttered. "Miss Fox, will we be paid for our time if we speak to the coachman?"

"Unfortunately, we don't have a client for this case," I said. "I can't pay you."

"I'm not available, anyway."

Goliath and Peter rolled their eyes.

* * *

I WENT in search of Flossy and found her moping in her suite. She brightened when I suggested we have afternoon tea together. "But first, tell me what's wrong," I said. "You look unhappy."

"It should be a fun time with all the social events starting," she said. "But Mother hasn't scheduled any daytime engagements for us."

"Perhaps you should set up your own."

"I suppose I am old enough now. Last year, I went wherever she went, but I'm nineteen now. I can do what I want."

"Within reason, Flossy."

She wasn't listening, however. She took a seat at her desk and made notes. I peered over her shoulder. She was listing the names of her friends. "I'm going to invite them all to afternoon tea," she said without looking up. "Not today, of course. It's too late. You and I can enjoy today together."

"Why not ask Amelia Livingstone?"

Her pen stilled. She looked up at me. "Is that a joke?"

"She could probably do with a friend."

"But not us."

"Why not us? If the rumors about her virtue have spread beyond the gentlemen, I imagine the invitations are drying up. She'll be upset, and without a mother to help navigate these stormy waters, she might drown."

"You feel sorry for her," she said flatly.

"She made a mistake, Flossy. I won't condemn her forever for desiring a man who turned out to be a scoundrel. It's not fair."

She placed the pen in the stand, leaving behind a dark ink blot on the paper. "It's not that, Cleo. If the rumor about her has indeed reached the ears of the ladies in the highest levels of society, I will be ostracized too if I associate with her."

"They'll overlook it. Everyone knows you're a virtuous young woman. They'll see that you're just being kind to her."

She jerked her head in the direction of her parents' suite on the other side of the wall. "Mother and Father would be appalled. They don't want me to do anything that might jeopardize my reputation. They'd forbid me from seeing her."

She was probably right. It wasn't fair of me to put pressure on her.

She caught my hand. "You're not going to see her, are you? Tell me you won't, Cleo. If my parents found out—"

"They won't unless you tell them." I patted her shoulder. "Now, I'm going to get ready for afternoon tea. I'm hungry."

She sighed. "So many secrets. It's exhausting keeping track of them all."

* * *

AFTERNOON TEA with Flossy was pleasant, but I had another motive. We watched ladies come and go. Some of the regular guests greeted us. Some joined us for a few minutes and asked after Aunt Lilian. I smiled and joined in, but all the while, I watched Mr. Chapman.

There were few men in the sitting room during afternoon tea. A small number accompanied their wives or mothers, but aside from the waiters, Mr. Chapman was sometimes the only one. He usually relished in his role of steward. He could be very charming. The middle-aged women in particular liked him. Like Mr. Hobart, he kept notes about the more important guests so that when he made conversation, he got the names of children and pets correct, and was able to ask how their renovations were proceeding, or how their elderly mother was feeling.

He wasn't so agreeable today, however. He didn't engage in conversation or smile, and he had the waiters show the important guests to their tables, instead of doing it himself. He remained near the door and studied the reservations book, or seemed to.

"Does Mr. Chapman seem pre-occupied to you?" I asked Flossy once we were alone.

"A little. I don't know. I don't take much notice of him. He's always just...there."

As if he knew we were talking about him, he suddenly looked in our direction.

Flossy and I dipped our heads and pretended to be deep in conversation.

She soon forgot about Mr. Chapman as other guests came and went from our table, but I watched him from time to time. He was certainly distracted, and not his usual self. Something was bothering him.

* * *

LADY QUORNE'S maid's favorite tipple was beer, which she claimed she drank "for her health". She sat with three men in a corner of the Hound and Fox but agreed to move to another table when we offered to buy her a beer.

It was a respectable pub, located in the well-to-do area of London. Its patrons were the servants of the big houses, however, not their owners. Most were men, but there were maids too. Women weren't a common sight at pubs, and I thought I'd feel conspicuous, but no one paid me any notice when I entered with Harry.

"What's this about then, eh?" Miss Docherty asked in a northern accent. She was a similar age to her mistress, but with a sagging jawline and the ruddy complexion of a heavy drinker. Her gaze wandered over us both then drifted off to a point in the distance. She was already three sheets to the wind and it was only ten-thirty.

"We work for a duchess," Harry said. "She wants to employ you, if you're free to leave Lady Quorne."

Miss Docherty's attention snapped back. "Course I'm free. I can do as I please." She put down her beer mug with a *thunk* on the table. "How did you find me?"

"The butler informed us you'd be here."

She snorted. "Course he did." She called the butler a few colorful names under her breath then took a long sip of beer.

While I didn't like to judge a book by its cover, my first impression of Miss Docherty was that she wasn't the sort of woman who'd be employed as a lady's maid. The ones I'd met were proper, sometimes more proper than their mistresses. Miss Docherty was uncouth. She wiped her mouth with the back of her hand and sat hunched over. She looked as though she'd spent hardly any time fixing her hair, a skill that many lady's maids prided themselves on. Perhaps she took more care with her mistress's than her own.

Miss Docherty's accent gave me hope that she'd known Lady Quorne before her marriage. Lord Quorne had met his future wife up north, so perhaps the women had known each other then. They might even have been close. That would explain why Lady Quorne continued to employ a woman who didn't seem suited to the position of lady's maid.

"Where are you from originally?" I asked.

"Manchester."

"Did you begin working for Lady Quorne up there or down here?"

She'd been about to take another sip but paused with the mug halfway to her mouth. Her lips tilted into a sardonic smile. "You ain't the first to ask me that."

"Oh?"

"I got into trouble from his lordship for speaking to him."

"Him? Who asked you about Lady Quorne?"

She sucked on her teeth as she thought. "I can't remember his name. But he's been in the papers recently on account of getting murdered."

CHAPTER 9

*H*arry sat back, as if Miss Docherty's words had pushed him. "Murdered? That's...unfortunate."

She shrugged a shoulder and downed more of her beer. "Sorry you wasted your time, but I can't tell you anything or his lordship will whip me. He threatened to, after the last time, but didn't do it. Her ladyship wouldn't let him, on account of us being close, once."

"In Manchester," I said, not posing it as a question.

She didn't correct me.

"You've known her a long time. You knew her from before she married."

Again, she didn't say anything.

I took that as a sign to go on. "If you're so close, you won't want to leave her for another position."

"I'd leave her for a duchess. I don't owe Lady Q anything. We stopped being friends when she stopped being nice to me. Marrying Lord Q turned her into a right snob. They warned me. Everyone warned me that Mary—Lady Q—wouldn't be the same once she became a lady, but I thought we had a bond. I thought we'd have great adventures here in London together, and that she'd tell me everything. But we drifted apart. She treated me like just another one of her servants, like we hadn't shared everything, once."

"You've been loyal to her, haven't you?" I pressed.

She downed the rest of her beer and held the empty mug

out to Harry, requesting another. "Ain't no one can fault my loyalty."

"You've kept her secrets, even about her past."

She lowered the mug. "You know about that?"

"Of course. The duchess employed private detectives to investigate you before sending us here. She can't hire just anyone for the role of lady's maid. She wants someone she can trust. Someone with integrity. Since investigating you inevitably meant investigating your mistress, she learned about Lady Quorne's past."

"I've been loyal," she said again, this time without meeting our gazes. No doubt she was recalling how she'd told Ambrose McDonald her mistress's secrets. He must have paid her handsomely.

"You're an honest woman," Harry went on. "Honest and hard working. That's the kind the duchess wants to employ. It's a shame your past is tainted too, because of what Lady Quorne did before her marriage."

His leap of faith got results. She was eager to defend her good name. "Me? Why should I get tainted because *she* was a dancer? I never trod the boards. I never met the gentlemen backstage for a bit of—" She winked at Harry. "That weren't me. That was all her. You tell your mistress that I'm respectable."

Harry signaled to the waitress for another mug of beer. "We'll make sure she knows."

Miss Docherty looked relieved. "It ain't fair that I should be tarred with the same brush because I was her friend. Then again, nothing in life is fair, is it? I was a shop girl, back then. I worked hard but I was satisfied. Mary was never satisfied. She worked in the shop too and danced at night. She liked the attention. She was real pretty, so she got a lot of it." She sighed. "You wouldn't understand. You're a man. But the pretty girls, well, they get whatever they want. They can marry lords. The rest of us are considered lucky if we get to serve them."

Harry signaled it was time to leave, but I had one last question. "Earlier, you mentioned the man who was murdered. I read about it. Nasty business. Was your mistress at the Bunburys' ball that night?"

"Aye."

"How did she seem when she arrived home? Was she upset about the murder? Did she seem worried?"

Miss Docherty lifted her shoulder in a shrug. "I don't remember."

"It wasn't that long ago."

"I said I don't remember!" She snatched the beer mug out of the waitress's hand and took a long drink.

Harry and I thanked her and left.

Outside, I flipped up the collar of my coat against the biting wind. "I don't think she connected McDonald's murder to her mistress's blackmail."

Harry agreed. "I don't think she's in any state to make that connection. I also don't think she was in any state to notice Lady Quorne's behavior upon her return home on the night of the ball."

It did seem likely that Miss Docherty would have been drunk if she spent the evening at the Hound and Fox. "They may have been friends in their youth, but Lady Quorne is very generous to keep her on. Most ladies would dismiss a maid who gets drunk in the local pub most evenings."

"Perhaps Miss Docherty was blackmailing Lady Quorne, too. Perhaps she'd agreed to keep quiet about her mistress's past if her ladyship continued to employ her."

He made a very good point. It explained much about their arrangement. "If Lady Quorne was being blackmailed by two separate people over the same thing, wouldn't she kill both to stop the truth leaking out? Why just kill Mr. McDonald?"

"Perhaps she couldn't pay McDonald what he demanded. In Miss Docherty's case, it's easy enough to continue to employ her. But if McDonald wanted money, perhaps Lady Quorne couldn't obtain it."

He was full of good points this evening. "So what do we do now?" I asked.

"Now I escort you back to the hotel and hope no one notices your arrival."

"You mean aside from the night porter?"

"I'll have a word with Philip."

"I can have a word with him myself, Harry. Philip is

discreet when it comes to keeping quiet about the family's comings and goings."

Harry's stride slowed before we turned the corner. "Floyd's different."

"Because he's a man?"

"Yes," he said matter-of-factly. "And I know you know that's the reason, so don't pretend otherwise with me."

I glanced at his firm jaw and uncompromising gaze as it swept the vicinity. Was he looking out for potential trouble? Or avoiding looking at me?

"I never pretend with you, Harry," I said quietly. "I can't. You always see right through me."

That got his attention. His pace slowed even more. "I've hurt your feelings."

"No. Not at all. You didn't make the world one that gives men more freedom than women. In fact, you do your best to accommodate me, even going so far as to accompany me to a pub when you know it would anger my uncle if he found out."

"He's already angry with me. What's one more reason?" He nudged me with his elbow. "Besides, if it's a choice between having you or Sir Ronald angry with me, I'll choose him every time. His temper may be worse than yours, but I don't like it when you give me the cold shoulder."

I nudged him back and laughed, but I couldn't think of anything to say. We were edging dangerously close to territory I no longer wanted to enter, and it was better to remain silent than tell him I didn't like him being angry with me either.

* * *

HARMONY LISTENED to my account of our meeting with Miss Docherty as she ate breakfast, and agreed with the theory that the maid may be blackmailing her mistress so that she could keep her job.

"It's what I'd do," she said.

"You wouldn't need to blackmail her. You're not a drunk, and Lady Quorne would be fortunate to have you."

"I'd ask for money to stay quiet, not employment."

C.J. ARCHER

I lowered my coffee cup to look at her. "You would?"

"Of course. Women like Lady Quorne use their beauty to raise themselves up, so why can't people like Miss Docherty and me use whatever means is at our disposal to do the same?"

"Are you saying you'd blackmail me if I had money to give? You know a lot of secrets about me that you could tell my uncle."

She picked up a fork and stabbed a sausage with it. "I wouldn't do that to you. We're friends. *They* stopped being friends because Lady Quorne turned into a snob. You'll never be a snob, Cleo. Besides, you're not going to marry anyone, let alone a rich man. You and I will always be friends."

"It seems I can't afford not to be friends with you."

She laughed. She understood my sense of humor.

"I have a report for you, too." According to Harmony, the Quornes' coachman was no help. He was too loyal to be bribed and too smart to be tricked. He didn't give up any of his master or mistress's movements. "If he drove them to a secret rendezvous with McDonald, he's not telling," she finished.

"Is that what Goliath reported to you this morning?" I teased, knowing full well she hadn't heard it from the porter.

"Not Goliath."

"Victor?"

She nodded without looking up from her plate.

"When did you see him?" I asked oh-so-innocently. "He wouldn't have been out of bed when you left this morning. His shift doesn't start for a few hours."

"I couldn't sleep without knowing what the coachman said so I waited up for him last night."

I smiled into my cup.

"You can wipe that smile off your face, Cleo. I needed answers, that's all. There's nothing going on between us."

"Yet," I muttered.

* * *

AMELIA LIVINGSTONE WAS at home to receive my personally delivered invitation to afternoon tea. I wasn't entirely sure

108

she'd receive me at first. The butler looked surprised when I asked for her. He disappeared for a few moments then returned and led me through to the drawing room where Miss Livingstone sat like a serene statue on the sofa. She looked as she had on the night of the ball, as if she were a queen surveying everything around her. It was as if nothing were amiss. It wasn't obvious from looking at this beautiful, elegant yet cool young woman that half of society was whispering about her liaison with Mr. McDonald and the other half was listening.

I admired her courage. I'd be cool with a newcomer under such circumstances too.

"I'm sorry we didn't have an opportunity to meet on the night of the Bunburys' ball," I began. "My cousin, Florence, told me all about you."

"That's sweet of her, but I'm afraid I don't know your cousin. Is she a Miss Fox, too?"

"No. She's a Bainbridge." At her blank look, I added, "The daughter of Sir Ronald Bainbridge, owner of the Mayfair Hotel."

"I've heard of the hotel." Her disinterest would have dented Flossy's pride. It was fortunate she didn't come with me. "Where do you fit into the family?"

"My mother and Lady Bainbridge were sisters."

"And your father?"

"A scholar at Cambridge University."

The pleasant smile tightened.

Well. I might as well get to the point. She hadn't offered me tea and didn't look as though she was about to. "My cousin and I would like to invite you to afternoon tea at the hotel."

"I'm afraid I can't today."

"Tomorrow, then. Or the next day."

"I'm very busy. That's the problem with being crowned debutante of the year by Lady Bunbury. All the invitations roll in and I simply can't refuse. I've been invited to so many things. It's very tiring." Her benign smile never wavered.

There was serenity and composure, and then there was rudeness. Flossy was right. Miss Livingstone was a dreadful snob, even now when her world was crumbling and she could do with a friend.

My sympathy for her was disappearing along with my window of opportunity.

"Thank you for your understanding, Miss Fox. The butler will see you out." She reached for the bell pull beside the sofa.

I had to act quickly, so I blurted out the first thing that came into my head. "You haven't been invited anywhere else, have you?"

Her fingers curled into a fist before touching the velvet cord. "I beg your pardon?"

Her butler had given me the clue when he'd reacted with shock to my presence. She'd received no callers since the Bunburys' ball. I was her first. "You're hiding away in here after the rumor about your liaison with Ambrose McDonald got out."

Her lips pursed until they turned white. It was the first crack in her composure. "You should leave."

"I don't care what you did with him. That's no one's business but your own. But Mr. McDonald has been murdered, and you must admit it looks bad for you considering the rumors, and the fact he had other lovers."

I watched her carefully for a reaction, but there was none. She must have known about the others. But had she learned about them on the night of the ball, or more recently? "A man has been arrested. It was nothing to do with me."

"McDonald used you," I pressed. "He enticed you to his flat in order to blackmail your father. Your father refused to pay, so McDonald spread the rumor. You must see how it looks, Miss Livingstone."

"How it *looks*?" she bit off, her voice a harsh rasp. "Miss Fox, when it comes to how things look, I am somewhat of an expert. Now hear this. No one has *used* me. No one would dare. I have many friends—*important* friends—and I will be in their favor again soon. It is simply a matter of waiting for them to realize their parties are dull without the most beautiful, most accomplished, and most graceful debutante present. *I* am what attracts the gentlemen, and without gentlemen, no lady of quality will bother to attend."

Her arrogance left me quite speechless. There was no sign

of her serenity anymore. It had completely disappeared, overwhelmed by her true nature. For a young lady of her stature to express such superciliousness was rare. They were taught from an early age to be demure and deferential. She must be under a great deal of pressure indeed for that façade to shatter.

Or she thought so little of me that she didn't care about my opinion.

I rose. "Thank you for enlightening me."

Her eyes narrowed to slits. "What do you mean by that?"

"Nothing." I headed for the door, not waiting for the butler to collect me.

Miss Livingstone dogged my footsteps. "He got what he deserved."

I stopped and turned to her.

She must have realized how her angry words sounded because she quickly added, "But I didn't kill him."

The butler appeared and waited for Miss Livingstone's directive. But she said nothing. She simply stared at me, waiting for me to acknowledge her statement of innocence.

"Good day, Miss Livingstone. I wish you well."

I followed the butler downstairs to the front door. Before leaving, I glanced back up the staircase to see Miss Livingstone watching me. Perhaps it was the angle, but she looked composed again, except for the slight sneer as she peered down at me.

* * *

"I'VE NEVER MET anyone like her," I told Harry as I sat opposite him at his desk. "I wanted to feel sorry for her, but she doesn't deserve my pity."

"Perhaps she doesn't want it and being rude is her way of rejecting it."

That was one way of looking at it, but I suspected Amelia Livingstone was merely a spoiled, immature girl who wanted everyone to admire and desire her. If the lack of invitations over the past few days hadn't changed her opinion of herself and her place in society, then a few more days would. Once it sank in that those invitations were never going to arrive again, she might learn some lessons in humility.

"All of this speculation is well and good, but we have no firm evidence," I said. "We have more motives and suspects, but no way of narrowing them down."

"What I'm about to tell you might help." Harry settled back in his chair and crossed his arms. He'd hung up his jacket and wore only his waistcoat over his shirt with the sleeves rolled up. He looked relaxed, except for the serious expression. "The coachman from Park Mansions called on me this morning. He claimed he frequently took McDonald to a club called the Portland in Marylebone." He arched his brows, waiting for me to say something.

I shrugged. "I don't know it. Is there something special about that club?"

"It's where gentlemen go."

"Like White's or Brooks'?"

His lips twitched. "No. It's where gentlemen go to find other gentlemen for...intimacy."

"There's a club for that? I thought it was illegal."

My innocence amused him. "It is, but the clubs are careful and have plans in place if the police show up. The Portland is very discreet. I sometimes directed hotel guests new to London there when I worked at the Mayfair, if they hinted they were after that sort of place."

That was a conversation I had difficulty imagining.

"We know Mr. McDonald earned his income through blackmail," I said. "What if he blackmailed someone he saw at the Portland? Someone with a lot to lose if his proclivities were discovered."

Harry nodded, clearly having already come to the same conclusion. He was holding something back from me, however.

"Go on," I urged.

He looked as though he was about to protest, but I tilted my head to the side and arched my brows, daring him to try. I wasn't going to believe him if he denied it. He sighed. "I didn't know whether to tell you this. It might change your opinion of him. But I see I can't hide anything from you."

"I'm glad you realize it."

He cleared his throat and fidgeted with his tie. I waited quietly until he was ready, and he finally rewarded me. "You know someone who attends the Portland, as it happens."

"I think I can guess, but go on."

"Chapman, the Mayfair's steward."

It came as no surprise. I'd suspected he preferred men over women ever since meeting him. "That explains why his name appeared in Mr. McDonald's coded blackmail register and why he seemed very interested in the newspaper articles about the murder."

"It does."

"I know we agreed to leave him out of this, but I don't think we can anymore. Perhaps now is the time to confront him. He could offer us some insights into who Mr. McDonald associated with at the club."

Harry shook his head. "He'd be horrified if you knew that about him. He'd also worry that you'd inform Sir Ronald. Your uncle would dismiss him on the spot if he found out. I think it's best if you don't let on."

I wasn't so sure. Mr. Chapman was in a unique position to tell us about Ambrose McDonald's close associates. I doubted he would confide in me, however. I suspected he'd prefer to see me fail. At least we could be certain he wasn't involved in the murder. He'd been on duty in the hotel dining room at the time.

"The coachman told me something else," Harry said. "As he got into the carriage to be driven to the ball, McDonald told the driver he was looking forward to the night because he expected it to be lucrative."

"He planned on blackmailing someone that night," I said, thinking out loud. "He met them in the library, told them what he knew and that he wanted money to remain quiet, and that person killed him." My gaze connected with Harry's. "We've been looking at this the wrong way. We've been looking for someone he was already blackmailing. But what if the killer was someone he was *about* to blackmail? Someone he saw at the Portland Club perhaps."

"It could have been anyone. There were a lot of people at that ball with a lot to lose. But I think you're right. I think it was someone he was about to blackmail."

I nodded, my mind racing. The pieces were starting to fall into place. "The maid from Searcys...I saw him give her something, most likely money. I think she's the key to this. I think she passed on information which he paid for then took to the library where he used it to try to blackmail someone."

Harry agreed. "Only that someone didn't want to be blackmailed. I think you're right. I think that maid from Searcys is the key. The fact that she gave a false name to her employer means she is up to no good. It may not be the first time she passed information to McDonald."

The problem was, how could we find her?

I suggested calling in at the Searcys office and telling the staff member that we needed to speak to the maid again and that we were to be informed when she returned asking for more work. Harry agreed and said he'd do it that afternoon.

"Speaking of maids," he went on. "I want to talk to the Bunburys' girl again. While you were searching Lady Bunbury's room, I got the distinct impression the maid knew something but held back. She may be concerned about speaking out in front of her superiors." He suggested he talk to her again in private considering she already knew him, but I had a better idea.

We agreed to go our separate ways, with him setting off to the Searcys office and me returning to the hotel.

I found Mrs. Short the housekeeper going over accounts in the office she now shared with Mr. Chapman. The steward wasn't there, thankfully. I didn't want him influencing Mrs. Short's decision.

She gave me her full attention as I informed her of a young girl of my acquaintance in need of work. "Her employer is in financial difficulty and the maid feels she needs to find something more secure. Could you take her on here?"

"We are always in need of hard-working, good girls. But I cannot hire her without a reference from her housekeeper. Not even on your word, Miss Fox."

"I wouldn't expect you to, Mrs. Short."

I agreed to return with the maid that afternoon for an interview. Now I simply had to get her to think it was a good idea too.

* * *

THE YOUNG MAID, Annie, answered the service door upon my knock. I decided to be direct with her and tell her why I'd found her a new position, if she wanted it. At the mention of Harry, she stood a little taller.

"He noticed me?" she said, wide-eyed.

"Mr. Armitage thought you wanted to tell him something when he was here but held back. Out of fear, perhaps, or loyalty."

She glanced over her shoulder into the depths of the house.

"Naturally, we'd very much like to know what you have to say but understand your predicament. If you're willing to talk then you'll have a position at the hotel. You'll need a reference from the housekeeper here, of course." I watched her carefully. "Is that something you'd like? Do you want to leave?"

She nodded quickly and leaned closer to me. She lowered her voice. "I haven't been paid for a month."

"The Mayfair always pays employees on time."

"Wait here, if you please, Miss Fox." She disappeared inside.

I waited for some time. I didn't dare return to street level lest Lady Bunbury see me. Last time she'd seen me outside her house, she'd made life very difficult for my family. I remained downstairs where she hopefully never looked. She didn't pass by, anyway.

Annie finally returned clutching an old carpet bag with broken handles to her chest. She announced with a grin that she was ready. Behind her stood the housekeeper, a thin woman with hollow cheeks who was old enough to be Annie's grandmother.

"You must be Miss Fox," she said, inspecting me from head to toe.

"I am. Thank you for letting Annie go."

She considered her response before answering. "It was the right thing to do. She's a bright, sensible girl and these opportunities don't come along often." She touched Annie's arm and her face softened. "Goodbye, child. Work hard and good things will come to you. I'm sure you will soon make friends amongst the other staff. And remember to say your prayers every night."

"I will, Mrs. Thompson." Annie patted her coat pocket. "And thank you for the reference."

The housekeeper gave her a wobbly smile as she squeezed Annie's arm.

Annie slipped past me and headed up the stairs.

I waited until she was out of earshot before speaking to the housekeeper. "I'll see she's taken care of."

The housekeeper dabbed at the corner of her eye with her apron. "Thank you, Miss Fox."

"One more thing. If her ladyship asks, would you be so good as to not tell her where Annie went. I don't want to cause friction between the Bunburys and Bainbridges."

"She won't ask."

I picked up my skirts and headed up the stairs. I told Annie all about the hotel and what her duties would entail on the walk, then I asked her about the Bunburys' ball and what she'd been holding back from Harry.

Annie's step faltered. She bit her lower lip. "I don't like to speak ill of my betters."

My heart sank. Had this all been for naught?

I needed to remind myself that Annie was better off at the hotel where she would receive a regular wage and could meet people her own age. If she never confided in me, then so be it. Perhaps she just needed time to realize she could trust me. After all, she probably saw me as one of her so-called "betters" and was afraid I'd tattle to Lady Bunbury or to her new employer.

Another idea began to form as we arrived at the staff entrance to the hotel. I entered with Annie and showed her to Mrs. Short's office. I left them then went in search of Harmony. I found her on the second floor, pushing her cart. She'd just finished her duties.

"I have a task for you, Harmony."

I told her what I required of her, and she agreed it was the best way. Annie would trust another maid before she trusted me.

"You have to go now," I urged.

"I can't just abandon my cart here."

"I'll take it. It goes in the basement, doesn't it?" I tried to shoo her away.

She refused to let go of the cart. "You can't! Someone will see."

"They won't say anything. Go on. You need to be the first maid Mrs. Short sees coming out of her office with Annie." Hopefully Mrs. Short would task Harmony with showing Annie to the residence hall and getting her settled.

Harmony reluctantly let go of the cart. "Are you sure you know where to take it?"

"Yes."

"The used sheets and towels have already gone down, so you just have to take the cleaning cloths. Refill any bottles that look low, swap jars of polish if they're nearly finished, and empty that." She pointed to the bulging linen bag full of rubbish attached to the front. "If you hurry, you'll be one of the first and won't bump into many of the other maids. What will you say if someone asks what you're doing?"

"I'm not sure yet. I'll think of something."

She gave me a dubious look then hurried off along the corridor to the service stairs. I followed her with the cart but took the service lift down to the basement. I avoided the kitchen area and headed for the laundry, leaving the cloths with the maids with flushed cheeks and chapped hands. I smiled as I handed the cloths over. They stared back, mouths ajar.

I pushed the cart into the housekeeping storeroom and refilled the bottles of cleaning liquid and replaced the empty jars before storing the cart in the allocated area. Only one other maid had already completed her rounds. When she recovered from her shock at seeing me, she asked if I was lost.

"I know exactly where I am." I smiled and headed out again.

Only to stop upon seeing Mr. Chapman round the corner.

CHAPTER 10

I froze at the same moment Mr. Chapman spotted me. He frowned and strode towards me.

"Are you lost, Miss Fox?"

"I, uh, needed a clean towel. I accidentally dropped the one the maid left in my bathroom and now it's dirty."

His frown deepened. "Then why are you walking away from the storeroom empty handed?"

I glanced over my shoulder. "I am lost, as it happens."

The maid I'd just seen in the storeroom approached with a fresh folded towel. "I couldn't help overhearing." She handed it to me and bobbed a shallow curtsy. "Have a good day, Miss Fox."

"Thank you...?"

"Martha."

"Thank you, Martha." I smiled at her, smiled at Mr. Chapman, and hurried on my way.

"Miss Fox!" he snapped.

I stopped, wincing. I'd almost got away with it. Mr. Chapman was no fool, however. He'd see right through my lie. The question was, what would he do about it? And if he did threaten me, what would I be forced to say to him?

He nodded at the towel in my hands. "Next time, call for service. Fetching towels is a maid's duty." He turned on his heel and marched off.

I mouthed "Thank you" to Martha and left, too.

I knew it would be some time before Harmony could rejoin me so I went in search of Flossy. We spent the afternoon together, going for a walk and then enjoying afternoon tea with some of her friends. Amelia Livingstone's social demise was on everyone's lips, not just within our group but the entire sitting room seemed to hum like a beehive with the whispers about her.

Even though I disliked her, I felt sorry for her. She'd lost so much, and all because she'd followed her heart. When I expressed sympathy for her plight, I was resoundingly admonished for it, however.

"She doesn't deserve your sympathy," said one of Flossy's friends. "She's not a very nice person."

"She thought she was above us all," said another.

"She refused to even acknowledge my existence," added a third. "I'm convinced it's because I'm plain."

Flossy patted her hand. "You have a beautiful character. That's all that matters."

The other two girls agreed somewhat half-heartedly.

Flossy plucked a tart off the tiered platter and studied the glacé cherry on top. "It goes to show that we must be careful who we give our hearts to. The gentleman must be beyond reproach. He must be quality." She turned to me. "Don't you agree, Cleo?"

She gave me an arched look, but I couldn't quite decipher it. Was she making a general statement, or indicating that she suspected something was going on between Harry and me? She couldn't know about the kiss, but she did know that we worked together. Perhaps she'd made an assumption based on the way I spoke about him.

I bestowed the sort of benign smile on her that Amelia Livingstone bestowed on the world. "I do agree, Flossy. He must be the sort of man who doesn't kiss and tell."

She wasn't sure what to make of that. She made sounds of agreement then pushed the entire tart into her mouth.

* * *

I WAS HEADING out with my family to dine with their friends, so I requested Harmony's assistance to arrange my hair before she did Flossy's.

"Well?" I asked when she closed the door to my suite behind her. "Did you have an opportunity to ask Annie?"

"I did."

"What did she say?"

"First, show me what you're wearing tonight."

I padded to my bedroom in bare feet and showed her the green chiffon and white lace evening gown I'd laid out on the bed. "It's one Madame Poitiers' seamstresses made for me."

She assisted me into my underthings and the dress, tying laces and securing fastenings before directing me to sit at the dressing table. "How would you like me to do your hair?"

I waved my hand at our reflections in the mirror. "I don't mind. You decide." I swiveled in the chair to look at her. "Well? What did Annie say?"

She gripped the top of my head like she was unscrewing a jar lid and turned me back to face the mirror. She removed pins from my hair and watched as the long brown tresses cascaded over my shoulders and down my back. "On the night of the ball she overheard an argument between Lady Bunbury and Mr. McDonald."

"What about?"

"She thinks it was a lovers' tiff. Annie heard Lady Bunbury use the word betrayal. She also said she wished she'd never trusted him and brought him into her confidence, and that her husband is furious with her."

She had to be referring to telling Mr. McDonald about their financial difficulty. He'd gained her trust in bed then she'd told him everything. Had he already suspected and therefore targeted her, charming her until she confided in him? Or had their relationship been based on mutual desire and he'd never planned to blackmail her but the opportunity was too good to ignore?

Either way, he really was a cad. "All these confidences betrayed and hearts broken. It's no wonder he was murdered. What did Annie say Mr. McDonald said to Lady Bunbury?"

"She couldn't hear his response, but he showed no emotion. Annie went so far as to say that Mr. McDonald didn't care for her as much as Lady Bunbury cared for him." She brushed out my hair, sighing over how easily the bristles passed through it. Her tight springy curls were the bane of her existence, so she'd once told me after I said I adored them.

"Now we know the source of the gossip for the Bunburys' blackmail," I said. "It's not the temporary maid who worked for Searcys. It was Lady Bunbury herself."

"She should have been more careful who she took into her confidence."

"You sound like Flossy."

She piled half of my hair on top of my head and studied the effect in the reflection. "Your cousin isn't as silly as she seems."

I watched as she secured my hair into place with pins and finished off with combs decorated in soft green enamel of the same shade as the dress and my eyes. My mind was elsewhere, however. I couldn't stop thinking about the case and what this new development meant.

We already knew the Bunburys were being blackmailed by Ambrose McDonald, but now we knew Lady Bunbury was the one who'd told him about their financial woes. He'd betrayed her trust in the cruelest way, just like he'd betrayed Amelia Livingstone. It was no wonder she was angry with him on the night of the ball.

Angry enough to hit him over the head with a candlestick in her own house at her own party?

Harmony stepped back and declared me ready. "I forgot to ask... Did you get stopped taking my cart to the storeroom?"

"Mr. Chapman saw me afterwards. I told him I was there to get a clean towel."

She wrinkled her nose. "Of all the people to find you, it had to be him."

I dearly wanted to discuss what Harry had told me about Mr. Chapman visiting the Portland Club and being blackmailed by the victim, but Harry was right. I couldn't confide in the staff. The steward's secret would have to remain with us.

But that secret connected Mr. Chapman to Mr. McDonald. Despite our reservations over confronting him, I knew deep down it must be done. Their relationship needed to be explored further, and I knew just the way to do it. Unfortunately it meant missing tonight's dinner.

I didn't inform Harmony of my plans. I let her go to Flossy's suite then waited until the last moment to inform my aunt and uncle that I had a headache and didn't feel up to dining out.

My aunt arrived in my suite with her bottle of tonic. She sat on the edge of the bed where I lay fully clothed on top of the covers, a damp cloth over my eyes. "You poor thing, Dear. Here. Try this. It helps."

I refused the tonic and bit back my lecture about its obvious addictive quality. Going by her twitching facial muscles, bright eyes, and busy hands, she was clearly already trapped in its dark embrace. She wouldn't want to hear my warning now. She wanted to enjoy the confidence and energy it gave her.

"I just need to rest tonight," I said. "I think I overdid it at afternoon tea with Flossy's friends."

She patted my arm. "You're not used to all this socializing. It does take a toll. I remember last year, in Florence's first season, she slept through the day a lot of the time. Perhaps you should too. There's no need to wake so early and do whatever it is you do. Where were you today?"

"The museum."

It wouldn't have mattered what I said. She wasn't listening. Her attention had been caught by the things on my dressing table. She moved them around, rearranging jars of creams, bottles of perfumes, and sifting through the box of combs.

"Are you looking for something, Aunt?"

She closed the box and smiled. "Just having a little rummage. Do you need help with your dress?" She returned to the bed and unfastened the back of my gown then kissed my forehead. "Goodnight, Dear. Promise me you won't read. It'll only make the headache worse."

"I promise."

She hurried out of the bedroom with brisk steps and I heard the suite's door close behind her. I breathed a sigh of relief.

I waited until nine when my family were well and truly gone and Mr. Chapman was in the dining room. He prided himself on attention to detail and personal service. Once the first guests arrived, he wouldn't leave until the last ones left.

Dressed in plainer clothes, I headed downstairs to the foyer. The night porter, Phillip, nodded a greeting but didn't question why I was there. The two doormen stood on duty at the front entrance where they would remain for a few more hours to welcome back guests returning from the theater or dining out. I hoped they wouldn't mention seeing me to my family upon their return.

I made a show of taking one of the newspapers from the stack at the post desk and reading the front page. When Philip wandered away to the far end of the foyer, I slipped past the smoking room and billiards room into the senior staff area. With the renovations in progress, much of the corridor was cordoned off, providing me with some coverage as I bent to pick the lock on the door to Mr. Chapman and Mrs. Short's office.

It took me longer than it took Harry and Victor to pick a lock, but I managed to get it open and slip into the office without Philip seeing me. *Thank you for the lessons, Victor.*

I pocketed the lock picking tools and removed the candle stub and match box I'd brought with me. I struck a match and lit the candle then went in search of clues.

The room was crowded with two desks crammed into it instead of the usual one. Mr. Chapman's desk was on the left. The desk surface was neat with everything in its place. The inkwell and inkstand were pushed towards the back, a notepad set to one side, the pencil lying diagonally across it. Blank stationary with the hotel's emblem of an M inside a circle at the top formed a small stack beside a ledger listing his department's expenses. The only personal items on the desk were an Egyptian pyramid paperweight in alabaster and a small metal globe. On closer inspection, the globe turned out to be a clever little traveling flask containing brandy.

The filing cabinet held employee records but none of the names were associated with our case. Old, completed ledgers occupied one shelf of the bookcase while Mrs. Short's books on housekeeping filled another. The top drawer of Mr. Chapman's desk contained letters from guests, thanking him for making their dining experience pleasurable. Once again, none were written by names associated with the case.

In the second drawer I found more stationary and a small diary. Daily entries listed meetings with suppliers, staff, and other names I didn't recognize. I skimmed the last few weeks then returned it. Most of Mr. Chapman's personal items must be at the residence hall. If only the renovations hadn't forced him to leave his private room here and move in there.

I closed the second drawer and opened the third and final one at the bottom. It was a mess and contained a lot of odds and ends. Broken pens, cleaning cloths, folded handkerchiefs, unfolded handkerchiefs, rulers, a measuring tape, shopping lists and, to my surprise, a painting of a man I recognized.

Reggie Smith.

It was a small painting, not quite a miniature, but no larger than my hand. It showed Reggie sitting on a chair. He didn't smile and his hair looked a little shorter than in the photograph we'd taken from his flat, but it was definitely him. What's more, the hands folded on his lap were poorly rendered. It must be a self-portrait. I couldn't read the small signature in the bottom right corner, but I suspected close scrutiny under a magnifying glass would show it was done by the sitter himself.

Had Reggie Smith given this to Mr. Chapman as a token of affection?

And was this the connection I needed between Mr. Chapman and Ambrose McDonald? Reggie clearly knew both men.

I was pondering what the painting meant when the door suddenly opened.

I froze.

"Miss Fox?" Mr. Chapman thundered. "What are you doing in here?"

I needed to think of something logical, and quickly. Unfortunately, my mind froze too and words failed me. There was no reasonable explanation for what I was doing in his locked office at night with the self-portrait of the main suspect of a murder in my hand.

CHAPTER 11

r. Chapman strode across the floor and snatched the picture out of my clutches. "Your uncle will hear about this." He dropped the portrait into the bottom drawer and kicked the drawer closed, all while glaring at me.

I felt the ice of it through to my bones. He would follow through with his threat. He would tell Uncle Ronald and then I'd have to explain myself and admit that I was investigating. He would probably guess that I worked with Harry.

"If you do that, I will be forced to tell him why I am in here. Is that what you want, Mr. Chapman? For my uncle to find out you met Reggie Smith, a man accused of murder, at the Portland Club?"

A ripple of shock passed over him. Perhaps he didn't think I was capable of resorting to dirty tactics, or perhaps the thought of losing his position here scared him. While I didn't like resorting to blackmail, I saw no other way out.

"Of course, my uncle may surprise us both and consider what you do in your own time is your own business. But do you want to find out?"

I wasn't sure what I'd do if he called my bluff. Fortunately, he didn't. He swallowed heavily, but that haughtily outthrust chin remained firm. "What do you want?"

"I want to know about your relationship with Reggie Smith."

Mr. Chapman hadn't turned on the light when he entered,

and the shadows cast by the candle's flame made him look like he hadn't slept in days. "I don't think I need to spell it out to you."

"I thought he was with Mr. McDonald."

"He was. And he was with me."

"Do you think he killed Mr. McDonald?"

"No! I know he didn't. He's a good person."

"But a painting taken from the Bunburys' library was found in his possession on the night of the murder. He admitted taking it."

"I don't know anything about that. I haven't had an opportunity to see him since..." He blinked rapidly and looked away.

"Did he paint it?"

"I don't know." He no longer sounded like he wanted to drag me into my uncle's office. He sounded defeated, sad. "I have to get back." He picked up a pen and pot of ink from the desk and waited for me to leave.

I passed him and headed for the door but paused before exiting. "Do you know where Mr. Smith was on the night of March thirtieth?"

He blinked in surprise at the question. "I think he was with me. Why?"

"Please try to remember. It could be important."

He opened the second drawer and pulled out the diary. He flipped back through the pages then turned it around to show me March thirtieth. There were two entries for the day. The first was at 11AM and simply stated Sir R. The second was two letters: RS. Reggie Smith. There was no time against it.

"This proves I saw him that night after I finished here," he said. "It would have been around one AM. That's when I usually leave, after the last diners have departed. You can ask Philip if you don't believe me."

"You were with Mr. Smith all night?"

"Until dawn."

That meant Reggie Smith had told the truth. He was with someone on the night the Grandjean was stolen from the Quornes'. We'd assumed it was Ambrose McDonald, but it seemed Reggie was having liaisons with both men around the same time. He hadn't given Scotland Yard the name of his alibi because he hadn't wanted to get Mr. Chapman into trouble. He knew it would cost him his job here at the hotel, ruin his reputation, and humiliate him. Whether Reggie had done it out of love, loyalty or for another reason, it didn't matter.

I wasn't sure what compelled me to ask my next question. "Do you think Reggie was in love with Ambrose McDonald?"

Mr. Chapman swallowed again and gave a slight nod. "Ambrose is—was—a force of nature. He was like a storm, wildly beautiful, but destructive for those in its path." He looked away, but not before I saw his eyes glisten.

"Thank you, Mr. Chapman. You've been very helpful."

His head jerked up to look at me again. "What happened on March thirtieth? Will me vouching for Reggie set him free?"

"I don't know, but it will help."

"Do I have your word you won't tell your uncle about the Portland?"

"I won't."

A look of relief washed over him. "Thank you."

"I don't care what you do in your spare time, Mr. Chapman, or who you're with. I just like to have answers."

The muscles in his jaw worked in an attempt to control his emotions. I left so he could compose himself before he returned to the dining room.

* * *

MY SLEEP WAS INTERRUPTED, first by Flossy, coming to check if my headache had gone. Despite telling her I was tired, and adding a yawn for effect, she slipped under the bedcovers with me and chatted about her evening for fifteen minutes. She started by saying it was dull without me there, then went on to tell me how much she enjoyed the company of the hosts.

The second interruption came in the form of Floyd knocking on my door at dawn. When I opened the door, he stumbled inside. I caught him and righted him. That's when I noticed Jonathon standing in the corridor, a sheepish look on his face.

"Sorry, Cleo," Jonathon said. "He insisted. I couldn't stop him."

Together we managed to prop Floyd against the wall. My cousin rested his hands on my shoulders and dipped his face to look me in the eye. His focus was a little off, and he reeked of cigars and brandy, but his earnest look worried me more.

"I'm doing this for him." I think he meant Jonathon, but I couldn't be sure. "He's a good friend. He wants to 'pologize."

Jonathon placed Floyd's arm around his shoulders and supported his weight. "I think it's time you go to bed before you say something you'll regret."

Floyd put up his finger to stop Jonathon speaking. His gaze focused on it, making him cross-eyed which in turn made him lose his balance.

I grabbed Floyd's other arm and helped Jonathon support him as we headed out of my room and down the corridor. Thankfully Floyd kept quiet until we had him inside his own suite with the door closed. We lay him on the bed and were about to leave when he flung his arm over his face and groaned.

"I'm ruined," he slurred. "If they don't kill me, I might as well be dead. Christ." The part of his face I could see screwed up, and tears slid down his cheeks, onto his pillow.

I appealed to Jonathon.

He heaved a sigh as he gazed down at his friend. "Sleep now, Floyd. Talk tomorrow."

Floyd wiped his eyes and opened them. He squinted at me. "Cleo? Go away."

There was nothing I could do. He was in no fit state to have a discussion, and I doubted he would confide in me anyway. I left and Jonathon followed me. We couldn't talk in Floyd's room or the corridor, so I indicated he should join me in my suite.

I asked him to sit on the sofa while I occupied one of the armchairs, keeping my distance. "I thought he had his gambling debt under control. He said he was going to ask the bank for a loan."

Jonathon sat forward and rested his elbows on his knees. He lowered his head and brushed his hair back, but it flopped forward over worried eyes again. If I'd ever felt anything for him, I would have gone to him in that moment and taken him in my arms. He'd never looked so vulnerable, so worried. But I didn't move.

"The bank refused," he said. "Floyd's not a good risk, apparently."

"So he can't pay his gambling debts?"

"He borrowed the money from the same gambler he lost to."

"Is he mad? Or just very stupid?" I'd never met the gambler, but it was obvious this was his strategy all along. Get the son of a wealthy man in his debt, threaten him if he didn't repay, then offer him a loan to cover it. "I assume the interest is exorbitant."

"Extremely." He swore under his breath. "The cur is also demanding the entire amount be paid back by the end of the week."

A hollow feeling in the pit of my stomach opened up. "Let me guess. Floyd thought he would be able to pay back the loan by winning. But he lost."

Jonathon nodded.

"Why didn't you stop him?"

"I tried! But when he's had a few drinks, he gets brazen. He doesn't think of the consequences. Not until it's too late. Besides, I was in another room at the time." This last he added in a mutter.

"How much does he owe?"

"Nearly eight hundred pounds."

I almost choked. "He'll never get his hands on that at short notice."

"I'd loan it to him, but I don't have it either. My allowance has been drastically cut this year."

I scrubbed my hand over my forehead where a real headache was beginning to bloom. "He'll have to go to his father—"

"No! He'll never do that. He's terrified of what Sir Ronald will think of him."

"He already thinks poorly of him."

"Precisely. Floyd can't afford to make it worse."

I almost called him out on his choice of words. "Can't afford to". Was Uncle Ronald nothing more than a source of

Floyd's allowance? Or was that Jonathon's interpretation of a father's role?

"I don't see that he has any other choice," I said.

"We'll think of something. We'll talk it through tomorrow." He looked around the room. "There must be something he can sell. Do you have any jewelry?"

"Not enough, and it was all given to me by my uncle anyway. If I stopped wearing it, he would ask why. And do not ask Flossy for her jewels. She's not to know about this. She looks up to Floyd."

"I wasn't going to ask her. She's not equipped for this sort of thing. Too innocent." He snapped his fingers as an idea occurred to him. "Lady Bainbridge will help. She must have money."

Aunt Lilian would indeed do anything for Floyd, including keep this secret from her husband. But she was fragile and I didn't want to upset her. "We'll go to her only as a last resort. Do you understand? We'll try to think of something else to get the money before the week is out."

Perhaps Jonathon was right and we could sell something that wouldn't be missed. I looked around the suite until my gaze fell on Jonathon.

He was watching me with that now familiar soft yet earnest look in his eyes. I regretted not sending him away earlier. "Floyd is right about one thing," he said, his voice warm. "I do want to apologize to you. Cleo...I am very sorry for upsetting you the other night. My behavior was deplorable."

"Apology accepted." I rose. "If you don't mind, I want to try to get some more sleep."

He rose too and caught my hand.

I withdrew it. "Jonathon, please. Don't do this."

He turned grave. "Hear what I have to say. Please, Cleo. I'm mortified and I want to make it up to you. Join me for dinner tonight."

"I'm afraid I have to decline."

"We can dine in the hotel restaurant, if it makes you feel more comfortable."

"It's not that." I drew in a breath and let it out slowly, stalling as I tried to think of a kind way to tell him. But I could only think of blunt words. "Jonathon, we can never be more than acquaintances. We're not compatible."

"You can't say that. We hardly know each other."

"I know enough."

My words stung. I could see it in the hard swallow and the slight narrowing of his eyes.

"It's not your fault," I hastily added. "I don't plan to marry anyone."

He relaxed and drew in a deep breath. He almost smiled. "Floyd did warn me, but I thought you might make an exception for…" He let the sentence drift like an unmoored boat, but I knew he was referring to his status as the heir to a viscountcy.

"I hope this doesn't make things awkward between us," I said.

"No more than they already were after my despicable behavior." He gave me a flat smile. "Goodnight, Cleo." He headed for the door, only to stop before opening it. He turned to me, frowning. "Blame the copious amounts of alcohol I drank tonight, but I'm going to die of curiosity if I don't ask."

Oh Lord.

"When you say you don't mean to marry, are you suggesting you want to be my mistress?"

"No!"

He put up his hands. "Sorry. Forget I said anything."

"Gladly."

He opened the door but paused again. "Don't tell Floyd I asked you that. He'd clock me if he knew."

"Perhaps you need to be clocked."

His shoulders slumped and he slunk away towards the staircase.

I closed the door behind him and returned to bed, determined not to think anything more about Jonathon or this strange night.

* * *

I SLEPT LATE. When I rose, I discovered Harmony had eaten her half of breakfast, cleaned my en-suite bathroom, tidied my sitting room, and left me a note telling me I snore. Under that was another note saying she hoped I was feeling better, but if I still had a headache, she'd make me a soothing tisane using an old family recipe.

I felt guilty that I couldn't tell her I didn't have a headache. She'd want to know why I'd come up with the story and I'd have to lie for Mr. Chapman's sake. I didn't want to lie to her. She'd probably see right through it anyway.

I ate my cold breakfast and collected my hat and gloves. That's when I noticed a piece of paper had been slipped under my door. It was a brief message asking me to call on my uncle in his office if I felt better.

I may have imagined the ominous tone in the written words, but I dreaded speaking to him. It could only be about Mr. Chapman finding me in his office. I forced myself to place one foot in front of the other, all the while thinking up an excuse as to why I'd broken in. But I could think of nothing that would sound reasonable. So be it. If Mr. Chapman broke his end of the bargain and informed my uncle, so I didn't have to keep mine.

I threw back my shoulders and knocked.

Uncle Ronald bade me enter and indicated I should sit and wait while he finished writing his letter. After a few minutes in which my stomach churned with anxiety, he signed his name and put down his pen. He set the letter aside for the ink to dry and clasped his hands on the desk in front of him.

"Are you feeling better this morning, Cleo?"

"I am, thank you. The long sleep did wonders."

"Good, good." He leaned back in the chair and moved his clasped hands to rest on his stomach. He regarded me with affection, setting my mind at ease. If this was about Mr. Chapman's office, I'd know by now. My uncle was the sort of man who wore his thoughts like an outer garment. "We missed you last night."

"That's kind of you to say."

"It's not a kindness when it's true. It's a truth." He smiled, pleased with his little word play. "The family weren't the only ones who missed you."

"That's sweet of Mr. and Mrs. Bracksley-Jones. I'll write to them and send my regards."

"I wasn't referring to Mr. or Mrs. Bracksley-Jones. I was referring to their son." His smile widened.

My heart sank. "I don't remember ever meeting their son. In fact, I've only ever met Mrs. Bracksley-Jones."

"You have met the son, as it happens. You danced with him at the ball. Richard Bracksley-Jones. Everyone calls him Dickie."

"I remember him now." He was a short man with bad breath and two left feet. "He knew a great deal about birds."

"That's the fellow. Loves to shoot birds at their country estate." He cleared his throat. "Usually Lilian would have this talk with you, but she seems to think you're old enough to orchestrate these things yourself."

"What things?" I asked carefully.

"Meetings with suitors."

"Uncle," I began. I blew out a fortifying breath. "Uncle, we've been through this. I am not interested in marrying."

"That's what Lilian said, but that was before the ball. You obviously didn't think there'd be this much interest. We all knew you'd be well received, naturally." He waved off his own compliment, as if he were embarrassed to give it. "Lilian informs me that Dickie Bracksley-Jones isn't the only one who wishes to get to know you better. There are others. As I said, you made quite an impression at the ball. You were very charming and one of the prettiest there, I might add."

"I am sorry, but I'm not interested in him. Or anyone. I'm quite content as I am."

I hadn't offended him. Indeed, he seemed as enthusiastic as ever. "It's wise not to express too much interest at this stage. Dickie is just the first to throw his hat into the ring. While the Bracksley-Joneses are a good family, I think you can do better. We'll see who else comes out of the woodwork in the coming weeks, shall we?" He winked at me then picked up the letter he'd just finished writing.

I rose and left, not bothering to say anything further. It would only fall on deaf ears. At least my aunt understood and seemed to be in my corner. I suspected I was going to need her.

Downstairs, I asked Frank if Floyd had left the hotel. He

hadn't. Not that it mattered. He wouldn't confide in me. Even if he did, there was nothing I could do to be of practical help.

I felt utterly useless.

It was Floyd's problem, rather than the investigation, that remained topmost on my mind all the way to Harry's office. I stopped in at Roma Café and ordered two coffees to take upstairs. With my hands full, I lightly kicked the office door with the toe of my boot.

Harry answered and relieved me of the coffee cups. "You're late this morning."

"I slept in."

"A ball? Dinner party?"

"An interrupted sleep." I sat and sipped my coffee. The warm liquid was far better than the cold brew I'd tried to swallow at breakfast. I sighed and cradled the cup between both hands.

Harry frowned at me. "Something's happened."

"No. Nothing. Why do you say that?"

"I can tell."

I shifted in my chair. I wanted to tell him about Floyd, but Floyd wouldn't like that. He didn't even like *me* knowing his troubles, he certainly wouldn't want an outsider, and a former employee at that, learning about his gambling problem. But Harry had a way of seeing through me. I couldn't continue to lie.

I changed the subject instead. "Annie the maid overheard Lady Bunbury and Ambrose McDonald arguing at the ball." I told him what Annie had told Harmony, that Lady Bunbury accused him of betraying her, and that she'd been the one to inform him of their financial predicament. "That information, at least, he found out from the original source. I'd be furious with him too, if he'd deceived me like that."

"Perhaps she was furious enough to kill him." He gave me one of his crooked smiles. "I have to admit, I was skeptical, but your idea to give Annie a position at the hotel was a good one. I thought she might be too loyal, but it got results."

"She couldn't afford to be loyal. She wasn't being paid regularly at the Bunburys."

"Their situation must be dire indeed."

"That's not all I learned yesterday," I went on. "Mr. Chapman was in a relationship with Reggie Smith."

A number of expressions flitted across Harry's face before it finally settled into a look of disapproval. "You confronted him," he said flatly.

"I broke into his office and he caught me holding a self-portrait of Reggie that I found in his desk drawer. I had to admit why I was there. Once he realized I already knew he was a member of the Portland Club, he admitted the rest."

"Cleo," he muttered with a shake of his head. "Did he threaten to tell your uncle?"

"That's your first question?"

He merely glared at me.

"We've come to a mutual agreement. He won't inform Uncle Ronald that I broke into his office, and I won't tell him that Mr. Chapman takes men to bed. Now, can we get back to what it means, please?"

He blew out a measured breath and I thought I was going to get a lecture about being more careful, but he refrained. "Chapman may have been jealous of McDonald's relationship with Smith."

"I think he was. He says Reggie Smith was in love with Ambrose McDonald, even after their relationship ended."

"That matches what Smith's neighbor and landlady said about him being in a low mood recently on account of him no longer seeing his artist friend with the studio."

"Speaking of art, Mr. Chapman is Reggie's alibi for the night of March thirtieth. He was with him from one AM until dawn. Reggie couldn't have stolen the Grandjean from the Quornes."

We both fell silent, considering the implications of that information on the murder. It may have none. The two events may not be linked.

At least, that's what I thought Harry was thinking about. I was wrong.

"You should confide in one of your cousins," he said.

"Pardon?"

"Whatever is bothering you...if you don't want to discuss it with me, you should talk to your cousins. A problem shared, *et cetera*."

My heart pinched. His concern was touching. So much so that I couldn't meet his gaze if it meant lying to him again. I went to sip my coffee, only to find the cup empty.

He reached across the table and rested a hand on my forearm. "Is it your uncle? Did he find out about your investigating? Or that you continue to see me?" His mouth set into a grim line. "It is, isn't it? That's why you don't want to tell me."

"No." I couldn't let him think that. I had to come clean. "My uncle still isn't aware of any of this. Nor can I talk it over with either of my cousins. Flossy is too innocent and it's about Floyd."

He released me and sat back. "Let me guess. He got himself into trouble and can't find a way out, so he asked you for help since you're clever as well as practical."

"He hasn't asked for my help. His friend, Jonathon, did."

Harry's gaze snapped to mine. "Hartly? You've spoken to him privately?"

"Unfortunately, yes."

It was meant as a joke about Jonathon's character, but Harry didn't find it amusing. "Why unfortunate? Has he done or said something to you that he shouldn't have?"

"Don't worry about Jonathon. I can handle him."

"You shouldn't have to handle him. Why does Floyd let him go near you?"

"Harry," I ground out. "I can handle Jonathon."

The muscles in his jaw worked as he bit back his retort. After a moment, he said, "What did Hartly confide in you?"

"Floyd is in debt to a gambler. He borrowed money at an exorbitant rate, hoping to win it back but of course he didn't. Now he owes even more and must pay it by the end of this week."

"What will happen if he doesn't?"

"I don't know." I'd been so worried about my uncle and aunt finding out, I hadn't asked.

"Do you know the name of the gambler?"

"No. It doesn't matter."

"It does," he shot back. "If I knew the name, I might know his reputation. Some are violent, others work in more civilized ways, but are no less nasty to debtors who can't pay."

I arched my brows. "How do you know the reputations of individual gamblers?"

"There are surprisingly few professional ones who operate at the level at which Floyd would be playing. I got to know them over the years working at the hotel. Guests confided in me. I had to help some by pointing them to private lenders, or ensuring they were safe within the hotel. It was not the most pleasant part of my job."

"Did Mr. Hobart know?" I couldn't imagine the manager dealing with the sort of characters who used violence to ensure debts were repaid. He was so proper and sweet.

"My uncle was probably aware of what went on, but the guests learned to approach me, not him. There must have been something about me that made the guests think I'd understand their plight and be comfortable dealing with dubious characters." He said it half-jokingly, but he was right. There was an air of capability and confidence about him that signaled that he could help. I always felt safer with Harry. I felt safe confiding in him too. He wouldn't betray a confidence.

"I'm afraid the fellow could be violent." There had been an occasion when Floyd had been roughly deposited outside the hotel by an unmarked carriage. That was when his problems began, a few weeks ago.

"Then your cousin needs to pay him back. Appealing to the gambler's gentlemanly nature won't work. I don't want to scare you, Cleo, but it's possible the fellow has threatened to harm one of Floyd's family members if he doesn't pay."

I gave a small nod. I'd already thought of that possibility. "If he can't raise the money he owes by the end of the week, I'm going to approach my aunt on his behalf. He's too proud to do it himself. I'm sure she'll have some money she can loan him by the deadline."

"And if she doesn't?"

I hadn't considered that. Nor had Jonathon. "Perhaps Floyd has friends..." I turned away to hide the sudden burn in my eyes as tears welled. I pressed my lips together.

Harry crouched before me. I hadn't even heard him rise and round the desk. He clasped my hand, resting on my lap, and gently squeezed. "I'll think of something."

"This isn't your problem, Harry."

"I beg to differ."

"I only told you to share the burden of it with someone. I wouldn't have mentioned it if you were going to take on the responsibility of fixing it. You can't fix it. Only money can." I heard my voice rise and was powerless to stop it. I hated that I'd thrown in the part about money, too, but it *was* the only way to fix Floyd's problem. And neither Harry nor I had the sort of money needed to pay back the debt.

We truly were powerless.

But Harry was a gentleman for trying to make me feel better, and I shouldn't snap at him. I folded my hand over his and offered him a weak smile. "Thank you anyway."

He slipped his hand out from between mine and stood. "We should pass on the information to my father about Reggie Smith being with Chapman on the night the Quornes' painting was stolen."

The change of topic was so sudden I needed a moment to refocus.

"Will it matter? Does your father have any sway in the case now? His superiors might ignore the information and continue with their persecution of Reggie. They want to close this investigation as soon as possible. And what if they decide to arrest Mr. Chapman for indecency? I could never live with myself."

Harry swore under his breath. He knew I was right.

I was about to suggest we do something drastic to nudge our investigation forward, but never got the opportunity. There was an urgent knock on the door.

Harry answered it. "Lady Treloar. This is unexpected." He stepped aside to allow the art gallery owner inside.

She swept past him, smiling in greeting, then spotted me. "Oh! How fortunate that you're here, too, Miss Fox." She sat in the chair Harry indicated and swept a hand over her skirt to smooth the wrinkles out of it. She wore a black and cream dress today with a tightly cinched waist and a flimsy chiffon layer over a daringly low-cut bodice. Her hair was elaborately styled with a wave set forward, covering one side of her forehead. She wore a little color on her cheeks and lips, and her lashes were darker than I remembered. They framed large gray eyes that she fluttered in Harry's direction.

He gave no indication that he noticed. "How may we help you, madam?"

"I thought I'd better tell you about a visitor to my gallery yesterday. He tried to sell me a painting. When I saw it, I immediately thought of notifying you, Mr. Armitage. It might be relevant to your investigation."

"Why is that?"

"The painting he tried to sell me was a forgery." She sounded pleased to be bringing us the news. "Not only that, I'm certain it was done by the same artist who did some of the Bunburys' pieces."

CHAPTER 12

"It's not often someone comes to the gallery carrying a painting by a well-known artist," Lady Treloar said. "In this case, it was a portrait of a young woman reading a book by the Dutch painter Johan de Klerk. I probably should have had my suspicions at that point, but I didn't. It wasn't until I studied the painting more closely that I began to wonder. You see, de Klerk is an excellent portrait painter, but this painting wasn't up to his standard. The face was good, as was the dress, but the hands were not. They were out of proportion and quite masculine."

Harry's gaze connected with mine.

"Is that detail important?" Lady Treloar asked.

"Who brought the painting in?" Harry asked.

"I don't know. He didn't give his name. I'm sorry I didn't find out, but I was so taken aback, I didn't think clearly. I let him leave."

"Did you indicate you knew it was a forgery?"

She shook her head. "I was careful not to."

"Can you describe him?"

The man was in his twenties, of medium height and build, with brown hair, a thick beard and whiskers. "Now that I think about it, I suspect the facial hair wasn't real."

"Do you know anyone who may now be missing that painting—the real one?" I asked.

She shook her head. "It's not a piece I'm familiar with. The original must belong to someone whose home I've never been in."

"He was rather daring to try to sell the copy to you, considering you might have known where the original hung."

"Unless he was sure she didn't," Harry added.

"Or he was just stupid," Lady Treloar said. "People often are, I find. When I was in Biarritz, a German duke tried to convince me he owned an unsigned Vermeer. When I pointed out that it looked nothing like a Vermeer, he told me I don't know fine art." The corner of her mouth kicked up in a sardonic smile.

I hardly heard her little story. I was thinking about something she'd said earlier. "You claim the painting is done by the same artist who did some of the Bunburys' copies."

"I'm almost certain, yes."

"How do you know? They were landscapes, weren't they? So it couldn't have been the hands."

"It's in the way the paint is applied, its thickness, the strokes, that sort of thing. Besides, a portrait still has scenery in it. The painting the fellow brought in had all the same qualities that I noticed in the Bunburys' art. I'm sure they're by the same artist." She looked from me to Harry and back again. "Does that help explain it?"

I nodded. "Do you know who the forger might be?"

"No. I don't know anyone who paints in that style and has difficulty with hands." She rose. "I do hope it has been some help and that if you find the artist, you'll get some of the answers you seek."

The paintings may have been done by Reggie Smith, but the thefts weren't. He had an alibi for the Quorne heist and was in prison yesterday. Someone else had approached Lady Treloar with the forgery. It may be that Reggie didn't know the fellow at all. Or he could be Reggie's accomplice. Did the seller know the painting was a copy? Or did he think he possessed the original?

Harry saw Lady Treloar out then closed the door. He turned to me, his eyes bright. "I see it now. I see the connection between the paintings and the murder."

So did I. "Reggie Smith painted the forgeries and Mr. McDonald found out. He blackmailed him, threatening to

141

expose him. Unable to pay and afraid of going to prison, Reggie killed him."

Harry nodded. "I admit it's a relief knowing the right man was arrested."

"I agree. But we need to be certain. So how do we prove it?"

"I can only see one way." He removed his jacket from the stand and put it on. "My father has to confront Smith in prison. If he tells Smith about this new evidence, he might admit everything. I'll go to Scotland Yard and speak to my father now."

"But he's no longer on the case. What if his superiors find out?"

"He can say he's tying up loose ends. It won't matter anyway. Lady Treloar's statement implies Smith is guilty and his guilt suits them."

I collected the cups and my bag and followed him out.

"What will you do?" Harry asked as we descended the steps. "Get ready for another ball?"

"I know you're being sarcastic, but I do have one tonight, as it happens. I've got hours before I need to get ready. I might as well come to Scotland Yard with you."

"It's not necessary."

"True, but you'll enjoy my company nevertheless."

He gave me a rueful smile and didn't disagree.

* * *

D.I. HOBART INFORMED us that Reggie Smith's trial was set for two days hence. We took a cab to the Old Bailey where he was being held in a cell beneath the courtrooms until his trial. We waited outside while D.I. Hobart spoke to him.

I imagined the Newgate Prison and Old Bailey courthouse buildings once towered over the surrounding streets with all the grim authority of a judge, but modern developments had diminished its stature. It wasn't surprising there was talk of it being demolished and replaced by something befitting the grand status of London's Central Criminal Court, but there was no sign of that happening soon. According to Harry, it could be years away.

To fill in time while we waited, he told me all about the building's history. He talked about the building itself, from its humble beginnings as a wooden Medieval structure before the Great Fire right up to when the neighboring Newgate Prison was closed to long-term prisoners a few decades ago. It was only used now as a temporary lockup for those prisoners awaiting trial.

When he reached the present day in his retelling, he suddenly stopped. "Sorry. I'm boring you. I tend to go on about buildings a little too much."

"I wouldn't expect anything less from an enthusiast of architecture and engineering. But perhaps you'll want to learn some stories about the prisoners themselves for dinner party conversation."

"Your dinner parties must be macabre affairs if that's what you talk about."

"What can I say? I'm an enthusiast of murder mysteries."

He chuckled.

I couldn't help smiling at his profile as he watched the Old Bailey's main entrance. I liked making him laugh.

"Speaking of dinner parties and balls," he went on, "where are you going tonight?"

"Our hosts are the Druitt-Poores. Do you know them?"

"I've met Mrs. Druitt-Poore. She often came to the hotel to have afternoon tea with Lady Bainbridge. They have daughters, if I recall correctly."

"You do. There are no sons."

"They'll be needing as many gentlemen there as they can muster. Floyd will be in attendance, I assume. And his friends."

"I suppose."

"Is Hartly going?"

"Jonathon? I have no idea."

He leaned against the lamp post and folded his arms over his chest. There was no evidence of his good humor anymore. He'd turned broody.

D.I. Hobart emerged from the Old Bailey and joined us on the pavement. He indicated we should climb into the waiting cab then directed the coachman to return to Scotland Yard before settling into the seat opposite Harry and me with a groan.

He rubbed his left knee as he gave an account of his meeting. "Smith finally admitted he was in a relationship with McDonald, but it ended ten days before the murder. This overlapped with a relationship he had with Chapman." He nodded at me. "He says the affair with Chapman was more casual in nature than that which he had with McDonald. His feelings for the murdered man ran deeper. Even so, he was worried about getting Chapman into difficulty so he wanted to keep his name out of it, hence he never told me his alibi for the night of the Quorne heist. I assured him there would be no repercussions for Chapman, as long as he doesn't turn out to be the murderer."

"You let Smith believe you think him innocent?" Harry asked. "Is that fair?"

"I do think him innocent. Even more so, now. We had a good conversation. An honest one. I believe every word he told me. Let me finish," he added when Harry opened his mouth to protest. "Smith admits to being jealous when he learned McDonald had other lovers. They fought and McDonald ended it with him."

"He's not innocent," Harry said. "He killed McDonald when McDonald blackmailed him after he learned Smith painted the forgeries. It's the only explanation that makes sense."

"He claims he didn't paint them."

"He must have. Lady Treloar says the painting that was brought to her had poorly rendered hands, and the style matched several of the Bunbury forgeries."

D.I. Hobart stroked his whiskers in thought. "He says he didn't paint forgeries for anyone and I believe him. He also continues to deny stealing the Quornes' painting on March thirtieth, and now we have Chapman giving him an alibi for that night anyway. Smith did admit that the theft gave him the idea to steal the painting off the wall of the Bunburys' library in retaliation for Lady Bunbury stealing McDonald away from him." He looked to me then to Harry. "The upshot is, he continued to deny murdering McDonald and I believed him. I don't want you to give up on him yet."

Harry shrugged and shook his head, but finally agreed. "The problem is, I don't know where to look next."

Nor did I. All the evidence pointed to Reggie Smith being the murderer, but if D.I. Hobart believed him innocent, then we had to continue to investigate. We needed absolute proof, one way or another.

* * *

AFTER LEAVING D.I. Hobart at Scotland Yard, Harry and I decided to drive to Upper Brooke Street. He would talk to Lady Bunbury, and I would remain in the cab, out of sight. I didn't envy him at all, but I would have liked to see her reactions to his questions. He was going to confront her over Annie's claim that she saw Lady Bunbury arguing with Ambrose McDonald on the night of the ball.

I watched as the butler let Harry into the house. That was already further than I expected him to get. A few minutes later, Lady's Bunbury's face appeared in the drawing room window. Her gaze arrowed down to me.

I flattened myself against the back of the seat, out of sight.

A few minutes after that, Harry opened the carriage door. He instructed the coachman to drive to the Mayfair, then climbed inside and sat beside me.

"Well?" I asked. "What did she say?"

"They were both there, Lord and Lady Bunbury. They didn't say anything."

The carriage lurched forward, causing me to shift in the seat and my knee to bump his. "Nothing at all? What was their reaction when you mentioned the argument with McDonald?"

His arm rested on the windowsill. His fingernail scraped the wood, drawing his attention.

"Harry?" I prompted.

He lowered his hand to his thigh. "They both looked surprised that I knew about it, then Lord Bunbury became hostile. He ordered me to get out. I asked who painted their forgeries and neither responded. Again, both looked surprised that I knew. Lord Bunbury then threatened to send for constables, so I decided to leave."

I could tell by the way he wouldn't look at me that there was more. "And?"

He heaved a sigh. "And as I exited, Lady Bunbury vowed retribution." He shook his head, slowly. "I've made it worse."

"Not you, we. Anyway, we knew it was a risk, but one we had to take. We had nowhere else to turn."

"We still don't."

* * *

THE DRUITT-POORES' ball wasn't as grand as the Bunburys'. For one thing, their ballroom was smaller, so not as many could fit inside. In every other way, I felt a strong sense of having previously experienced the evening before. I danced with the same gentlemen, I had the same conversations with the same ladies, and the refreshments were the same. Even Miss Hessing's plight was the same. She tried to separate herself from her mother only to be reeled back in by that domineering parent. She melted into the wallpaper, and those men who did see her, snubbed her. At least no one neighed as they passed her this time. And once again, Floyd rescued her by asking her to dance. Afterwards, she was asked two more times by other gentlemen. I considered it a triumph. She considered it greed.

"They're only doing it because they saw Floyd dance with me," she said. "They think I must be someone important if he is paying me attention."

I looped my arm through hers. "You are important."

"I'm wealthy. That's not the same thing."

"There are many girls from wealthy families here. They could have their pick considering there is a distinct lack of men."

Her gaze tracked around the room. "I suppose…"

I squeezed her arm. "Have you told the gentlemen that your mother is keen to stay in America if you happened to find an English husband?"

She laughed softly. "It's not an easy thing to drop into a conversation. If a man does show more than a passing interest, I will be sure to try." She eyed her mother, standing a few feet away with a gaggle of ladies who'd spent all night talking loudly, sometimes over the top of one another. "She acts as though I am not even here, but whenever I move away, she crooks her finger and beckons me to her to tell me some piece of gossip or other. Honestly, it's like I'm connected to her by a piece of string."

"You could always pretend you don't notice."

"I couldn't."

"If you don't look her way, she can't admonish you for not doing her bidding."

"She can and she will. The only time she doesn't mind me going off is when I'm dancing."

"Then we shall attempt to find you more partners." As I said it, I smiled at two passing gentlemen.

They stopped and asked us to dance. I accepted the offer from the shorter one, since the taller fellow was more of a match for Miss Hessing's height. My partner was pleasant enough and I enjoyed the dance.

Until I noticed Jonathon watching me from the edge of the ballroom. I hadn't seen him arrive.

When he saw me looking, he smiled and made a little hand signal, indicating writing on my dance card. Not wanting to appear rude, I nodded back.

When the music ended, I asked my partner to escort me off the floor in the opposite direction to Jonathon. Miss Hessing and her partner joined us, and the four of us conversed for a few minutes before the men declared they were both engaged to dance with other women.

Miss Hessing watched them leave from beneath lowered lashes. "It was kind of him to take pity on me."

"He didn't dance with you out of pity. Didn't you notice his smile as he led you off? He seemed quite pleased."

She sighed. "He only danced with me because you took the other one."

"Nonsense. Look. He just turned and smiled at you."

Her cheeks flushed and she dipped her head to hide her face. "Oh!"

I surreptitiously looked around for Jonathon, wanting to avoid him if he approached. I saw Flossy heading our way, her steps purposeful, her eyes bright with the gossip she wanted to impart.

"Have you noticed?" she said when she reached us.

"Noticed what?" I asked.

"Amelia Livingstone isn't here."

"What of it?"

She leaned in and lowered her voice, forcing us to lean in too to hear her over the music. "Meredith Druitt-Poore says the invitations were sent out weeks ago, before the scandal. Miss Livingstone had accepted. But she's not here."

"Can you blame her? She would be the subject of gossip all evening. Everyone would stare." Although I hadn't liked Miss Livingstone when I met her, I still felt sorry for her. She was a young woman who should be enjoying herself, but she was enduring a self-imposed exile. She must be miserable.

Flossy glanced around then leaned in again. "Apparently she didn't even send a note to Mrs. Druitt-Poore to say she felt unwell and couldn't attend tonight. It's the height of rudeness."

Miss Hessing agreed. "A brief note should have been sent to the hostess."

"I must admit that her absence is in our favor. She isn't hogging all the gentlemen, leaving them free to dance with us." Flossy grasped my hand. "Don't look now, Cleo, but Lady Bunbury is over there, glaring at you."

I didn't look, but Miss Hessing did. "She has quite a fierce scowl on her face," she said. "Did you say something to upset her, Miss Fox?"

"I, er…"

"She dislikes us," Flossy said matter-of-factly. "Cleo discovered the Bunburys are poor, and Lady Bunbury is mortified. She's terrified it will get out."

I glared at Flossy, but she barreled on.

"She doesn't realize how discreet Cleo can be."

"Unlike some," I muttered.

Flossy clicked her tongue. "Miss Hessing is a friend, Cleo. She won't tell a soul, will you, Miss Hessing?"

Miss Hessing made a locking motion at the corner of her mouth and pretended to throw away the key.

Flossy patted my arm. "See? No need to worry. Oh look, here come Floyd and Jonathon. Are you up to seeing him, Cleo?"

"Why wouldn't she be?" Miss Hessing asked.

"He has all but declared himself."

Miss Hessing gasped.

"Hardly," I said, looking around for the nearest exit. Unfortunately, I'd have to pass Jonathon to get to it.

"Are you not interested in him, Miss Fox?" Miss Hessing asked.

"No."

"But...why not?"

"We're not suitable."

"I see." She didn't sound like she saw, but there was no time to explain it. Jonathon and Floyd were almost upon us.

At least I wouldn't be alone with him.

Jonathon smiled at me. "May I have the next dance, Cleo?"

Ugh.

I was about to tell him I had sore feet when a commotion near the door had us all turning towards it. Someone was shouting and some of the men were trying to get the fellow to leave. It wasn't until the music quieted that I could hear what the newcomer was saying.

It was Mr. Livingstone.

"You call yourselves gentlemen!" He lurched forward with the effort of his shout, and his words slurred. "But none of you are!" He stabbed his finger at the nearest man then the one next to him. The two men exchanged confused glances.

Mrs. Druitt-Poore forged a path through the crowd like a steam engine at full pace. "Mr. Livingstone! Dear Mr. Livingstone, do come with me and we'll hang up your coat."

He put up a hand, warding her off, but almost tipped forward. "You! You women are the worst!" He wiped his mouth with the back of his hand. "You pretend to be nice, but you bite and snap behind my Amelia's back like crocodiles." He made a biting motion with his thumb and fingers. "Snap, snap, snap. Bitches, the lot of you."

Several of the women gasped. Mrs. Druitt-Poore stilled, shock etched into every groove on her face. It was as though his accusation had turned her to stone.

Someone behind me snickered.

"Drunken idiot," muttered another.

Near the exit, several footmen closed around Mr. Livingstone, like poachers attempting to snare a wild animal. The butler stood back with Mr. Druitt-Poore, directing the footmen with subtle hand signals and whispered orders that everyone heard and saw, nevertheless.

Mr. Livingstone pushed away the closest footman. "My daughter is a good girl! She is the prettiest! The most 'complished. Most elegant!" He pushed away another footman who drew too close. "Lady Bunbury says so!" He pointed at her. Well, in her general direction. He was too drunk to point straight.

I'd never seen Lady Bunbury look so mortified, as though she wanted to sink into the floor and disappear. She'd just realized that by bestowing her so-called awards on Amelia, she'd aligned herself with a disgraced girl and her drunken, belligerent father.

I couldn't help but feel delighted at her plight. I'd avoided her all night but the glare she bestowed on me from the other side of the room was so cold it sent shivers down my spine. Harry's report of her threat of retribution had weighed on my mind all afternoon.

A footman urged Mr. Livingstone to come away, but Mr. Livingstone shoved the fellow in the chest. The butler stepped in and said something quietly in Mr. Livingstone's ear, but Mr. Livingstone pushed him, too. The poor man fell over and landed on his backside.

Mr. Druitt-Poore himself stepped into the breach next. I hardly knew him, but he seemed to be a gentle and somewhat comical fellow whose large belly shook when he laughed, which he did often and heartily. But when he tried to discreetly urge Mr. Livingstone to leave, he received a punch on the nose.

The ladies gasped again. A few of the younger ones shrieked.

Finally stirred to action, four of the closest gentlemen took matters into their own hands and captured Mr. Livingstone. They forced his arms behind his back and marched him out of the ballroom.

He shouted all the way. "You'll regret this! Mark me, I will have my revenge! The last fellow who wronged Amelia found his way to an early grave!"

Good lord. That was quite a statement. Or was it a confession?

Beside me, Flossy grasped my arm. "Cleo, did you hear that?" she whispered. "Do you think he did it? Do you think he murdered that man at the Bunburys' ball?"

I shook my head, but I was thinking the same thing.

I hurried off towards the door, but both Jonathon and Floyd caught up to me. Floyd blocked my exit.

"No, Cleo. Not here."

I tried to see past him but he was too tall. "It's the perfect opportunity to question him."

"Everyone is watching," he hissed.

He was right. All eyes were on the exit through which Mr. Livingstone had gone, but they weren't watching me. They were waiting to see if he returned, and whispering to their friends about the shocking display. I heard Amelia's name several times. Those who didn't know about her disgrace before, certainly knew about it now. Mr. Livingstone had made sure of that.

He would regret his outburst in the morning. It would be a better time to speak to him then, once he'd sobered up and calmed down.

I assured Floyd I wouldn't go after him and headed back to where Miss Hessing and Flossy were standing. I passed near Lord and Lady Bunbury, talking to one another in harsh whispers, seemingly oblivious to those watching on. It would seem the Livingstones weren't the only topic of gossip in the ballroom.

"Poor Mrs. Druitt-Poore," Flossy said.

I followed her gaze to where our hostess was being supported by my aunt while another woman vigorously flapped her fan at Mrs. Druitt-Poore's pale cheeks. A helpful bystander offered her a cigarette from his silver case. She shook her head. It wasn't until Aunt Lilian dipped her little finger into the case that I realized it didn't contain cigarettes but snuff or some other powder. Aunt Lilian sniffed it off her finger with a deep inhale.

The middle Druitt-Poore daughter, the one whose debut

we were here to celebrate, was in tears, consoled by her sisters and friends. A dazed and bloody-nosed Mr. Druitt-Poore was being supported out of the ballroom by two other gentlemen.

"What a to-do," Miss Hessing said. "For once, I am glad to be a wallflower. We can cry over our misfortunes without being ogled and discussed."

"You're not a wallflower," Floyd cut in.

Jonathon agreed, albeit a moment too late and without conviction.

Miss Hessing blinked back at Floyd, smiling shyly.

The music struck up a lively tune and I was too slow to move away. Jonathon took my hand and ushered me onto the dance floor. Floyd led out Miss Hessing. To avoid looking up at Jonathon, I studied the other guests. Many earnest conversations were in progress. Lord and Lady Bunbury had disappeared.

Most interesting of all, the gentleman who'd danced with Miss Hessing earlier now watched her with Floyd, a rather curious look on his face. Indeed, if I wasn't mistaken, it was the look of a man enamored.

* * *

THE BALL DIDN'T SURVIVE the incident much longer. A mere half hour after Mr. Livingstone was escorted from the premises, most of the guests had departed. Mr. Druitt-Poore was not to be seen, his middle daughter had taken to her bed with a headache, and Mrs. Druitt-Poore wore a smile so false and so hard it looked painted on.

We left a little after one. Floyd and Jonathon claimed they had another party to attend, but from the scowl on Jonathon's face, I suspected it wasn't a party, it was a gambling venue, and he wasn't happy about going. My uncle wasn't happy that Floyd was going out, but he didn't stop him. He merely lectured him about not lazing in his rooms all the next morning.

As they were talking on the pavement, I sidled up to Jonathon. "Look after him."

"I'll try, but he makes it difficult."

Their cab arrived and they climbed in. Before it drove off,

movement up ahead caught my eye. The door to a waiting cab opened and a man climbed in.

My breath caught in my chest.

I knew that figure. The light cast by the streetlamps and the carriage lamps may be poor, but I'd know that tall frame anywhere, and the way he moved, with easy athleticism and an abundance of self-confidence.

Harry.

What was he doing here?

CHAPTER 13

*H*arry wasn't in his office the following morning when I arrived at ten-thirty. Nor was he in Roma Café. Luigi hadn't seen him.

"Where do you think he could be?" I said to no one in particular. "It's not like him to be this late to the office."

Luigi picked up a cloth and began wiping one of the cups he'd just washed. "Maybe he slept in."

"Maybe he has a woman," said one of the old men in a thick accent.

His companion nodded knowingly and said something in Italian. The first one chuckled. They both looked at me, smiling like naughty teenaged boys.

"Your English is better than I thought," I muttered.

"Ignore them," Luigi said to me. "They don't know Harry."

I considered asking him if Harry had ever mentioned a woman to him but decided against it. I didn't want to know the answer. Well, I didn't want to know if the answer was yes.

That didn't stop my mind from wandering in that direction. Perhaps he'd been waiting outside the Druitt-Poore's house to collect someone from the ball. A pretty widow, perhaps, or a maid finished for the evening. She would be pretty, too, of course. He might have met her when he went to the Searcys office without me. The maids and footmen must go there from time to time to collect their pay and ask about future work.

"Miss Fox?" Luigi said. "Did you hear me?"

"No. Sorry. I was miles away. What did you say?"

"Do you want me to give him a message?"

"No, thank you. I'll come back later."

My plan for the morning didn't require two people. Indeed, it might be better if just one of us confronted Mr. Livingstone.

* * *

LAST TIME HARRY and I called on him, he'd sent us away with blustery anger. I'd hid my face by lowering my hat brim, but this time I kept it up. I wanted to see his reactions and that meant allowing him to see me.

He tried to have his butler send me away this time, too, but I insisted. I told the butler to tell Mr. Livingstone that I would inform Scotland Yard of his accusation from the previous night. I was shown up to his study without delay. I was very glad not to be shown into the drawing room where Amelia was more likely to walk in.

Mr. Livingstone did not invite me to sit, but I sat anyway. Some things couldn't be discussed standing up like a soldier. I wanted to be delicate, gentle, and a picture of feminine sympathy. Honey was better at catching flies than blunt hammers.

I left the door open and could hear the butler shuffle his feet just outside.

"Thank you for seeing me, Mr. Livingstone. I'm sorry to arrive unannounced like this."

If my polite, ladylike manner caught him off guard, he didn't show it. Although he was clean shaved and superbly dressed, he looked like he'd only just crawled out of bed. A gentleman who'd drunk himself into a state the night before can look immaculate of a morning thanks to an efficient valet, but he couldn't hide the pallor of his cheeks or his bloodshot eyes.

"You again," he snapped. "Is your superior not with you this time?"

"Mr. Armitage is my associate and no, he is not here." Despite his hostility, I felt immeasurable relief that he didn't recognize me from the ball. I'd deliberately worn plainer clothes today, knowing I was coming here. "Regarding last night's outburst—"

"That's none of your affair."

"On the contrary. Scotland Yard are very interested in what you had to say, and as I consult for them, I was duty bound to inform them. They know I am here, speaking to you on their behalf."

He leaned forward, eyes narrowed. "Who are you? I swear I know you."

"I work for Searcys as a temporary maid. I've been hired by the hostesses of several balls you've attended, including the Druitt-Poores."

"You don't sound like a maid."

Drat. The dress hadn't been enough to fool him. I should have put on a Cockney accent. "You shouldn't judge a book by its cover, Mr. Livingstone. To the matter at hand. Last night, you barged in on the Druitt-Poores' ball."

"I didn't *barge* in. I was invited."

"As was your daughter, I believe."

"How does a temporary maid know that?"

"Miss Livingstone failed to attend, however. Did you deliberately leave her at home, knowing you would be involved in an altercation?"

He sat back heavily, all the fight having suddenly left him, as if my accusation had punched it out of him.

"Mr. Livingstone, did you mean what you said last night?"

He swallowed heavily. "Wh... What did I say?"

"You said you would have your revenge on the gossipers, and that the last person who wronged your daughter found his way to an early grave"

He closed his eyes and groaned.

"Mr. Livingstone, you must see how it looks. You implied that you killed Ambrose McDonald after he spread rumors about Amelia. We know you met with him in the library just a short time before he died. Is that when you did it?"

His eyes sprang open. "It wasn't me! I have an alibi."

He remained seated, allowing me to relax a little. Accusing him in his own office had been a gamble, but one I'd been prepared to take. It could have gone terribly wrong, however, hence I'd left the door open.

I flexed my fingers around the knife I held inside my pocket but did not release it. "You didn't mention an alibi last time we spoke. Nor did you deny going to the library."

"That's because I did go to the library to speak to McDonald. But someone saw me leave and must have also seen McDonald alive at that time. I didn't mention the witness last time because I was hoping to keep his name out of it. We met outside the library and went to a sitting room. The room was decorated in a lot of pink." He wagged a finger at me. "I remember seeing a large stuffed ginger cat by the sofa. Ugly looking thing. That's why I remember it."

"Rooms don't make very good alibis. I'm afraid you'll have to tell me who you were with and why."

"He's a gentleman who wanted to negotiate terms for the marriage of Amelia to his son. A fine, noble gentleman of upstanding character; determined too. He was prepared to agree to very favorable terms. You see, there were several others vying for Amelia's hand, so he wanted to work quickly." A flicker of pain crossed his face and he lowered his head. He pressed his fingers into his eyes. "I cannot believe this is happening. It was all going so well. The suitors lined up to dance with her. They were captivated by her beauty, her wit and charm. And with my money, she could have had her pick of them. I managed to secure the best for her. With the deal as good as sealed, I refused to bow to McDonald's demands for his silence. I refused to pay him."

"You told him that when you met with him in the library?"

"Before that. At the beginning of the night. It was much later when I asked to meet him in the library. As soon as I heard the first rumor blackening Amelia's good name, I knew I needed to do something quickly. So I met with McDonald again and promised to pay his dirty money if he stemmed the tide of his vile gossip. Then I left the library and that's when I met my daughter's future father-in-law."

"You sealed the deal with him."

He gave a nod, but it was not convincing. I suspected the terms of the agreement required Amelia to remain pure. Mr. Livingstone knew the deal had been snatched from his grasp at the last moment.

It sounded like a business arrangement because that's precisely what it was. For people like the Livingstones, emotions rarely mattered when finding a marriage partner. Feelings counted for nothing. The best deal for both parties was all that counted. Last night's outburst had been a result of Mr. Livingstone knowing the deal was off.

"Who was the gentleman?" I asked.

"I'm afraid I can't tell you. I haven't seen him since..." He cleared his throat. "I haven't seen him lately. I need to speak to him before..."

"*I* need to speak to him to verify your alibi."

He picked up his pen and dipped it into the ink. "No. Out of the question. I can't have you badgering him."

I stood. "I understand. Unfortunately I'll have to inform Scotland Yard of your reluctance to co-operate. They'll return shortly, at which point one of two things will happen. You will give them the name of this so-called alibi—"

"'So-called!' But he exists!"

"And your neighbors and staff will see the uniformed policemen and wonder why they're here. Or you will refuse to answer their questions so the police will be forced to interrogate the guests at the Bunburys' ball and discover which gentleman you met. Again, the uniformed officers may cause a stir."

His nostrils flared. "You know how to get your way."

Honey be damned. Sometimes hammers were the only thing that got the job done. I waited patiently for him to write down a name and address on a notepad. He tore off the page and handed it to me.

The name came as a surprise. I knew it, although I'd never met him. I schooled my features so as not to give away to Mr. Livingstone that I was a guest at the ball, not a maid, and was familiar with the family.

I headed back to Harry's office. I wasn't sure I wanted to confront Mr. Livingstone's alibi on my own. Indeed, I wasn't sure I should confront him at all.

What if Jonathon was there? What would he do if he saw me speaking to his father?

I spotted Harry in the café through the window, chatting to Luigi at the counter and sipping coffee. They both looked around upon my entry.

"Ah, there she is," Luigi said, as if they'd been talking about me. "Coffee, Miss Fox?"

"Yes, please." I asked Harry to join me at one of the tables. "You're in late today."

"I slept in."

"Late night, was it?"

He lifted a shoulder in a shrug. He showed no signs of tiredness so he must have got some sleep.

"Did your late night have something to do with the investigation?" I asked.

"No."

"Did you attend a party?"

"Nothing like that."

"So you were at home? Or someone's home, if not your own?"

His gaze narrowed. "No."

"A gentlemen's club?"

"Can I not sleep late from time to time without being subjected to an interrogation?"

"I wouldn't be a good detective if I didn't at least try to get some answers."

"A good detective knows people don't always answer truthfully. She would try to get her answers elsewhere then confront her suspect with them."

Luigi deposited a cup of hot coffee in front of me. I waited until he left before I spoke again.

"Is that an admission that you're going to lie if I ask you what you were doing last night outside the Druitt-Poore's place?"

He lifted his cup to his lips and sipped, but I saw the flicker of surprise pass over him before he schooled his features.

When it became clear he wasn't going to answer, I pressed on. Even if he remained silent, I might read something in his face. "Were you there for me?"

He laughed. "I never guessed you to be so arrogant or vain as to think a man would wait for you on the slim chance you'll happen to pass by and see him."

I held his gaze for a long time without speaking. He didn't look away. At first, I was a little put-out by his teasing dismissal. Perhaps he *did* think me arrogant and vain. But then I realized he had said that to distract me from pursuing the truth.

"I see," I said. "Nicely done."

"What is?"

"You haven't answered my question." I picked up my cup with the fingertips of both hands. "Very well. I'll allow you to keep your secrets."

He smiled. "How magnanimous of you."

"It's none of my affair anyway."

His smile faded.

I sipped my coffee, relishing the bitterness on my tongue. It was just what I needed after a night out.

Clearly Harry's night had finished later than mine. Perhaps it had only really begun when he collected his companion from outside the Druitt-Poores' house.

"Luigi tells me you were here an hour ago looking for me," he said. "Sorry I missed you. Did you learn something at the ball?"

"I learned that Mr. Livingstone has a violent streak when he's drunk. He also threatened anyone who gossiped about his daughter, saying the last fellow who did went to his grave. It sounded like an admission."

"It does."

He didn't seem like he'd just heard about the incident for the first time. There wasn't even so much as a ripple of his eyebrow in surprise. He must have already heard the details from the companion he met last night.

Harry drained his cup and indicated mine. "Finish up and we'll pay a call on Livingstone."

"I already have."

This time his brows arched. "Without me?"

"You weren't in yet, remember?"

He scowled. "You know where I live. You could have found me there."

"And interrupt your...sleep?"

His scowl deepened.

My hesitation might have sounded like suggestive teasing, but I was genuinely interested in whether he'd taken a woman back to his flat after the ball. Interested and somewhat jealous, if I was being honest.

I shook off the thought. Jealousy was ugly at the best of times. It was even uglier when I'd purposely placed physical and emotional distance between us. I had no right to be jealous.

I focused on the investigation and told him about Mr. Livingstone's alibi. "The fellow met Livingstone outside the Bunburys' library. They had some important matters to attend to. Livingstone claims the gentleman would have seen McDonald alive then. I think we should confirm with him."

He nodded. "Who is he?"

"Lord Cremorne."

"Jonathon Hartly's father?"

"You know him?"

"I know of him. Hartly is a regular at the hotel, and I made it my business to know everything about everyone, even if they didn't stay with us."

"Even though he was just my cousin's friend?"

"He still expected the finest service. If Hartly wanted his shoes polished at midnight, I organized it. If he liked strawberries out of season and the kitchen didn't have any, I rang all the nearby markets and restaurants in search of hothouse fruit. If he stayed overnight in a drunken state, I made sure his family were notified and a cab collected him in the morning."

"That was kind of you."

"Kindness had nothing to do with it. That's what I was employed to do."

Talk of him working as assistant manager for the hotel had me wondering what it would have been like if he was still employed there. The situation between us might be awkward now, but it would have been doubly so if he'd never been dismissed.

We paid Luigi and left the café. It wasn't until we were

climbing into an omnibus that Harry asked me why Mr. Livingstone met with Lord Cremorne at the ball.

"Apparently they were negotiating terms for the marriage between Amelia and Jonathon."

He stopped. I stopped too when I realized. "Hartly is marrying?" he asked.

"Not anymore. I doubt it will go ahead, considering her reputation has been smeared. I'm sure Lord Cremorne would have put it in writing that she must be above reproach."

He indicated spare seats near the back. "I thought he was pursuing you."

"So did I, in his own dreadful way."

His head tilted to the side to look at me as he sat beside me. "Dreadful?"

I sighed. "He seems to think his title and wealth make him irresistible to someone without those things. It sometimes makes him unbearable to be around."

"Unbearable is putting it lightly," he muttered. "He shouldn't have tried to court you while his father was in negotiations with Livingstone."

"I don't think he knew."

He merely grunted.

Lord Cremorne lived on Chapel Street, a stone's throw from the grounds of Buckingham Palace. The townhouse was handsome rather than elegant, however, and not overly large compared to some I'd been in, but it would have cost a fortune to purchase. I tilted my head back to take it all in.

"They only moved in five or six years ago," Harry said. "I recall Hartly complaining to your cousin about its size. The house they owned before it, around the corner on Grosvenor Crescent, was much larger."

"Why did they move?"

"Why does anyone move into a smaller residence? Because they were having financial difficulties. Still are, if the rumors are true. Apparently Lord Cremorne might need to sell up and move permanently back to his estate if things don't turn around for them soon."

"No wonder his father was trying to marry Jonathon to the wealthy Amelia Livingstone."

I could feel Harry watching me, but when I turned to look at him, he pretended to study the door knocker.

"Imagine if I'd encouraged Jonathon... I could have been mistress of all this." I indicated the house. "Well, until the money disappeared entirely." I couldn't help laughing at the absurdity of it. "Lord Cremorne would have been livid to be saddled with a poor nobody for a daughter-in-law."

I thought it was all rather amusing, but Harry merely grunted.

He stepped up to the door and slammed the brass knocker down. Even if the butler was nearly deaf and at the back of the house, he would have heard it.

The door opened and Harry introduced us as consultants for Scotland Yard. The butler checked with his master and returned a few moments later to escort us up to Lord Cremorne's office.

I kept my head low while trying to look out for Jonathon. It wouldn't be a complete disaster if he saw me. He already knew that I was investigating Ambrose McDonald's murder. Even so, I didn't want to explain my presence to him. I didn't want to see him at all. He was most likely still in bed, anyway. It wasn't yet midday.

If I wanted to know what Jonathon would look like in twenty-five years' time, I only had to look at Lord Cremorne. Their features were arranged the same, and they both possessed piercing blue eyes. His hair was mostly still blond except for two gray patches at his temples. It was thin, however, not lush like his son's. But idleness and indulgence had caught up to Lord Cremorne, as they would one day with Jonathon if he didn't curb his excesses. The lines across his forehead were deep, and pouches of skin sagged beneath his eyes and jowls. He sat sprawled in the chair, his girth testing his waistcoat buttons.

"This is about the murder of that fellow at the Bunburys'?" he asked, giving Harry his full attention.

"It is." Harry introduced us without naming me. While I didn't recognize Lord Cremorne, and he clearly didn't know me, it was safer to keep my name out of it. I doubted he would have remembered it anyway, just as I doubted he would remember me after we left. He didn't even look at me.

Lord Cremorne was grave. "The murder was an unfortunate occurrence, but I don't understand why you're here. I thought the police arrested the murderer."

"There are still some loose ends. One of which is vouching for where all the guests were at the time of the murder."

"Including me?" He sounded amused, as one is when a child asks a foolish question.

"Everyone."

"When I heard the scream, I was in a sitting room having a conversation with an acquaintance. He can vouch for me. Livingstone's his name."

"And before that?"

"Here and there, but I can assure you, McDonald was very much alive when I went into the sitting room with Livingstone. I saw him in the library. Livingstone was just leaving him, as it happens."

"What was your conversation with Livingstone about?"

"I don't see what that has to do with anything."

Harry waited.

After a moment in which the men stared at one another like prize fighters in the ring, Lord Cremorne said, "Ah. I see. You've come from Livingstone's and wish to test my story against his, looking for inconsistencies. Eh? Good man. You've clearly done this sort of thing before. Since I like to see an enterprising young fellow choose an honorable career path, I will answer you, even though it goes against my instincts to discuss a private matter with a stranger." He shifted his weight in the chair. "Livingstone and I were discussing the marriage of his daughter to my son. However, we could not come to terms. There you have it. All above board."

"Thank you, sir."

"Keep that between ourselves, shall we? No need for the world to know our business."

Harry nodded. "Of course. Miss Livingstone has endured enough gossip lately. There's no need to add to it."

"She has only herself to blame."

My blood rose, hot and thick. I couldn't stay silent any longer, even though some part of me knew it was futile to voice my opinion. "Does Mr. McDonald deserve none of the blame for seducing her?"

Lord Cremorne frowned at me, seeing me for the first time. "A girl worthy of being the future Lady Cremorne doesn't allow herself to be seduced. My son's wife must be beyond reproach."

"Pity your son isn't."

Lord Cremorne leaned forward and studied me closely. "Do I know you?"

"No," Harry said as he ushered me past the waiting butler and out of the office. His firm grip on my elbow didn't loosen until we reached the ground floor entrance hall.

The door opened just as the footman reached for the door-knob. Jonathon strode in but stopped upon seeing us. His jaw dropped and his gaze slid from me to Harry.

"You again," he snapped.

Again?

Jonathon turned to me. "What are you doing here with him?"

Harry's grip tightened once more. "We were just leaving."

"Kindly release Miss Fox and allow her to speak for herself. She doesn't need anyone else to speak for her, let alone a former employee of her uncle's."

Harry tensed, although he did release me. He clasped his hands at his back. I wondered if that was to stop himself from punching Jonathon's nose.

Considerable diplomacy was required to diffuse the situation. Unfortunately, I was still annoyed by Lord Cremorne's comments and diplomacy was beyond me. "Do stop the chest beating, Jonathon."

He stiffened.

"To answer your question, we're here to speak to your father about the night of the murder."

He made a scoffing sound in his throat. "You're still continuing with this ridiculous endeavor?"

"Investigating a murder isn't ridiculous."

"The police have arrested the killer. You're wasting your time, Cleo. Not to mention, it's unworthy of you. Not just the activity, but spending all your time with..." He jutted his jaw in Harry's direction.

"Just as I am capable of speaking for myself, I'm also capable of deciding what—and who—is worthy of my time."

Jonathon pressed his lips together and drew in a deep breath. Reining in his temper perhaps? "Cleo, can we talk in private?"

"No. I have to go."

"I'll wait for you outside," Harry said, his voice dark but no longer angry.

I must have looked as though I wanted to throttle him for abandoning me, because he added, "He's right. You need to talk." To Jonathon, he said, "Cleo helps me from time to time when I have to question someone of your father's caliber. I find they open up more in the presence of someone with gentle breeding. She's never in harm's way and her reputation is always foremost on my mind, and hers. Be assured, there's no need for alarm."

Jonathon looked as shocked by the speech as I felt. Neither of us had the presence of mind to respond.

Harry left but paused in the doorway. He mouthed "Be nice" to me. With his back to Harry, Jonathon didn't see. The footman closed the door then melted away into the shadows.

While I understood why Harry was worried, he didn't need to be. Jonathon may not like me investigating, but he wouldn't do anything about it. If Floyd was willing to let it slide, Jonathon had no reason to interfere. It wasn't his place, and a gentleman never overstepped.

"Come into the sitting room," he said.

"No. We have nothing to say to one another." He winced and I regretted my unkind tone. "I like you, Jonathon. You're a good friend to Floyd, and he certainly needs friends right now."

He looked down at his feet.

"But we're not suited. You need someone who was born and raised in your world. Someone who appreciates all this." I indicated the large entrance hall with the crystal chandelier hanging above our heads, the gilded clock on the table and paintings on the walls. "Your father understands that."

He frowned. "What do you mean?" It was odd to me that he didn't seem to know about the arrangement his father tried to broker with Mr. Livingstone, but perhaps Lord

Cremorne wanted to be absolutely sure an arrangement could be brokered before breaking the news to his son.

"If you intend to court a woman in future, you ought to speak with your father first so there's no...confusion." Before he could ask me to clarify, I added, "Let's remain friends, and we'll laugh about this in years to come."

He glanced at the closed door. "You can do better than him."

"There is nothing going on between Harry and me, nor will there ever be. But that doesn't mean there will be anything going on between us, either." I pointed at him then myself. "The sooner you accept that I am determined never to marry, the happier you'll be. It's not personal, Jonathon."

"I see now that you are determined. Does he see it too?"

"Harry accepts that we are merely associates." I gave a dismissive wave. "We're not even friends. Neither of us could bring ourselves to be friendly with the other. I had him dismissed from his position at the hotel, for goodness' sake. It's hardly a solid foundation for a friendship." I bit down on my tongue to stop myself rambling. It was a sure clue that I was lying. Not that Jonathon would know that about me. He hardly even knew me.

He opened the door. "You should go." It was said without heat or bitterness, thankfully.

I stepped out. "What did you mean when you said 'You again?' Are you referring to when you saw Harry with me in the hotel a few days ago?"

He opened his mouth to speak but closed it again. He looked past me to Harry, waiting on the pavement. "Good day, Cleo. Perhaps I'll see you later." His attempted smile was unconvincing, but at least he tried.

I tried too, hopefully with more conviction. I was certainly relieved that he wasn't angry anymore. My little speech about not being Harry's friend must have worked.

"All's well," I said when I joined Harry.

He fell into step beside me. "Are you sure? He didn't look like he'd accepted you investigating with me."

"He hasn't and he won't, but that doesn't mean he'll do anything about it. He's a wretch, but he's not cruel. He's no Ambrose McDonald."

Harry glanced sideways at me. "What did you say to him?"

"I explained how things are between you and me. Or, rather, how things aren't. As far as he's aware, you and I barely put up with each other."

"He believed that?"

"I think so. He's arrogant enough to assume I wouldn't be interested in a former employee of my uncle's."

"Indeed," he muttered.

CHAPTER 14

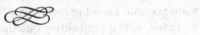

e parted on Piccadilly outside the hotel. We'd once again come to a dead end in our investigation. While Mr. Livingstone had an alibi for the time of the murder, Amelia did not. I couldn't recall seeing her dancing the entire time. She was still a suspect.

As I often did when an investigation stalled, I talked to Harmony and the other staff. We made lists in the parlor and talked through what we knew about each of our suspects. It amounted to a lot of motives, but no proof.

"You need to speak to all the staff who worked on the night of the ball," Harmony pointed out.

"We have. The only one we haven't spoken to is the maid calling herself Jane Eyre. I suspect she'll know something, considering she was the one who accepted payment from Mr. McDonald, but unless she shows up at Searcys office asking for more work, our hands are tied. We have no way of finding her."

"You should use your detective skills."

I arched my brows. "And where do you suggest we start?"

"I don't know. You're the detective, not me."

Victor frowned. "Jane Eyre...the name sounds familiar."

Harmony rolled her eyes. "It's fake. Jane Eyre is a character from a book."

Goliath chuckled. "If you read books, you'd know that."

Victor glared at him. The baby-faced cook could look quite

menacing when he wanted to. The scar helped, as did the hand resting on his knife belt.

Goliath gulped.

"You've read it, have you, Goliath?" Peter said with a smirk. "So what's your favorite part?"

Goliath pulled a face. "You haven't read it either."

"I might have." Peter lifted his chin. "I'm assistant manager now. I want to better myself."

Frank, who'd been sitting quietly in the corner sipping tea, snorted. "By reading gothic romances?"

Victor stood to refill his cup from the teapot. He stopped beside Frank and glared down at him. "There's nothing wrong with gothic romances. I like them."

Frank's gaze slid to Harmony. "Right you are."

Harmony pretended to be above the childish exchange. "So what are you going to do now, Cleo?"

I sighed. "Get ready to go out for the evening. I believe I'm attending a dinner somewhere, although I'd much rather curl up in bed with a gothic romance."

"You say that now, but you'll enjoy it once you get there and the gentlemen start flirting with you."

"Flossy's the one they flirt with. I'm merely her accessory."

She collected the empty teacups, placing them on a wooden tray. She passed the tray to Goliath. "Take these to the scullery for washing. I have to do Cleo's hair while I explain to her that she is just as popular as her cousin."

"You're just being kind," I said.

She thrust a hand on her hip. "When have I ever said something just to be kind? I speak the truth, plain and simple."

"Sometimes too much truth," Frank muttered. He dodged Harmony's swipe and beat a hasty retreat from the parlor.

No one else dared say a word.

* * *

AFTER HARMONY FINISHED DOING my hair, she went to Flossy's rooms to assist her to get ready. I went in search of Floyd. He wasn't coming with us tonight, and I wanted to make sure he wasn't going to do anything foolish like play cards with dangerous gamblers.

"How do you get out of these things?" I asked as I swanned past him and entered the sitting room.

"Do come in, cousin," he murmured.

"I'm serious. I want to know why I have to go and you don't. You're a Bainbridge. You ought to be invited ahead of me."

"I'm older and male. I don't have to do what my parents say."

"Is your father aware of that rule?"

He huffed. "He's doesn't care about social dinners. He only cares about the hotel. If our hosts tonight were people he needed to court in some way for the benefit of the hotel, he'd make sure I attended and put on a good show as the Bainbridge heir. But they're just friends of Mother's and not well connected. Tomorrow night will be different when we host dinner."

His view was rather cynical, but I couldn't fault it. From what I knew of my uncle, it was a true observation. If the other dinner guests were investors, potential investors, guests or potential guests, then it would be a different story and Floyd would have to attend. He wasn't yet at an age where his parents wanted to marry him off either, so he was safe on that score too.

"Brandy?" he asked, waving a half-full decanter at me.

"Isn't it a little early?"

"Yes." He poured two fingers worth into a glass and downed it in one gulp. He refilled the glass.

"Steady on, Floyd. It's going to be a long night." I lifted my gaze to his. "Isn't it?"

He ignored me and sat on the armchair opposite. "So, what's going on between you and Armitage?"

I clicked my tongue and rolled my eyes.

"Tired of hearing the question?" he went on. "Then perhaps you shouldn't see him so much."

"I'm not tired of it. You and Jonathon are the only ones asking it."

"Others would, if they knew you saw him most days."

"As I explained to Jonathon, we investigate together from

time to time. This is one of those occasions. It means nothing. There is nothing *going on*, as you put it. And if you value our relationship, you'll not ask again."

He put up his hands in surrender, making the liquid slosh in the glass. "Jonathon made out that there's more than the investigation. And, to be perfectly honest, I wasn't sure. I know how women are."

I arched a brow. "And how are we?"

"I've seen the female guests with him, Cleo, so don't pretend to be offended. They would flirt and flutter their eyelashes at him. It wasn't just the young women, either. I still get asked which hotel he now works at. We're lucky he didn't take a position with one of our rivals or we'd lose a third of our regulars." He laughed softly, so I wasn't sure if he was joking or not.

"There is nothing between Harry and me," I said again, this time with emphasis. "Nor will there be. So stop acting like the protective older cousin and more like the lazy good for nothing everyone else believes you to be, but I know is just a ruse."

He stared at me for a moment then chuckled again. Perhaps he was already halfway to being drunk. "I like you, Cleo. You're more fun than Flossy."

"You might change your mind when you hear what I have to say. Tell me, why did you see Harry last night?"

He lowered his glass to his lap. "Ah. You know about that."

I hadn't, not for certain, but now I did. "I know he met you outside the Druitt-Poores' house. Was that an arranged meeting or did he just show up?"

"I can't tell you. We have a gentleman's agreement to remain silent."

"You made an agreement?"

He nodded. "Armitage thought you might find out we met and ask why, so we agreed not to tell you anything. Seems he knows you rather well. Better than me. I said you'd never know. How *did* you find out?"

I drummed my fingers on the sofa arm and stared at the decanter. Perhaps if I got him drunker, he'd tell me what Harry was up to.

"That won't work." He pointedly set the glass down on the table beside him.

"Very well. I understand some things between gentlemen are sacred. But your agreement was only about last night. It doesn't cover tonight. Are you meeting Harry again?"

He crossed his arms, tucking his hands away under his armpits. He tilted his chin up and turned to give me his profile. He might be acting like a ten-year-old, but it was a stubborn ten-year-old.

I sighed and stood. "Have it your way."

He whipped around to face me again. "You won't get answers from Armitage."

"I never said I would try."

"But I know you will. He won't give in either. He's as stubborn as a mule. Trust me on that," he added in a mutter.

I let myself out and closed the door, just as the lift door opened and Jonathon stepped out. He stopped upon seeing me. With his head tilted and the blond mop of hair dripping over his eyes, he looked unsure of himself. Considering he was usually so arrogant, it endeared me to him a little.

"It's all right," I assured him. "I don't hold a grudge. We are friends again."

He looked relieved. "Good. I don't like arguing with you, Cleo."

"Nor I with you." I glanced at Floyd's door then signaled for Jonathon to step a few paces away from it with me. I didn't take him all the way to my suite, however. I would never willingly be alone in the same room with him again, just in case he misread the situation.

"Is something the matter?" he asked. "You have a curious look on your face."

There was nothing for it but to come right out and say it. I should have asked this morning when the idea first formed, but it wasn't the right time. He was too upset, as was I. I only hoped the gentlemen's agreement didn't encompass him, too. Although if it did, he was the weakest link.

"Why did Harry Armitage meet you and Floyd outside the Druitt-Poores' last night?"

He expelled a long breath, as if he'd been expecting the

question but hoped not to be asked. "I'm not supposed to say..."

But it was clear he wanted to tell me. A little encouragement should make him confess. "If this is in relation to Floyd's predicament then I should know about it. You already involved me so I should be kept up to date. Otherwise, how do I know what part I can play?"

"Very well. It's not as though it matters. Armitage made no difference to the situation. In fact, he was quite useless."

"Harry?"

He nodded. "Armitage was waiting for us outside the Druitt-Poores'. Apparently you'd told him about the ball."

"Just in passing."

"He followed us in a cab from there to our destination. He intercepted us outside the house and told Floyd he could help him pay back what he owed Dutch."

"Dutch?"

"The gambler. I guessed that you told him about Floyd's debt, but I know I never gave you the name. I can't work out how Armitage knew it."

"Because he's good at what he does."

"Meaning?"

I dismissed the question with a wave. "Was Floyd angry that Harry knew?"

"At first, but Armitage calmed him down by making him think all would be well. Floyd seemed almost relieved for Armitage to be involved. He should have got more details about Armitage's plan before letting him inside. It was a private party, you see, and only guests of invited guests were allowed. Floyd vouched for Armitage and Dutch agreed he could join in. Well." He made a scoffing sound. "Your associate clearly just wanted to help himself. He probably assumed playing with the big boys would earn him big money."

"I don't understand. Harry played cards?"

He nodded. "And won, naturally. That's always Dutch's way. Let them win the first time so they get cocky, then the next time, take them for all they've got, and more. Last night was the first instalment so Armitage won a tidy sum."

"That's good, isn't it? If he won, he can give it all to Dutch on Floyd's behalf?"

He shook his head. "One has to declare beforehand that one is playing on another's behalf. It's a gentlemanly thing. You wouldn't understand."

"But Harry can just give Floyd the money now and Floyd can take it tonight. Dutch needn't know where it came from."

"First of all, Floyd wouldn't accept money from Armitage."

"A gentleman's thing again?"

"More of a former employee thing. And secondly, it wasn't nearly enough to cover what Floyd owes Dutch. He would have to return again and again, but Dutch won't let him win a second or third time."

I chewed my lip, trying to think as Harry would. But I couldn't. It didn't make sense. Why was he even helping Floyd at all?

"That's why I was trying to urge you not to associate with him anymore." At my blank look, he added, "Armitage clearly wanted to splash around in a more exclusive pool than what he's used to. He enjoyed his evening, met some important people, flirted with a pretty actress, and left with his pockets full." He waited for that to sink in. "He used Floyd, Cleo. He's probably using you too. While I would never tell you what to do or who to see—"

"You already have, actually."

"I'm urging you to be careful. At best, Armitage has simply failed in his aim to help his former employer's son. At worst, he has another agenda that involves you."

I stared at the closed door to Floyd's suite, not quite sure what to make of Jonathon's story. If it was true, what was the point of Harry going at all? He'd not succeeded in helping Floyd. Was he trying to impress me? If so, why make Floyd and Jonathon agree to a code that dictated they couldn't tell me? I doubted Harry was out to impress me anyway. He'd never given me an encouraging sign.

Perhaps Jonathon was right and Harry had done it for his own selfish reasons.

But that wasn't the Harry I knew, and I refused to accept Jonathon's version. I'd considered thanking him for informing me. But I wouldn't thank him for attempting to disparage a good person's name.

"Harry is a better man than you give him credit for. I'm sure his intentions will become clear soon enough."

I walked away, but not before I saw my words wipe off his smirk.

* * *

DINNER WAS a distraction from my thoughts about Harry's motives, but not in a good way. It began inauspiciously enough with the host and hostess greeting me warmly. I'd met them before. They were a friendly couple, entirely without guile. Their other guests were another matter, however.

Two more families dined with us. My aunt and uncle knew them, but I did not. Instinct warned me something was amiss during the introductions in the drawing room before dinner. They were stiff and brief, and I was given a thorough going-over by more than one set of eyes. While it's not unusual to take one's measure upon an introduction, it is unusual to do it openly and with the top lip curled in a sneer.

It would seem I wasn't good enough to be in their presence. I thought it was because of my lack of fortune and breeding, but a whispered word caught my ear just before the dinner gong sounded. "Bluestocking," one of the older women said to the other. From the way the second woman looked down her nose at me, I suspected she agreed with the first. In their eyes, my education was as appalling as Amelia's loss of purity.

My aunt and uncle didn't notice. Uncle Ronald was oblivious and Aunt Lilian was still scatter-brained from the dose of tonic she took before leaving the hotel. I did my best to ignore the two dragons, but it became clear during dinner that the gossip had spread.

Guests at the other end of the table began looking at me oddly, as if seeing me for the first time. Some wore assessing looks, but most regarded me with disappointment, or even disgust.

After the women left the men to their port and cigars and

returned to the drawing room, the whispers continued. It was only a matter of time before my aunt heard them.

Flossy already had. She took my arm and steered me to a corner. "Now don't get upset, Cleo, but there is a rumor going around about you."

"So I gathered. Does it have something to do with being educated?"

"It does." She studied a cluster of three women seated on the sofa who were deep in conversation, their gazes flicking to me.

"And that is cause for gossip because…?"

"Because it is unbecoming for a young woman to be so intelligent."

"Is that all?"

"Don't be so dismissive, Cleo. It's a very damaging rumor. No gentleman wants a lady who is cleverer than he."

"If all the gentlemen at this party have deemed me more intelligent without getting to know me then they are indeed stupid." There was no point telling her yet again that I had no intention to marry. She clearly didn't believe me.

"It's not a joke, Cleo. You won't get invited anywhere important."

"You're not making your point as convincingly as you think you are."

"And, by extension, nor will I."

I took her hand and squeezed. Poor Flossy. She had just recovered from Lady Bunbury's previous attempt to ostracize us, and now she was going through it again. Only this time I couldn't prove it was Lady Bunbury and so my aunt couldn't blackmail her. Besides, it was too late for that. The damage was already done.

"Don't jump to that conclusion yet," I said. "Me being labeled a bluestocking may not affect you." I could have gone on to say that no one who knew her would mistake her for being too clever, but I couldn't bring myself to be cruel, even though she would probably take it as a compliment.

The entire situation was absurd. I would have laughed if she hadn't looked like she wanted to cry.

"Who would do such a thing?" she murmured. "Who is so jealous of you that they want to stifle your opportunities?"

I didn't respond. It would make no difference telling her it was Lady Bunbury. Indeed, it might upset her more knowing London's leading socialite still held a grudge against me.

"Oh dear," Flossy said on a sigh. "Now Mother has heard, too."

Aunt Lilian had been in a quiet conversation with the hostess. They both suddenly looked at me with twin expressions of concern and sympathy. At least I had allies in that quarter. Indeed, some of the younger women also looked at me anew, not with sneers but with curiosity.

The daughter of the hostess invited me to sit with her on one of the sofas where we were soon joined by another woman of Flossy's age. We fell into a conversation about Cambridge University, and how I'd been allowed to attend lectures but not earn a degree. They were enthusiastic about the idea of being educated like a man, and wished their parents were as progressive and encouraging as my grandparents had been.

By the time the gentlemen joined us, I felt happier than I had all night. I didn't care if the men thought me strange or dull. I was only disappointed for Flossy's sake. She seemed to think it was the end of *her* social life.

My aunt and uncle didn't raise the topic of the gossip on the way home, although both were silent. In my aunt's case, it was probably because her head ached after her tonic wore off. In my uncle's, it could just be that he was in a morose mood.

I managed to avoid them the following morning. I went down to the foyer, umbrella at the ready, but did not leave the hotel. I wasn't sure where to go. The investigation had stalled so I had no reason to see Harry. As much as I wanted to confront him about joining Floyd and Jonathon at the gambling house, I decided against it. There was no point. I knew him well enough to know he would honor his gentleman's code and refuse to speak to me about it.

I was considering going for a walk, despite the drizzling rain, when Mr. Hobart approached. There were several hotel guests milling about to check out, but he bypassed them all to speak to me.

Something was wrong.

He confirmed my suspicion when he asked me to join him

in his office. "I just had a telephone call from my brother," he said as he sat behind his desk.

My heart sank. I could tell from his face that it wasn't good news.

"He has been forced into retirement, effective immediately. His superiors sent him home after he arrived for work this morning."

"Didn't they even give him the opportunity to say goodbye to his colleagues?"

He shook his head sadly.

"I am so sorry," I said. "This is all my fault."

"I don't see how."

"Lord Bunbury must have pulled some strings with his friends at the Metropolitan Police. If I hadn't questioned him and his wife over the murder of Ambrose McDonald, this wouldn't have happened. He's doing it in retaliation."

He gave me a sympathetic look. "Do not blame yourself, Miss Fox. My brother asked you and Harry to investigate, and you did the right thing by questioning Lord and Lady Bunbury. No one is above the law. Not even them. And if Stephen's superiors don't believe that, well..." He parted his hands and shrugged. "Stephen was going to retire soon anyway."

"Yes, but on his own terms. This way isn't fair. He has had a long and successful career and deserves a proper send-off."

He clasped his hands and tapped the thumbs together. "Hmmm."

"Did D.I. Hobart say anything about Harry and me and the investigation? I assume we have to end it. Not that there is anything more we can do. We've reached a brick wall, and I can't see a way over or around it."

"Ordinarily I would advise you to pull down the wall." He offered a weak smile. "But not this time."

I left Mr. Hobart's office feeling flat. I was in no mood to battle the elements for a walk, so I returned to my room and stayed there until after lunch. Harmony joined me after her shift ended and loaned a sympathetic ear. I felt a little better after sharing D.I. Hobart's plight with her and gorging on sandwiches sent up from the kitchen.

Flossy arrived after Harmony left and reminded me that

we had an afternoon tea party to attend, and that her parents were hosting dinner that night and I was expected to be there.

"Even though I am a social pariah?"

She blinked her big eyes at me. "Oh yes. Showing up is the best way to end the gossip. When people see you are unaffected by it, they'll see no sport in spreading it and just stop. It's a pity Amelia Livingstone didn't understand that. It's too late for her now, but not for you, Cleo." She patted my hand.

I drew her into a hug. "You are so wise sometimes, Cousin."

"I know. And I didn't even go to university to get this way."

* * *

AFTERNOON TEA WASN'T AS dreadful as I thought it would be. For one thing, the hostess didn't rescind my invitation, as I'd worried she would. For another, Aunt Lilian and her friends sat at one end of the drawing room while their daughters, Flossy's friends, sat with Flossy and me at the other.

Most of the mothers gave me circumspect looks, worried I would corrupt their girls just by sitting with them. Their daughters were altogether different. Out of the four of them, only one tried to ignore me. The other three wanted to talk about Cambridge, university, and the future of women's education. The one who clearly abhorred the thought of an educated female did brighten when the conversation turned to the ratio of men to women on campus. All of a sudden, a university education didn't seem quite so horrid in her eyes. I wasn't sure whether to be appalled by the reason for her change of heart or amused.

Afterwards, I couldn't help pointing out how much Flossy had enjoyed the day. Even she seemed interested in hearing how free my life in Cambridge had been, how I'd been able to go about the city alone, join clubs and societies, and meet with whomever I wanted. It was quite a different life to the one she lived here.

"It wasn't a complete disaster," she agreed as we approached our waiting conveyance outside.

I didn't mention the gossip to my aunt and she pretended nothing was amiss as we chatted all the way home. She seemed to be only half listening, however.

Flossy pointed out some homes of people they knew through the window to me. She paused when our carriage slowed due to the traffic and sat back in the seat. "I don't know anyone who lives in this part of Portland Place."

As she said it, a small white plaque on a black door caught my eye. There was no writing on the plaque, just the symbol of a blue dove.

I'd seen that symbol before.

"Did you say this is Portland Place?" I asked.

Flossy nodded. "There are some nice buildings along here, although the traffic is a nightmare this afternoon."

"Indeed."

My mind raced through what we knew about the case so far and how it fit in with that symbol on the plaque. Portland Place...the Portland Club... It must have been named after the street on which it was located. And behind that door with the plaque must be the club itself. The symbol couldn't be a coincidence.

All I had to do now was convince Harry that we should continue with the investigation, even though his father no longer worked at Scotland Yard. I couldn't think why he'd refuse. He must be as interested in seeing this investigation through to its end as I was. If he did refuse, I'd continue the investigation alone. As an independent, educated woman, it was my right. It was also expected of me now.

CHAPTER 15

$\mathcal{I}$ had very little time before I needed to start dressing for dinner, so I didn't divert to Soho and collect Harry from his office. If he wasn't there, it would be a wasted journey.

I was disappointed to find that Mr. Underwood wasn't at the boarding house when I arrived. My disappointment faded, however, when I realized I could obtain answers from the landlady. Mrs. Rumble was a chatty woman and quite without guile. She was surprised to discover that my questions weren't about Reggie Smith but about his neighbor.

"Why do you want to know about Mr. Underwood? Is he somehow tangled up in the murder, too? Good lord, I hope not." She pressed a hand to her breast. "It's awful enough thinking that Mr. Smith is guilty, but to think there have been two murderers under my roof!"

I quickly threw water over the idea before it caught fire. "Don't fret. Mr. Underwood is not under suspicion." At this point, I could have added.

But the more I thought about it, the more suspicious I became. Ambrose McDonald often visited the Portland Club, a discreet place where men who liked men frequented. The club's symbol was a dove inside a circle. I'd seen that same symbol on a card in Mr. Underwood's possession. It couldn't be a coincidence. If he also visited the club, it was likely he

182

knew Ambrose McDonald. Yet he denied it the first time we'd met.

Mrs. Rumble was still looking anxious about my interest in Mr. Underwood. I needed to set her mind at ease or she might never open up. "He may be a witness without even realizing it. I wanted to question him about Mr. Smith again." It was a clumsy effort, but it seemed to assuage her fears a little.

She wrung her hands in her apron. "Yes, of course. I don't think Mr. Smith is guilty, you know. He was such a polite young man. Always paid his board on time. Never gave me any trouble. I'd like to see him released, and if knowing more about Mr. Underwood helps you, I will tell you what I know."

"I'm pleased to hear it. Would you say Mr. Underwood is a good fellow, trustworthy?"

"Oh yes. He's a quiet, private man. Never makes a fuss."

"Have you ever seen anything in his room that gave you pause?"

"I don't go in. He cleans it himself."

"Isn't that odd?"

"It's not common, but some are happy to clean themselves. It saves on the board, you see."

I would have liked to look inside to search for private letters or some other connection to McDonald, but I suspected it would be a step too far for the landlady. "Do you have a curfew here?"

She shook her head. "The doors are locked at eleven, but the boarders all have their own key to come and go as they please. Some work late, you see. Mr. Smith often worked well into the evening when he was hired as a footman for parties."

"And Mr. Underwood? Does he come and go late into the night?"

She nodded. "Thursdays through Sundays. He leaves just before midnight and comes home before sun-up. He's very quiet, but there's nothing wrong with these old ears." She chuckled, but it quickly faded. "Why is that relevant?"

"It's not. I just wanted to know when he was home so I could ask him about Mr. Smith's movements, if he heard anything through the walls, that sort of thing." I removed a piece of paper from my bag and showed it to her. When I'd got home, and before I left, I'd drawn a dove inside a circle, the symbol from the door on Portland Place. "Have you seen this before?"

"Can't say I have."

I thanked her and left. By the time I arrived back at the Mayfair, I had my next moves all planned in my head. It was Thursday. According to Mrs. Rumble, Mr. Underwood regularly left the boarding house near midnight every night from Thursday to Sunday. I suspected he went to the Portland Club, but I wanted to make sure. That meant following him.

I stopped at the post desk at the Mayfair Hotel to organize a message to be sent to Harry. Then I headed downstairs to the kitchen before returning to my rooms to tell Harmony my plan while she arranged my hair for dinner.

She thought it was dangerous but conceded it was the best way to get answers; perhaps the only way. In the end, she agreed I should do it. I didn't tell her I was going to do it anyway, whether she liked it or not.

* * *

AUNT LILIAN WAS the perfect hostess at dinner. She was capable and generous, beautiful and elegant, and full of life and energy. I knew the latter wouldn't last long, and I worried it would drive her to take more of her tonic at some point in the evening.

The guests were almost thirty in number and consisted of some of my aunt and uncle's friends as well as important hotel guests. Mrs. and Miss Hessing were among their number. The mother was seated beside a quiet, mousy gentleman who didn't seem to mind that the woman on his left didn't stop talking. Miss Hessing was seated between two middle-aged gentlemen who carried on polite conversation with her. I knew one of them was a widower, openly seeking a new wife. My aunt knew precisely what she was doing when she thought up the seating arrangements.

Her single seating failure was me. I found myself next to a highly educated gentleman who'd studied in Cambridge. On paper, we were well suited. He'd traveled widely, and I was interested in learning about the world. He was handsome and friendly, neither too meek nor dominating. Unfortunately, when he discovered I attended lectures in Cambridge and was an advocate for opening up higher education to women, he turned cold. It was as if I'd told him I liked to roll around in mud.

I wouldn't have mentioned it at all, but the woman on his other side did. Although she seemed genuinely interested, there was a gleam in her eye when the gentleman seated between us railed against women taking up positions in universities that should have gone to men. No amount of pointing out that the women didn't replace men, merely added to the overall number, had any effect. He talked over the top of me. He then turned to the woman on his other side and chatted to her for the rest of the night.

Good riddance.

The gentleman on my other side was older and offered little in the way of conversation so I spent much of the evening thinking about how to make an early exit.

I caught sight of my aunt, watching me from the other end of the table, a troubled look on her face.

After the men adjourned to the smoking and billiards rooms, we ladies moved into the private sitting room. Aunt Lilian steered me towards a corner.

"I am sorry, my dear," she said. "You didn't seem to get along with your dinner partners."

"My education came up."

Her gaze narrowed and slid towards the girl who'd been seated next to my Cambridge partner. "Little snake. I should have known she'd be jealous of you. It's not that she wants him for herself; she just doesn't like seeing other women succeed. I should have put her between two elderly men."

"Don't worry about it, Aunt. I was glad she mentioned it. Imagine if I'd enjoyed my evening with him, and he'd taken that the wrong way? It would have become very awkward."

She pressed her lips together and blinked severely at me. It was as much of a chastisement as she'd ever given me. "You will want to marry when you find the right man. He just wasn't it. And you're right. It's fortunate you discovered that early." She huffed out a frustrated breath. "Honestly, I had no idea he would be so against women being educated."

"Most men are."

"And some women, too." She sighed. "I cannot believe you've become the topic of conversation. There are far more interesting things to discuss than your education. I don't understand all the fuss about having a bluestocking in our midst. It's not as though you're a bore. Indeed, you can be charming and agreeable. My sister knew what she was doing when she raised you."

It was the best I could hope for from my aunt. She didn't understand the importance of education for women either. But at least she didn't try to censor me at these dinners, nor did she blame me for the guests not turning up. Four places had been quietly and quickly removed by the waiters before the first course was served. I suspected their absence had something to do with not wanting to dine with me. It seemed like an over-reaction, but these people never ceased to surprise me with their snobbery.

I almost told my aunt that Lady Bunbury was to blame for the rumors. Aunt Lilian had come up against her before and won. But she couldn't win this time. Indeed, the rumor was out now. We had already lost, and it would only upset my aunt more. Besides, it would blow over soon enough. It was hardly a scandal on par with Amelia Livingstone's, for example.

Indeed, Amelia's plight was the main topic of the whispered conversations in the sitting room. With the gentlemen gone, they didn't hold back. I wondered if the men were having the same conversation. I'd have to remember to ask Floyd later.

I spent the next half hour talking to Miss Hessing and a few other young women who told me they admired me for getting an education. Some clearly didn't believe their own words, but others did. I then retired, claiming a headache, and returned to my suite where Harmony was waiting for me.

She quickly helped me change out of my evening gown and into a plain black dress. We snuck out of my rooms and took the staff exit near the kitchen. It led to the lane beside the hotel where Victor stood, leaning against the wall, smoking.

He stubbed the cigarette into the bricks and gave us a nod. Without speaking, we left the lane, avoiding the brightly lit front entrance of the hotel where guests dressed in furs and silks returned from an evening at the opera, theater or private party. Some of the men would leave again to go to a gentleman's club. Floyd would probably be among them.

I tried not to think about him getting further in debt, or of what Jonathon had said about Harry's attempt to help Floyd —that he'd only done it to impress me. He was wrong. He must be. I was already impressed with Harry; he didn't need to try to extricate my cousin from his self-inflicted problem for my benefit.

I gave him no sign that he'd risen in my esteem when he joined us outside his building. Indeed, I didn't feel like having that sort of conversation with him right after he scolded me.

He stood underneath a streetlamp, arms crossed over his chest, his expression dark and forbidding. "I could have gone alone." His voice was low, almost a growl. "There's no need for you to come, too."

"It's my investigation as well as yours," I shot back. "Harmony and Victor escorted me here, so I was perfectly safe the entire time. Now, are you coming with me, or do you want to stand there and brood?"

He walked alongside me, Harmony and Victor behind. We parted ways with them at the corner and headed in opposite directions. On our way to the boarding house, I filled Harry in on the Portland Club's door plaque, and the matching symbol I'd seen on a card in Mr. Underwood's case.

He agreed it was a very strong coincidence.

"Your uncle told me about your father's forced retirement," I said as we walked. "How is he taking it?"

"In his stride, as he takes most things; although I think he's a little upset with the speed of it. My mother is furious with his superiors for the way they handled it."

"I'm sure she is, and I don't blame her."

Harry's mother was a formidable woman who still held a grudge against me for getting Harry dismissed from the hotel. I suspected she'd never forgive me, even if he made an enormous success of his detective agency.

"She's planning to cook his favorite meals every night this week," he said. "Naturally I'm going to dine with them."

"Naturally."

"I wouldn't want them dining alone and my mother always cooks too much when it's just the two of them."

"You're a good son. I'm sure they appreciate both your company and the lack of waste." After a moment's silence, I added, "The dismissal is Lord Bunbury's doing."

"Most likely." He turned sharply to look at me. "Have you suffered any repercussions?"

"No." Being ostracized for my education wasn't a repercussion that affected me greatly, and not one I thought worthy of a mention.

"Your family?"

"They're fine."

"Good."

"Why 'good?'"

"Because family is important."

It was the perfect opening to ask him about helping Floyd, but I didn't. Whatever his motive for going to the gambling house, it had ended without success. It was done now and it might only serve to embarrass him if I brought it up.

We arrived at the boarding house but did not go in. We waited opposite and, just as Mrs. Rumble had said, Mr. Underwood slipped out at a quarter to midnight. Harry set off to follow him, but I held back.

"What's wrong?" he asked.

"I want to see inside his room. I've got a feeling there's something in there he doesn't want anyone to know. You follow him, I'll catch up."

"I'm not leaving you." He watched the retreating form of Mr. Underwood then nodded at the house. "We'll go in. Your instincts are rarely wrong."

"I believe that's the nicest thing you've ever said to me." I crossed the road, leaving him in my wake.

I lit the candle I'd brought with me and kept watch while he used his lock picks to open the door. It took a few minutes, but he managed to get it open with a soft click of the lock. He insisted on going first, peeking through the gap before opening the door wider.

It was dark inside with all the curtains closed and no lights on. With only the light from my candle to guide us, we tiptoed up the stairs to Mr. Underwood's room. Harry once again picked the lock, and moments later, we were inside.

We didn't have to look very hard to find what Mr. Underwood was hiding from the landlady. Indeed, we didn't have to look at all. It was obvious from the smell of turpentine that he painted in the room. The small room contained a bed, trunk and dresser, but instead of a table and chairs, there was an easel, brushes and paint palettes. An incomplete painting occupied the easel while two finished ones leaned against the bed. They looked good to my untrained eye.

We searched through his things but found nothing else of interest and no letters from Ambrose McDonald. We headed back down the stairs. At the bottom of the staircase, Harry suddenly stopped. I bumped into his back and had to catch myself with my hand to his shoulder. He put his finger up, listening.

I heard it too. Voices coming our way. I recognized Mrs. Rumble's but not her male companion. They would be upon us in moments.

Harry grabbed my hand and pulled me with him. We raced out through the front door and ran along the street, not stopping until we turned a corner. I was breathing heavily, unable to expand my lungs fully thanks to my corset.

Harry propped me against the wall then peered around the corner. "No one is following." He frowned. "Are you all right?"

"Bloody corset."

His gaze dipped to my chest. I wished the light had been brighter so I could see if he blushed, but the lamps were few and far between. "I'll give you a few minutes."

"I'm all right. Walking is fine." I set off in what I assumed was the direction of Portland Place. Harry didn't stop me.

"I think Underwood is the forger, not Smith," he said as we walked.

"I'm not so sure. He has skill. But that's the problem, in a way. Someone tried to sell Lady Treloar a fake portrait with poorly done hands. That clearly points to Reggie Smith."

"The Quornes' stolen painting was a landscape," he pointed out. "Do you know what the Bunburys' forged paintings looked like?"

"All landscapes too, from what I saw."

"We could have two forgers. The main one, Underwood, painted the landscapes. The other, Smith, painted the portrait."

"I think it's a possibility but unlikely. What are the chances there are two forgers embroiled in this case?"

"Highly unlikely, I agree. And yet...instinct is telling me Underwood is somehow involved."

"And your instincts are rarely wrong, too." I smiled at him, but he wasn't looking at me. "Very well, we'll both keep an open mind. Perhaps we'll learn more about Mr. Underwood at the Portland that will help shed light on his character."

Most of Portland Place was lit up as bright as day. The streetlamps were spaced close together and none were broken. Lights blazed in the windows of the mansions and private clubs, and welcoming lanterns brightened porches. Footmen greeted guests with lanterns held aloft. Most guests were gentlemen, but some had ladies accompanying them. Going by the amount of makeup they wore, the ladies were not their wives.

The Portland Club was different. The front porch was only illuminated by a single lantern and all the curtains were closed so that it seemed as if no one was inside. But men entered the building. No women, just men. We watched for almost an hour, but no females graced its colonnaded porch.

"What do we do now?" I asked. "I can't get in and you're not...that way inclined."

Harry was unperturbed, however. "Wait here." He moved away before I could stop him.

I watched as he handed the footman something then spoke to him for a few minutes. The footman disappeared inside and Harry returned to me.

"Why the surprised face?" he asked. "Did you expect me to go in?"

"Well...yes. Did you bribe him?"

He nodded. "I asked him about Underwood. Apparently he works here."

I was about to ask what work he performed but decided against it. I could guess. "And why has the footman gone inside?"

"To fetch him, of course. We need to speak to him."

I eyed the closed door. "He won't come."

Harry leaned back against the fence railing and crossed his arms. "He will."

A few minutes later, the door opened and the footman emerged. He was alone.

"I should have put a wager on it," I said.

"I didn't say he'd come straight away. But he will."

Fifteen minutes later, a person climbed the external stairs from the basement and approached us. If it wasn't for the man's hat, worn low to cover the eyes, and the man's coat with the collar flipped up to hide the lower half of his face, I'd have thought it was a woman. His walk was feminine, but that could have been because he wore heeled shoes and what appeared to be a woman's skirt going by the crimson hem peeking below the coat.

"What do you want?" The voice was Mr. Underwood's.

"We just want to ask some questions," Harry said. "Answer them truthfully or I'll follow through on my threat."

Mr. Underwood glared at Harry from beneath eyelids painted pale blue and lashes daubed with charcoal. There was no sign of the affable man who'd helped us on the day we'd first searched Reggie Smith's room. Before us was a man who spoke in angry, defensive tones, but whose hunched stance told me he was embarrassed to be caught wearing makeup and women's clothes.

"We want to know if you painted the forgeries," Harry said.

The fingers gripping Mr. Underwood's coat at his chest tightened. "I don't know what you're referring to. I paint to amuse myself. The days are long, otherwise."

"Did you meet Ambrose McDonald here at the Portland Club?"

Mr. Underwood hesitated before nodding. "He was a patron."

"Did you have a relationship with him outside of the club?"

"Not the kind you're thinking of."

"What kind was it?" Harry asked.

"Purely business."

"The business of forging paintings?"

"I told you, I don't know anything about forged paintings."

"I think you do."

Mr. Underwood swallowed heavily. If he was lying, I couldn't tell. He might simply be nervous with Harry bombarding him with the same question.

I decided to ask a different one. "Did Reggie Smith work here?"

"He used to. This is where he met McDonald. They continued their relationship outside of the club. And yes," he said to Harry, "it was *that* kind of relationship, not the business kind. After they got together, Reggie ended his employment here. He didn't need to work anywhere else. He just painted. Although he never said, I think McDonald supported him."

"Until their relationship ended," I pointed out.

"I don't know why it ended. Reggie never confided in me. But I can make a guess, if you like."

"Please do."

"McDonald wasn't faithful. When Reggie found out, it upset him."

"Enough for him to kill McDonald?"

"I wouldn't say that."

"But you think it?"

He lifted a shoulder in a shrug. His coat slipped a little, revealing a black ribbon choker around his neck. He quickly recovered himself. "May I go now?" He addressed the question to Harry. "Or is the information I've given you not enough to stop you informing Mrs. Rumble?"

"You may go," Harry said.

Mr. Underwood hurried back to the Portland Club, but the floral scent of the perfume he wore lingered.

Harry and I set off down the street. "You told him you'd tell Mrs. Rumble about...?" I indicated the club.

"I told him I'd inform her that he painted in his room. I didn't mention the Portland."

Blackmailing Mr. Underwood with that and not his nocturnal occupation was all right with me. "Do you think he's lying about not painting the forgeries?" I asked.

"I'm unconvinced."

We both fell silent. Something troubled me and I tried to think back to when I'd first met Mr. Underwood. Something troubled Harry too, but it wasn't the same thing.

"Did seeing him like that...disturb you?" he asked.

I frowned at his profile. "In women's clothing? No, except that it's not fair he can wear obvious color on his cheeks and lips and I can't. One evening the lights went out in the hotel as I was getting ready for dinner and I had to dress by candle-light. I put a little too much rouge on my cheeks. When the lights came back on, I was with my aunt. She ushered me back to my room and made me take it off before my uncle saw."

He laughed. "Perhaps one day you can dress however you want and wear as much rouge as you like and no one will bat an eyelash."

"I think we're some way off from that day."

It began to rain, so Harry suggested we take a cab the rest of the way to the hotel. Once inside the dry cabin, I told him what had been on my mind. "Did something seem odd about his answers to you?"

"In what way?"

"When we first met him, I recall telling him that Reggie Smith was arrested for the murder of McDonald. After that, he seemed to open up a little. He was more forthcoming about Reggie, even hinting at his relationship with McDonald and that he thought McDonald was Reggie's patron. He also mentioned their relationship ending. Of course, he never named McDonald. He let us come to that conclusion on our own."

"And tonight he *did* name McDonald," Harry said.

"Indeed." I frowned, trying to make sense of the strange feeling I'd got from Mr. Underwood. "He made quite a point of repeating everything he'd already told us. Perhaps too much of a point."

Harry nodded slowly. "Is he trying to make Reggie Smith look guilty to divert our attention from himself?"

"Because *he* is, in fact, the murderer?" I finished.

It was an intriguing notion, and not out of the realms of possibility. I wasn't sure I believed Mr. Underwood when he claimed to know nothing about the forged paintings.

Harry stifled a yawn and checked his watch. "We'll talk about it more tomorrow. Come to my office at ten-thirty."

"Why not earlier?"

He showed me the watch. It was two-thirty. "It's late. I'll let you sleep in."

"How sweet of you." I smiled, all the while watching him for signs he intended to head out again after returning me to the hotel.

But if he was meeting up with Floyd at the gambling house again, he hid it well. He seemed more concerned about getting me back inside the hotel where I ought to be tucked up in bed.

"Philip is on duty tonight and he won't say a word to my uncle," I assured him as he assisted me down from the carriage.

"I know," he said tightly. "But I won't be satisfied until you're in. Even then there's a chance your uncle or cousin will still be up, roaming the halls."

"Floyd will be out getting drunk somewhere, or gambling."

He glanced around before pushing the door open. "Are you still worried about him?"

I was about to tell him that I was but thought better of it. I didn't want him thinking the situation still needed fixing. "He's an adult. He can take care of himself."

He studied my face and I tried to school my features, but I suspected I failed. A sudden chill of concern for Floyd rippled through me.

"You're cold." He opened the door wider and nodded a greeting at Philip. "Go in, Cleo. And don't worry about Floyd. You just need a little patience with him. He's not such a fool as I thought; he'll come out the other side of this eventually."

He sounded so confident that I immediately felt better. How could I not believe him when he seemed so sure?

I entered the hotel and turned to thank him, but the door was already swinging shut. "Goodnight, Harry," I said in case he was still there on the other side. "And thank you."

CHAPTER 16

$\mathcal{T}$he woman who opened the door at the base of the staircase leading up to Harry's office was beautiful with the hourglass figure so many women tried to create with tightly laced corsets but few actually achieved. It wasn't the dark luster of her hair or the creaminess of her skin that made my heart lurch in my chest, however. It was the secret little smile she sported as she headed past me. It was the sort of smile a woman gave after flirting with a handsome man.

Instead of going up to Harry's office, I diverted to Roma Café and ordered two coffees. "Have you seen that woman before?" I asked Luigi.

He turned the handle of the coffee grinder and the noise of crushing beans filled the otherwise silent café. "I see many women come and go from Harry's office, but none are as beautiful as you, *Bella*."

"Many women?"

He winced. "I also said none are as beautiful as you."

I rolled my eyes. "I can see I'm not going to get a serious answer from you."

He smiled. "Are you jealous?"

"Not at all. Just curious if he's getting many clients." There was no money in the current investigation, so it was only natural that he would work other cases at the same time.

I balanced the two cups in one hand and headed up the stairs to Harry's office.

"Back already?" He looked up from his paperwork and his smile evaporated. "Cleo! It's you."

"Don't look so disappointed."

"I'm not!" He cleared his throat and accepted the coffee cup. "I thought you were someone else."

"You mean a beautiful brunette who can afford you?"

He choked on the coffee. "Afford me?" His face reddened, but I wasn't sure if he was blushing or simply recovering from the choke.

"The woman who just left here. I assume she's a client."

"Ah." He turned the notepad around to show me the name and a time he'd written down. "Cassandra Morris works at Searcys. I met her the other day when I returned to their office to make inquiries about Jane Eyre. She's the one who said she'd notify me when Jane Eyre came looking for more work. When Miss Eyre showed up at the office yesterday, Miss Morris told her to return today at eleven to discuss further employment opportunities. She came here to suggest I show up at the same time."

"Just you?"

"I didn't mention your name, but you can come along, if you like."

I wondered if Miss Morris would be disappointed to see me.

Harry pulled his watch out of his waistcoat pocket. "It was a clever idea of Miss Morris's."

"Indeed."

"This could be the breakthrough we need."

"I hope so."

He narrowed his gaze. "You're annoyed I didn't tell her about you."

"Not at all."

His gaze narrowed further. "I never mentioned you because it didn't seem important to tell her about an associate who occasionally works for me on an unofficial basis."

"I understand." I rose, still smiling. "And I work *with* you, not for you."

He smiled back. "That was a test. I see you haven't let go of your desire to get your name on my door."

I opened the door and studied the bold lettering:

Armitage and Associates Private Detectives. "You sound like you're coming around to it."

"I'm not. I like my door the way it is. Besides, there's no point adding your name when we only occasionally work together."

It seemed more than an occasional arrangement lately, but I didn't say so. I just kept smiling.

* * *

MISS MORRIS LET her disappointment show in the tightening of the smile she bestowed upon Harry when we entered the Searcys office a few minutes before eleven. To her credit, she quickly recovered and greeted me warmly. She greeted Harry with even more warmth.

He pretended not to notice. "Miss Fox suggested we don't tell Miss Eyre who we are until absolutely necessary. We don't want to scare the maid away."

Miss Morris hesitated then shook her head. "I prefer you to declare yourselves and your reason for wanting to speak to her. It's not fair to trick her."

"She has tricked you by giving a false name," I pointed out.

"We don't know yet if it's false."

"It must be. She gave you a false address."

Miss Morris clasped her hands in front of her. She looked even more beautiful up close, with skin like porcelain and bright blue eyes that regarded me with a directness that I found a little unnerving. "There could be a valid reason for that." She turned to Harry. "Perhaps you could pretend this is your first visit here to the office. That way I'm not implicated."

"Of course," Harry said.

She indicated the chairs. "Would you and your assistant like to take a seat while you wait?"

"Miss Fox is my associate, not assistant."

Her eyes widened. "A lady private detective. How remarkable. But if it's just the two of you, why isn't this agency called Armitage and Fox?"

I arched my brows at him and pressed my lips together to stop myself smiling.

He cleared his throat. "It's complicated."

The door opened and the redheaded maid from the Bunburys' ball stepped inside, her slight limp making her gait jerky. "My apologies." Her gaze fell on Harry and her eyes widened. "I—I'll wait outside."

"Wait." Harry pulled out a chair and asked her to sit. "My name is Harry Armitage and this is Miss Fox." He glanced from me to Miss Morris. A beat passed, two, while he made his decision. In the end, he simply said, "On the night of the Bunburys' ball, you spoke to a man named Ambrose McDonald."

The maid took a step back through the doorway. She held onto the brim of her hat and dipped her head.

"They're private detectives," Miss Morris explained. "They just want to talk."

The maid turned and fled.

Harry hesitated, so I went after her instead. Despite the limp, she was quicker than me. Harry was too, and he soon passed me on the stairs.

He chased her all the way to the ground floor and outside where she raced onto the road to catch up to a passing omnibus. She darted in front of a carriage. The coachman swore but the vehicle missed her.

Harry waited until it passed him. By the time it did, I'd caught up to him. But Jane Eyre, if that was her real name, had caught up to the omnibus. She stood on the bottom rung of the ladder and blew Harry a kiss.

He swore under his breath then ran after the omnibus.

I marched back up the stairs and into the Searcys office. "She got away."

"Drat," Miss Morris muttered.

"You shouldn't have told her we are private detectives."

She stiffened. "I am not a liar, Miss Fox."

"No one asked you to lie, just not speak."

"Withholding the truth is still a lie." She glared at me and I glared back. "You should have identified yourselves."

"We would have, but only *after* Harry blocked her escape."

Miss Morris gave a small gasp of shock and clutched her throat.

"This is a murder investigation, Miss Morris. Jane Eyre could be a witness, accomplice, or the murderer. We may not know which of those she is yet, but we do know she was our only hope of finding out more. And now she's vanished into thin air with no hope of finding her. If my methods of getting answers concern you, then so be it. I won't apologize."

Miss Morris went a little pale. She blinked furiously back at me.

Harry returned, holding his hat in his hand and breathing heavily. His gaze switched back and forth between us, clearly sensing the tension. He suggested we leave then thanked Miss Morris for assisting us.

I followed him out, too frustrated to say anything further to Miss Morris.

By the time I reached the pavement, my temper had cooled. I was still frustrated, but I regretted my tone. "Wait here." I picked up my skirts and headed back up the stairs. Before pushing open the door to the Searcys office, I drew in a deep breath, swallowed my pride, and practiced my apology in my head.

I pushed open the door, catching Miss Morris dabbing at the corner of her eye with a handkerchief. It threw me off-kilter. I'd been harsher than I thought.

"Yes?" she said, her voice trembling a little.

"I wanted to say I'm sorry. My tone just now…it wasn't nice considering you helped us. You were right. We should have told Jane Eyre who we were from the start, and blocking someone from leaving a room—and a woman at that—was a poor suggestion on my part. I'm not proud of it."

She folded up her handkerchief and tucked it into her sleeve. "Thank you for the apology, Miss Fox. It's appreciated. I know how much you wanted to speak to her, and I know I am to blame for her running off. I didn't think she would, you see. I thought her innocent in all this. Her flight makes it seem as though she has something to hide, and now you'll never know what that is." She lowered her head and shook it. "I thought…"

"Go on."

"I thought I was being clever by asking her to come back today and Mr. Armitage, too, but it seems I'm a gullible fool. I should have bowed to your expertise and let you question her in your own way."

Now I felt even worse. She was being so understanding and forgiving, and I wasn't sure I deserved it. "I'm no expert. If I were, I'd have more evidence and wouldn't have to rely on one witness." I turned to go, only to turn back again at the door. She offered me a peace offering in the form of a tentative smile. "Harry's a good man. He's also free...if you're interested."

I raced down the stairs, my heart thundering so loudly in my chest I couldn't hear the sound of the midday traffic. Nor could I hear Harry. He was speaking to me, but the pounding of blood between my ears drowned out his voice. I nodded numbly, not sure what I agreed to, and followed him through the throng of pedestrians crowding the pavement.

By the time my heart calmed and all my senses returned, I realized we were heading to the Mayfair. He was escorting me home. Was my behavior that bad that I required an escort all the way?

As we drew closer, Harry looked around, checking the vicinity. He didn't depart at the door, but approached Frank. "Are any Bainbridges in the foyer?"

Frank crossed his arms over his chest.

"Please go and see," I said on a sigh.

Frank lowered his arms and disappeared inside.

"You're coming in?" I asked Harry.

He frowned at me. "Did you hear anything I said back there?"

"Actually, no. Tight corset," I added when his frown deepened.

"I have no idea why that would affect your hearing, but I'm a gentleman and I never discuss a ladies' underthings." He smiled that disarming, charming smile of his.

I stared back, trying to anchor myself in the moment and the conversation. I drew in a deep breath and let it out slowly. It helped me re-focus. "Why are we here?"

Frank returned and announced that no Bainbridges were in the foyer. He opened the door for us, all the while scowling

C.J. ARCHER

at Harry. Frank was a Bainbridge man through and through, and if my uncle didn't like Harry then Frank wouldn't like him either. I knew it cost him to bow to my wishes while disobeying my uncle's.

I patted his arm as I passed and thanked him.

Harry strode up to Peter in the foyer. "Have you seen my uncle?"

"Mr. Armitage! Um, Mr. Hobart is in a meeting with Sir Ronald." He glanced at me. "Everything all right, Miss Fox?"

"I think so. Harry, perhaps you can repeat what you said to me outside the Searcys office."

He glanced at Peter.

"Peter knows about the investigation."

The lift door opened and Flossy emerged with two friends. They headed towards the sitting room and didn't see us.

"We can't talk here," Harry said. "We'll go to my uncle's office."

Peter blocked Harry's path. "I can't let you do that, sir. No one should be in Mr. Hobart's office without his permission."

Harry drew himself up to his full height and looked down at the man who'd replaced him as assistant manager. Peter swallowed.

"We'll talk in the staff parlor," I said. "You should come too, Peter, if you have the time."

"I shouldn't leave my position on the floor if Mr. Hobart is absent."

"You might be able to help," Harry said. "I'm trying to recall a former employee, one of the maids. Red hair, has a slight limp."

"You recognized her!" I blurted out.

"I think so."

"Why didn't you say?"

"I did, but you weren't listening."

"I mean before that."

"I wasn't sure at first, until I noticed the limp. Then I was too busy chasing her."

Peter ushered us towards the staff parlor. "You two go in before someone sees you. I'll fetch Harmony. She'll remember a former maid better than anyone."

202

Once inside the parlor, I poured us tea from the pot warming on the portable gas stove. "Do you think Jane Eyre recognized *you*? Of course she did," I muttered, answering myself. "That's why she ran."

He accepted the teacup with a wry smile. "It's my height."

I kept my teasing retort about his looks to myself. The last time I'd teased him about it, he became cross.

Peter returned with both Harmony and Goliath in tow. Harry described the maid known as Jane Eyre and told them why we needed to find her, although none of the staff showed any surprise. They were already well informed. Goliath sported a smirk, however.

"You remember her?" Harry asked him.

"Not really. I just find it amusing you couldn't catch a limping girl."

Harmony punched him in the arm. "Even limping girls can get away from athletic men if they're smart. She was clever, if it's the same limping redhead who used to work here as a maid."

"How many can there be?" Peter said.

"She was too clever for this work, but that was her lot in life." Harmony turned to Harry. "Her name was Mercy. Mercy Price or Prince, something like that. She didn't work here long before she was dismissed. It would have been two years ago, at least."

"Where did she go after leaving here?" Harry asked.

"I don't know. She left suddenly under a cloud. Mrs. Kettering said she was dismissed for unbecoming conduct, but didn't say what exactly Mercy did." Mrs. Kettering was the former housekeeper, before Mrs. Short.

I could see Harmony was holding something back. "What did the other maids think happened?" I asked.

"We heard that Mercy was caught going through the guests' things."

Harry frowned. "I would have heard if she stole from the guests."

"She never took anything."

"You mean she was never *caught* taking anything," Peter added.

Harmony shrugged. "It's all just rumor. Only Mercy and Mrs. Kettering know for certain what she did."

"Did Mrs. Short retain Mrs. Kettering's employee records?" I asked Peter.

"She threw out some things when she moved offices," he said. "But I'm sure she kept all the old employee files."

"It's hotel policy to keep them," Harry added. "If someone applies here again, we'll know why they left, any circumstances or traits that made them unsuitable employees, that sort of thing." He didn't seem to notice that he'd said "we". Perhaps being back here made him feel as though he'd never left. "I'll go through the housekeeper's files—"

"You'll do no such thing," I snapped. "It's too much of a risk for anyone but me to be caught going through the files."

"It's a risk for you too, Cleo."

I ignored him. I wouldn't entertain an argument on the matter. "Harmony, can you keep Mrs. Short away from her office for a while?"

She glanced at the clock. "I'm supposed to be on the second floor now. I'll tell her there's a problem with one of the beds up there. But she shares an office with Mr. Chapman so someone has to distract him, too."

"I'll do it," Peter said. "I wanted to speak to him about a particular guest's dietary requirements anyway."

"I'll stand by the door and keep watch," Goliath added. "I'll whistle a tune if someone comes."

We filed out, but instead of staying in the staff parlor, Harry followed. I thought he would leave the hotel altogether and wait outside, but he sat in one of the leather armchairs, picked up a newspaper and pretended to read.

"I don't suppose you would leave if I suggested it," I said.

He snapped the paper to straighten it. "You suppose correctly. I'll keep watch out here."

"And what will you do if my uncle sees you?"

"I'll think of something."

"Don't get into a row with him."

He peered at me over the top of the newspaper. "It would be a good distraction and give you time to get out of Mrs. Short's office."

"Don't get into a row with him," I said again, adding a stern glare for good measure.

He lifted the newspaper to hide his face.

I waited until I saw Mrs. Short leave her office with Harmony. Peter looked in and re-emerged immediately. He shook his head at me and shrugged. Mr. Chapman wasn't there.

I crossed the foyer then slipped into the office and closed the door. The employee files were in a cabinet behind Mrs. Short's desk. I searched for Mercy Price then Mercy Prince, but there was no one by either name. I flicked through all of the surnames beginning with Pr and found her listed as Mercy Prentice.

According to the file, she'd worked for a mere six weeks before being dismissed. One of the guests had caught her looking through the dressing table drawers in their suite. Although nothing had been taken, Mercy was dismissed immediately. As with most of the maids, she'd lived in the staff residence hall, but an address for her parents had been written down in Mrs. Kettering's neat hand. I committed it to memory then returned the file to the cabinet.

I opened the office door a crack and peered out. My view was blocked by the large form of Goliath. At that moment, he began to whistle off-key. Without being able to see past him, I didn't know if it was Mr. Chapman or Mrs. Short returning to their office, or merely someone else passing by.

"Goliath," I whispered. "Who is it?"

His whistling stopped. "Mr. Bainbridge. It's safe to come out. Mr. Armitage stopped him and is now speaking to him. Mr. Bainbridge has his back to us."

I quickly stepped out and hurried into the foyer to rescue Harry from my cousin. Harry had angled himself so that Floyd had to face away from the staff office area to speak to him. I approached Floyd from behind and quickly schooled my features.

"Harry, this is a surprise," I said. "Have you come to visit Mr. Hobart?"

Floyd turned to me and crossed his arms over his chest. "Of course he has. Why else would be here? Christ, Cleo, stop interrogating everyone all the time. We know you like to fashion yourself as a sleuth, but there's no need for the constant questions. Leave the man alone."

I blinked at him as he strode off. Frank couldn't open the front door fast enough and received a glare from Floyd as he waited.

"What did you say to him?" I asked Harry.

"We were just talking. So did you find an address for Mercy?"

He wasn't going to elaborate on the conversation he'd had with Floyd any more than he was going to tell me why he'd gone to the gambling house with him. I let the matter go and told him what I'd learned as we left the hotel.

* * *

MERCY PRENTICE's parents lived in a working class area on the other side of the river. After convincing her mother that we wished to speak to her daughter about working at the hotel again, she finally told us where to find Mercy.

It was mid-afternoon by the time we reached the residence hall that housed the Palmerston Hotel staff. We waited in the small sitting room near the entrance while the matron fetched Mercy Prentice. Harry couldn't sit still, however. He strode around the room, shaking his head at the peeling paint, the rising damp, and the electric wire dangling from the ceiling. He was so tall he could touch it, but was wise enough not to.

"This place is a disgrace," he muttered. "The staff deserve better."

Mercy entered, took one look at him, and turned to flee. But the matron unwittingly blocked the doorway with her bulky frame and Mercy had the good sense not to order her to move. The matron didn't look like someone who'd take kindly to one of her residents telling her what to do.

"Miss Prentice, may we have a private word about your parents?" Harry asked.

Mercy was caught off guard. "My parents? What's happened? What's wrong?"

Harry eyed the matron until she left and closed the door. "Nothing," he told Mercy. "I had to say something to get rid of her yet not raise her suspicions." He stepped around Mercy and stood in front of the door. "This is Miss Fox, and I'm Harry Armitage."

"I know. I remember you."

"I no longer work for the Mayfair Hotel. I'm a private detective now, and I need to ask you some questions about Mr. Ambrose McDonald."

Mercy swallowed.

I invited her to sit, but she refused. "You're not in trouble," I assured her. "We're investigating Mr. McDonald's death, and if you don't fully co-operate, we'll be inclined to believe you had something to do with his demise."

"I never! His death ain't on my conscience."

"Then you won't have any problems answering our questions."

She folded her arms over her chest and pursed her lips.

"Why did you run when you saw me this morning?" Harry asked.

She sniffed and lifted a shoulder in a shrug.

"Miss Prentice," he said with a tone that was somehow both gentle and insistent. "I know why you were dismissed from the Mayfair. This isn't about that."

"I never stole. You know that, don't you, sir? I never took nothing from the Mayfair and I take nothing from the Palmerston. I ain't a thief."

"I believe you."

She looked relieved. "I thought that's why you were at the Searcys office. I thought you wanted to blame me for something that went missing from back then at the Mayfair. But if something did go missing, it weren't me who took it. I swear to you."

"It's all right, Miss Prentice. As I said, I no longer work for the hotel. This has nothing to do with your time there. This is about Ambrose McDonald. We need your help to understand what happened to him on the night of his murder."

She let out a measured breath. "I don't know nothing about his death. I don't know who done him in. I thought someone has been arrested."

"The case isn't closed," I said. "Tell us, why did he give you money on the night of the Bunburys' ball?"

"How do you know 'bout that?"

"I was there. I saw you."

She looked at me anew, her assessing gaze taking in my well-made dress, my hair and bag. "You're a friend of Lady Bunbury's?"

"No. I don't like her." She smiled wryly at that. "Tell us how you came to know Ambrose McDonald."

She lowered her arms and finally sat beside me on the sofa. "I met him a few months ago at the Palmerston Hotel. He was a guest there while his flat got repainted. He caught me...taking an interest in his things when I was supposed to be tidying up." She cleared her throat and didn't meet our gazes. "He threatened to tell the housekeeper unless I did something for him. I couldn't afford to lose my position. It took an age to find work again after I left the Mayfair. It ain't easy with no reference, you see. So I agreed to do what he wanted."

"And what did he want?" I asked gently.

"He wanted me to tell him anything I learned about the other guests that he might find useful."

"Useful?" Harry prompted.

"Something they wanted to keep a secret. He'd tell them he knew their secret and they'd pay him to keep quiet. It might be a conversation I overheard, or private letters, or that they're keeping a mistress at the hotel. I'd pass on the information to him and he'd pay me thirty percent of what they paid him."

"Is that why you took the work at Searcys?" I asked. "So you could pass on the information to him without anyone being suspicious?"

She shook her head. "I got the extra work for the money. It doesn't interfere with my work at the Palmerston, and it pays well."

"Did you pre-arrange to exchange information that night or was meeting him at the Bunburys' purely coincidental?"

"It was a coincidence, but I didn't have any information to give him. Not at the start of the night, anyway."

Harry sat forward. "You learned something that night that you thought might interest him?"

She nodded. "I recognized someone from the Palmerston. She looked different, but that's because she was wearing a wig when she stayed at the hotel. She also checked in under a different name. I asked around among the staff at the ball and learned she has a flat here in London. She didn't need to stay at the hotel. I thought Mr. McDonald could use that information to get money from her. I reckoned she wouldn't want anyone to know she was at the Palmerston, otherwise why wear a wig and give a fake name? It seemed real suspicious to me, so I told him. He was real interested and got all excited. It was like I told him he'd inherited a mansion. He paid me right away instead of waiting to get money from her. He said the information was worth it."

"Who was it?" I asked on a rush of breath.

"She checked into the Palmerston as Mrs. Tidmarsh, but at the ball I heard them call her Lady Treloar."

CHAPTER 17

*L*ady Treloar! Why had the gallery owner checked into a hotel under a false name? Why would anyone do that, let alone a successful businesswoman? Did she rendezvous at the Palmerston with a secret lover? Was she hiding from someone?

I looked to Harry but he was looking at Mercy. There was none of the confusion on his face that I felt. Hotel guests checking in under false names was his territory. He must have some ideas as to what Lady Treloar was doing.

"When was she at the Palmerston?" he asked.

Mercy raised her gaze to the ceiling, calculating. "She left the day before the Bunburys' ball. She'd been there for a few weeks."

Now it was beginning to make sense. We'd been right all along. Or, rather, Detective Inspector Hobart had been right. The murder was related to the stolen art. Not the painting Reggie Smith had removed from the Bunburys' library wall, but the first one, taken from the Quornes on March thirtieth.

We thanked Mercy and left, but got no further than the pavement.

"Lady Treloar did it," I said, hardly able to contain my excitement. "She pretended to travel to Biarritz but in actuality, she stayed at the Palmerston Hotel. During that time, she stole the Quornes' painting. When Mercy recognized her at the Bunburys' ball, but heard she was using a different name, she knew something was amiss and passed that information on to Ambrose McDonald to see if he could make something of it. McDonald knew the art theft had happened in that time and put two and two together. He guessed Lady Treloar was the thief. He confronted her that night, hoping to blackmail her, but she killed him instead."

My excitement was reflected in Harry's eyes. "An excellent deduction."

"You deduced it, not me. You asked about the dates of her stay, so you must have had an inkling. My first instinct was an affair with a married man. How did you make the connection to the theft?"

"We sometimes had guests stay at the Mayfair under false names in the first quarter of the year. My uncle was the only one who knew their true identities. The reasons they stayed were always the same, and it was rarely an affair of the heart. They stayed with us because it was cheaper than traveling overseas."

"I don't understand."

"They couldn't afford Biarritz or any of the glamorous resorts on the continent. But they wanted people to think they could, so they closed up their townhouses here, if they had them, and moved into the hotel for a few weeks. They laid low, some rarely leaving their rooms to avoid being seen."

"But the Mayfair is expensive."

"Not as expensive as traveling to Biarritz, and they still enjoy a level of luxury they're used to. When Mercy said Lady Treloar stayed at the Palmerston under a false name, my first thought was that she was hiding from her friends too, merely *pretending* to travel to the continent. Then I remembered her claiming to be in Biarritz when the Quornes' painting was stolen. Once I realized she was in London at that time, there was a good chance she stole the painting, considering the business she's in."

"Ambrose McDonald certainly seemed to think so."

We still stood in the narrow street that housed the Palmerston Hotel's staff. Scotland Yard was in one direction and Lady Treloar's gallery in the other. Did we confront her or take what we knew to the police?

As much as I wanted to involve them, I suspected they

would dismiss Mercy's evidence. It was her word against Lady Treloar's. With Lord Bunbury putting pressure on his friends at Scotland Yard to wrap the case up quickly, they'd be reluctant to keep it open based on the word of a maid who'd been dismissed from her prior position for unbecoming behavior.

"We need proof," I said.

"We do." Harry nodded at the door to the residence hall. "We could ask the other members of staff if they remember the guest named Mrs. Tidmarsh and then ask them if they recognize Lady Treloar."

I could tell from his tone that he didn't think it would help the case against her. "Or we can find other evidence," I said. "We need to find something that connects her to the theft without any doubt. Let's think…why does someone steal an expensive painting?"

"To sell it."

"Exactly. She must have contacts in the art world and know of wealthy people prepared to purchase stolen art. Perhaps there's a bill of sale in her gallery or some correspondence between her and the buyer."

Harry gave me a skeptical look. "Thieves don't usually draw up bills of sale or leave crucial evidence lying around."

"Then what do you suggest?"

He thought about it a moment then said, "I think we should look around the gallery and see what we can find."

"That amounts to the same thing I suggested, only I was being more specific."

"Then it seems we're in agreement." Harry set off, his steps determined.

I picked up my skirts and hurried after him. "What should we say to her? We don't want her to suspect that we know. Not yet."

"I'll think of something."

I was beginning to realize when Harry said he'd think of something, it meant he was planning on using his charms. I wasn't sure it would work this time.

As it turned out, we didn't need to make up excuses or use charm. The gallery was closed. I checked my watch. It was a little after four o'clock.

Harry stood with hands on hips, glaring at the locked door as if it were to blame for the delay. "If it was dark, I'd break in."

"You will do no such thing. Not tonight." I crossed my arms. "Not without me anyway."

"You're not invited."

"It's not a party, Harry. This is my investigation too, and I want to be here when you break in. But I'm busy tonight. I suppose I could leave early…"

"Where are you going?"

"To yet another ball." I sighed. "Blasted things."

"It is the Season."

"Yes, but why so many? It's getting rather tiring, not to mention it's interfering with the investigation. Why do I even need to go?"

"Because you're being put on display. The more balls you attend, the more admirers you gather." He made it sound like a game where the participants collected points as they moved around the board. Only this game wasn't a lot of fun for me.

"Don't be absurd. Flossy is the one on display. She's the one looking for admirers."

He continued to glare at the door. "If you say so."

"I do say so." I glared at the door too. "Why does everyone continue to think I want a husband when I've mentioned many times that I do not?"

"I didn't say *you* wanted a husband. But your aunt and uncle want one for you. That's why you're being paraded in front of the right people—your family's idea of who is right for you, that is."

The fact that I wanted to make my family happy only made me feel so much worse for being unable to do as they wanted. I heaved another sigh.

"Not all marriages are bad," Harry said quietly. "My parents are happy. My aunt and uncle, too. You just need to find the right person." His profile was rigid as he studied the doorknob, as if willing it to turn. Or perhaps he was simply avoiding looking at me. "The more balls and parties you attend, the more chance you have of finding him. It's simple mathematics, Cleo."

"Probability. My father taught me all about it." I smiled

wistfully at the memory of my professorial father listening in to this conversation about marriage.

Then my smile faded. My father had been the smartest person I knew, but he'd not known how to make a successful marriage. He and my mother had argued often. Indeed, their final conversation had been spoken in anger, right before their cart rolled over, killing them both and injuring me.

"Cleo?" Harry touched my elbow. "I'm sorry. I've upset you."

"No. Not at all." I tried to give him a reassuring smile, but I suspected I failed. His concerned frown remained firmly in place. I was about to say something more, but the door to the gallery suddenly opened.

"Oh!" Lady Treloar paused in the doorway. "It's you two."

Harry recovered from his surprise first. "We do apologize, madam. We didn't realize you'd closed."

"I'm closing early today. I have a ball to attend tonight, and I need to pick up my gown from the seamstress."

Although Lady Treloar knew my name, she didn't know my connection to the Bainbridges and hadn't recognized me from the Bunburys' ball. If she was attending the same event as me tonight, she would see me there. I wouldn't be able to hide from her all evening.

I couldn't decide whether to reveal myself or pray that she was going to a different ball.

Harry made the decision for me. "Miss Fox is also attending a ball tonight."

"The Heathertons," I added.

Lady Treloar blinked at me. "As am I! I didn't realize we moved in the same circles, Miss Fox. Are you a friend of Lady Heatherton?"

"An acquaintance."

I didn't need to look at Harry to know he was delighted to know she was out all evening. He would already be calculating the best time to return to break into the gallery. Now that he knew Lady Treloar wouldn't happen past, it was the perfect opportunity. It was even more perfect—for him—because I was also occupied and couldn't join him.

"How can I help you today?" Lady Treloar asked. It was

difficult to reconcile this woman as the murderess. She was friendly and composed, cultured and intelligent.

But it was Harry's father who'd taught me that murderers came in all forms, from the lowest in society to the highest. One's outward appearance could hide a multitude of emotions and a cruel heart.

"We wanted to speak to you about Biarritz, as it happens," Harry said. "Specifically, the cost of traveling there."

"Oh."

She wasn't the only one who thought it an odd question. Where was Harry going with this line of interrogation, if that's what it could be called?

He bestowed a curious smile on me. "Cleo and I want to go, but..." He shrugged, letting her fill in the rest of his sentence.

And fill it in, she did. Her eyes lit up. "I knew from the moment I met you both that you were more than colleagues. How romantic."

My face heated and my pulse quickened. I didn't dare glance at Harry to see his reaction, although I dearly wanted to know.

Lady Treloar opened the door wide. "Come in. Let me show you something." She crossed the gallery floor to the door that led to the rear staff room.

We followed her. The room wasn't very large. The three of us barely fit. We certainly couldn't move past each other unless we got embarrassingly close.

While Lady Treloar looked through a box containing scraps of paper, I took the opportunity to glance around the room again, but this time with an eye to her being the killer. Everything was the same as on my previous visit—the bench with the same blue and white teacup, a kettle on the portable stove, the same books on art, and catalogues, and even the same paintings sat on the same scuffed section of the floor, leaning against the wall.

My heart stilled. The scuff marks were in an arc. I'd noticed them last time, but now I wondered if they'd been caused by a door opening. It couldn't have been a very large door, but big enough for someone to slip through. The same size as the wall panel, in fact.

The right size to hide a painting in the secret room beyond.

"Ah, here it is." Lady Treloar handed a piece of paper to Harry. "I didn't travel first class this year, but don't tell anyone."

Harry smiled and handed the slip of paper to me. It was a train ticket for a French railway, dated March thirtieth. The price in francs was printed in the corner, below the station-master's stamp.

"Quite affordable," I said as I handed back the ticket. I sounded cheerful, but my heart was sinking. The ticket was evidence that she'd been in France on the thirtieth. She couldn't have been in London stealing the Quornes' painting.

"Indeed." She returned the ticket to the box and indicated we should leave the room ahead of her. "Now, if you don't mind, I must get to the seamstress before she closes her shop. I'll see you at the ball tonight, Miss Fox." She touched my arm. "Rest assured, your secret is safe with me."

"Thank you."

It wasn't until we were well away from her gallery and walking in the opposite direction to Lady Treloar that I uttered a rather unladylike word. "I don't believe that ticket is real for a moment, but the police will believe it."

Harry agreed. "It won't help our case against her, but I'm even more suspicious of her now than I was before."

"Because of the scuff marks?"

"What scuff marks?"

As we walked to the omnibus stop, I told him about the floor in the back room and how I suspected the wall panel hid a door to a secret storage chamber.

"A brilliant observation, Cleo. Now I'm doubly sure she's guilty of the theft, at the very least."

"Are you? She was quite convincing with the ticket. She seemed to believe our story about running away together to Biarritz."

We climbed onto the omnibus and took our seats. "She didn't believe it," Harry said. "Did you see how quickly she showed us her ticket? She knows we're fishing for information and she had that on hand just in case the police asked for proof of where she was at the time of the Quornes' theft. It was too convenient."

I knew he was right, but being too eager to produce a French rail ticket wasn't proof against her. We needed something solid.

The conductor tore off two tickets from his roll and punched a hole through each before handing them to us and taking our money.

I held mine up and peered at Harry through the tiny hole. I could just make out his eye. "Her ticket wasn't punched."

He studied his ticket with its hole. "It was not. But it had a stationmaster's stamp on it."

"Shouldn't it also have a hole punched through it from the conductor on the train?"

He shrugged. "Perhaps they do things differently in France."

"Perhaps. Or perhaps her ticket is a forgery, but the forger forgot the hole. A fake ticket must be a relatively easy thing to obtain if one knows a good forger."

"Underwood," Harry muttered.

He was my first thought too. "He's a painter who either forged the Bunburys' paintings or knew who did, and she's an art dealer." I gasped as something else occurred to me. "Do you remember the forged painting she claimed someone tried to sell her? She specifically mentioned the odd hands. She knew that was a trait of Reggie Smith's paintings so she added that detail to further point the finger of blame at him."

"And to point it away from herself," he added, nodding. "The painting never existed. She made it up after we went to her gallery. She was worried we might be onto her so she made up a fake painting and a fake seller to throw us off and implicate Smith because she knew he was already in custody. It was her way of making absolutely certain she wasn't a suspect."

It all made sense now. I knew we were on the right path. But proving it was going to be difficult. Difficult, but not impossible.

"Harry, will you please do something for me?"

"Anything."

"Tonight, when you break into the gallery to look inside

that hidden room, will you take your father with you? I hate to think of you doing it without someone watching out for you. If a constable happens by, D.I. Hobart can use his authority to persuade him not to arrest you."

He crossed his arms and arched a brow. "Very well."

"And don't make it too late."

"Why not?"

"Because while she's at the ball, I can watch her. But I can only keep her there for so long. Besides, I'm sure you have somewhere better to be late at night. I wouldn't want to keep you from a prior engagement."

His only response to that was to purse his lips and narrow his eyes at me.

As we parted ways, he caught my wrist. My skirts brushed his legs and heat surged between us. My cheeks flushed. His gaze connected with mine in a long moment that was both excruciating and thrilling. He was going to confide something to me. Something important.

His chest rose and fell with a deep breath. "Be careful at the ball. Don't be alone with her. Not for a moment."

I swallowed my disappointment. "Oh. Yes. Of course."

He let go of me, but not before his thumb caressed the bare skin at my wrist.

* * *

ACCORDING TO PETER, Floyd was in the smoking room. "He's in a sour mood," he warned me.

"Thank you. I'll be as quick as I can and avoid all delicate topics."

"Any update on the investigation?"

"I'll tell you after I've spoken to Floyd."

"Miss Bainbridge was looking for you earlier. Apparently you're supposed to be getting ready for the ball."

I checked the clock on the wall behind the front desk. "I've got time."

I found Floyd alone in the smoking room, slumped in an armchair by the fireplace, a cigarette dangling from between his lips and a tumbler in hand. The liquid in it was dangerously close to spilling. He was staring at the carpet, eyelids at half-mast, and didn't even look up upon my entry.

"You shouldn't keep your own company when you're feeling like this," I said.

His lashes barely flickered as he lifted his head. His gaze focused on me then became distant again. He sucked on the cigarette.

I touched his chin. "Are you drunk?"

He jerked away from my touch. "You shouldn't be in here." It was said without conviction. Unlike most men, he didn't care if I was in the smoking room. It was supposed to be the domain of gentlemen only. My presence would shock some and anger others. It would be unwelcomed by all.

Floyd was too drunk to care. He went to sip from the glass but I snatched it out of his hand. I poured the contents into the unlit fireplace. The liquid soaked into the ash.

"You know I can just get another whenever I want. Peter keeps them filled." He indicated the decanters on the sideboard with a tilt of his chin.

"You can't go like this to the ball tonight."

"I'm not going to the bloody ball."

"Have you told your parents that?"

"I'm an adult, Cleo. I don't need to tell them what I'm doing every minute of every day."

"But you do have to attend events if they want you to."

"Because they pay for all this?" He waved half-heartedly at the ornate furniture, thick carpet, and the decanters.

"No, because you're part of this family." I crouched before him and took his hand. "Floyd, I know you've got yourself into some difficulty."

He grunted.

I took it as a good sign that he didn't remove his hand from mine. It could have been that he was simply too drunk to notice, but I liked to think it was because he found it comforting. "You'll get through this. You'll find a way to pay back Dutch and all will be well again. Trust me."

He blinked furiously at me, as if trying to blink away grit in his eyes. "How do you know about Dutch?"

I let go of his hand and stood. "You've been to France, haven't you?"

He squinted into the light above my head. "Yes. Why?"

"Did you travel by rail there at any point?"

"Yes."

"Do you recall if they have conductors on their trains who punch holes in the tickets, like we do here?"

"They do. Cleo, what does this have to do with Dutch?"

"Nothing. It's a clue in the investigation."

He thoughtfully drew on his cigarette and blew out a ribbon of smoke. "I'm in no position to lecture you about your affairs. But as your older cousin it's my responsibility to remind you to be careful. Don't get caught playing detective with Armitage. You're already the subject of gossip. Don't make it worse."

I laughed softly. "If the worst is being talked about as a successful investigator, then I am quite all right with being the subject of gossip. You, on the other hand, have a more delicate reputation."

He snorted. "Very amusing." He flicked the empty glass in my hand. "Another, dear Cuz."

I picked up the decanter, pulled out the stopper, and poured the contents into the fireplace. Some of it leaked out of the grate and onto the carpet.

"That wasn't nice," he muttered.

"It's still early. Go and nap for an hour before the ball. That way you'll be able to face Dutch afterwards with a clear head." I put out my hand.

He took it and lurched to his feet. "How *do* you know about Dutch?"

"I'm a good detective."

He grunted. "I think it has more to do with being a pretty female who knows how to manipulate a man infatuated with her."

"Jonathon isn't infatuated with me."

"So it was Jonathon was it? Traitor."

I smiled as he followed me out of the smoking room. I was a good detective. I may have fallen into his trap and inadvertently told him who'd broken his confidence, but he'd fallen into my trap too. He hadn't denied it when I suggested he was meeting Dutch tonight after the ball.

It only remained to be seen if Harry was going with him again.

* * *

THE HEATHERTONS' ballroom wasn't as large as the Bunburys', so there were fewer guests. I couldn't have hidden from Lady Treloar for long so it was fortunate that Harry had taken the bull by the horns and told her I'd be here. We nodded at one another as we passed at the edge of the dance floor, but her gaze quickly flicked to Flossy on one side of me and my aunt on the other. If she recognized them, she gave no indication and glided by without acknowledging them.

Despite being under the influence of her tonic, Aunt Lilian noticed our exchange. When it came to socializing and gossip, she was the most observant person I knew. "How do you know Lady Treloar?"

"I've been in her gallery."

"Why?"

"I like art."

Fortunately, a friend approached and drew her away, otherwise she would have persisted with her interrogation.

Flossy and I continued with our circuit of the room to gauge the mood of the guests. While greeting acquaintances and writing names on my dance card, I kept an eye on Lady Treloar. She was all smiles and easy countenance with her friends, but I caught her watching me more than once.

Harry must be right. She'd guessed we'd returned to her gallery to gather evidence against her, and that's why she'd been keen to prove her innocence with the railway ticket. I must be careful not to let on that we suspected it was fake. I must also be sure not to be alone with her tonight.

"Have I left it too late?"

The voice behind me made me jump. "Jonathon! Don't sneak up on a lady like that."

"I didn't sneak. You were a miles away." He opened my dance card, dangling from my wrist. "I see I'm not too late, after all."

Flossy peered at my card. "That is a surprise. Why so many free dances, Cleo?"

"I think it has something to do with my education."

She rolled her eyes.

Jonathon wrote his name down twice. "Some men are intimidated by women with big brains. Not me. I find smart women interesting. Well. One in particular." He bestowed a sweet smile on me.

I scanned the room, searching for an escape. "Excuse me, but Miss Hessing is signaling to me." I strode away. I didn't turn back to see Jonathon's face. I didn't want to know if I'd hurt his feelings. Part of me wanted to quip that he had no depth of feeling, but that wasn't fair. It was quite possible that he truly cared for me. I just didn't care for him in the same way. Extricating myself from an exchange that could turn embarrassing was kinder to us both.

Miss Hessing looked relieved to see me. She drew me away from her mother and the ladies she spoke with, but not before some peered down their noses at me. I suggested we take a turn around the room. It was mostly an excuse to go in search of Lady Treloar. She'd disappeared while I was speaking to Jonathon.

I found her moments later, chatting to another guest.

"They're still gossiping about that Livingstone girl," Miss Hessing said to me as we continued past Lady Treloar. "The poor thing may never live down her humiliation."

"I suspect she'll be fine. She's the sort who'll rise above it out of sheer force of will. Trust me on that, Miss Hessing. I've met her. She'll look down on the likes of you and me for the rest of her life because we don't have as many God-given virtues as her."

She sighed. "She isn't the only one. My card is quite empty." She showed it to me. One name had been written three times, but it was otherwise blank. I recognized him as the fellow who'd danced with her at the last two balls.

I showed her my card. "Mine is looking like a wasteland too."

She huffed a breath. "Hardly a wasteland, Miss Fox. A little emptier than usual, perhaps. Never fear. I see Mr. Hartly has put his name down. I'm surprised it's only twice, though."

"Twice is enough, thank you."

She laughed, thinking I was joking.

We spent much of the night together, talking and occasionally dancing with partners brave enough to take us on, or perhaps desperate. We were emerging from the refreshments room a little after eleven, when two gentlemen passed us. I'd danced with both at the Bunburys' ball, so was obliged to greet them and introduce them to my companion. It would be good for Miss Hessing to meet some gentlemen while her mother wasn't nearby.

But they merely nodded at me and kept walking. As they passed, one said to the other in a loud voice, "I find a lady with an education to be dull indeed, don't you?"

"I do," the other chimed in, a laugh in his voice. "Not only that, it's a waste of her time. What could a lady possibly need with all that knowledge?"

I felt Miss Hessing stiffen and was about to tell her to ignore them as I wasn't bothered with their petty comments, but an extraordinary thing happened. A defense came from an unexpected quarter.

I hadn't noticed Floyd and Uncle Ronald nearby with a group of gentlemen, some of whom I recognized as hotel guests. My uncle suddenly turned and addressed the rude men who'd snubbed me.

"You're mistaken, sirs. An intelligent woman is an asset, particularly for a man in business." He clapped one of them on the shoulder and turned him to face me. "My niece is a prime example. Cleopatra has taken a great interest in the hotel business and made some excellent suggestions for improvement. I value her opinion highly."

The gentlemen muttered words of half-hearted agreement then extricated themselves from the situation. Uncle Ronald winked at me and returned to his friends who laughed and congratulated him on offering sound advice to the "young pups".

Floyd strode away.

I couldn't decide whether to go after him or if that would make him feel worse.

I never made my decision. As he walked off, I spotted Lady Treloar glancing at her watch. She closed its case and slipped out of the ballroom.

I caught Miss Hessing's hand. "Come with me."

"Where are we going?"

"I need some air."

"Oh dear. Did those men upset you?"

I steered her through the ballroom, avoiding people I knew who might stop us to talk. More guests milled about in the adjoining room, but I couldn't see Lady Treloar. There was only one other exit and it led to the staircase. She must be leaving the ball altogether.

If she suspected Harry was going to break into her gallery tonight, she might head there to catch him in the act. The notion wasn't out of the realms of possibility. She already suspected we were onto her. I had to stop her.

I tugged Miss Hessing along with me to the stairs.

"Are we going out the front door?" she asked. "Why not go onto the balcony? The air will be fresher there on account of the height."

We reached the landing between the first and ground floors. Just as I was about to step down onto the final flight of stairs, Lady Treloar emerged from the shadows of the large potted palm in the corner. She rushed towards me and, before my gasp had time to escape, shoved me.

I lost my balance and felt myself falling.

CHAPTER 18

With one foot in the air and the other about to lose connection with the floor, all my momentum was propelled forwards. The flight of stairs filled my vision and my heart filled my throat. I could do nothing to break my fall.

With an almighty wrench on my arm, I was jerked back from the precipice. I tumbled into Miss Hessing instead. She wrapped her arms around me, hugging me so fiercely I could hear her thundering heartbeat. I'd been tethered to her tall, solid form by our joined hands.

She gasped. "Miss Fox! Are you all right?"

"I am, thank you. You saved me." I would thank her properly later. Right now, I had a murderess to stop.

Lady Treloar was getting away. I raced down the stairs after her, but she was too far ahead of me. I'd never reach her. The footman put out a hand to open the door for her.

"Don't let her leave!" I cried.

The poor man looked confused. He hesitated.

Lady Treloar opened the door herself.

But she did not exit. She stumbled back as a constable and a sergeant barreled inside, followed by a man in plain clothes. I recognized him as a detective who'd worked with D.I. Hobart on previous cases.

"That's her," I told him.

He ordered his men to arrest her.

"What is the meaning of this?" thundered our host from the top of the stairs. "Unhand my guest!"

"Lady Treloar is under arrest for the murder of Ambrose McDonald and the theft of Lord and Lady Quorne's artwork."

Lady Quorne appeared beside Sir Gregory Heatherton. "My painting! *She* took it?"

Several guests had followed the sound of the voices and joined them on the stairs. Others streamed down the staircase towards us, now on the ground floor in the entrance hall. The front door still stood open, but the footman had melted away, replaced by an indignant butler.

Sir Gregory and Lady Heatherton pushed through the crowd and demanded to know what was going on.

I took a leaf out of the footman's book and drew Miss Hessing into the background. Lady Treloar watched me go through eyes narrowed to slits. Despite her captured wrists, she stood magnificently defiant, her jaw firm and her shoulders thrown back.

The detective calmly closed the front door. Clearly D.I. Hobart wasn't coming. I hoped he might, but given he no longer worked for Scotland Yard, it was understandable. Harry's absence wasn't a surprise either.

I looked around for Floyd and spotted him halfway up the staircase, watching proceedings. He didn't see me standing behind him; nor did his parents. As far as they were aware, I had nothing to do with this incident.

Miss Hessing, however, stared at me. Besides the police and Lady Treloar, she was the only one who'd heard me point out Lady Treloar to the detective.

Everyone else listened to what he had to say. "The painting stolen from the Quornes' house on the night of March thirtieth was found hidden in Lady Treloar's gallery."

The crowd gasped.

"You sold it to us in the first place," Lady Quorne said to Lady Treloar. "Why did you steal it back?"

"For money, of course," her husband said.

The detective shook his head. "For her reputation. The painting was a forgery."

Lady Quorne clutched her throat and collapsed into her husband's arms. Another guest tried to revive her by fanning her face, but it wasn't until Lord Quorne lightly tapped her cheek that she opened her eyes.

"You sold us a forgery?" Lord Quorne growled at Lady Treloar once his wife had recovered.

Lady Treloar lifted her chin further and refused to speak.

"Not knowingly," the detective said. "She didn't learn that it was a fake until Ambrose McDonald informed her."

The final piece now clicked into place. She hadn't stolen the painting to sell to a secret collector. She'd taken it so no one else would find out it was a forgery. If they did, her reputation would have been ruined and her business with it. Harry must have found it in her gallery, behind that hidden door. She was probably waiting for a good time to destroy it. The discovery was the definitive proof we needed.

"And how did McDonald know?" someone asked.

"The forger himself told him," the detective said. "The forger confirmed as much tonight." Even though he was speaking, they were Harry's words. Harry had found the painting earlier and must have taken it to Underwood. Underwood admitted he'd painted it. Harry passed all of this on to the detective, probably in the presence of his father, who'd given him the name of a trustworthy colleague.

The guests had fallen silent, stunned by the presence of a thief and murderer walking amongst them. "My god," one woman muttered. "Did you kill Mr. McDonald just because you inadvertently sold one forgery?"

Lady Treloar swallowed heavily. "Take me away now, please."

But the detective didn't give the order. He wasn't finished with the theater. Indeed, this was rather more theater than an arrest usually warranted. I got the impression he was enjoying himself. "That's not why she killed him. The victim learned of the forged painting several weeks ago through his friend, the forger. He informed Lady Treloar, who attempted to dismiss it. She said the same thing you did, madam. It was just one painting and she hadn't known it was a fake. But a few nights later, she stole it off the Quornes' wall so that no one else would realize it was a copy. The crime went unsolved for a few weeks, until McDonald learned that Lady Treloar wasn't in Biarritz as she claimed, but was here in

London at the time of the theft. He guessed why she'd lied about her whereabouts and confronted her on the night of the Bunburys' ball. He threatened to inform the police unless she gave in to his blackmail demands."

Murmurs filled the entrance hall and stairwell, all the way up to the next two levels, where guests leaned over railings to hear.

"What of the footman they arrested?" someone asked.

"Didn't he try to steal the Bunburys' painting?" said another. "Isn't he involved somehow?"

The detective put up his hand, calling for calm. He puffed out his chest, and I was reminded of a blustery actor on the stage before his scene-stealing monologue. He was relishing this. "He's largely innocent, as it happens, and will be released."

Lady Bunbury clapped her hands. "We are all relieved to hear it. Shall we return to the music and dancing now? It has been quite enough excitement for one evening."

She appealed to Lady Heatherton who appealed to her husband. But Sir Gregory didn't notice her. "I don't understand. A painting that didn't belong to him was found in his possession. Why would you release him?"

"He claims he was about to put it back," the detective said.

Lord and Lady Bunbury exchanged terrified glances. They knew their carefully constructed world was unraveling, yet they were powerless to do anything about it.

"It was fake, you see," the detective barreled on. "He realized once he saw it in a better light."

The audience turned to Lady Treloar.

"I didn't sell it to them!" she cried.

"Oh, no, it wasn't her," the detective agreed. "Apparently the same fellow who painted the Quornes' forgery also painted all of the Bunburys'. He admitted as much during an interrogation."

"*All* of them?" my uncle piped up. "Good lord. How extraordinary. How could one painter manage to swap all of your masterpieces without your knowledge, Bunbury?"

I could kiss him for pointing out the absurdity of the Bunburys not knowing. He'd come to my aid earlier with the rude gentlemen, and he was doing so again, but this time for Aunt Lilian and Flossy's sakes as well as mine.

Aunt Lilian looped her arm through his and bestowed a warm smile on him. He patted her hand and looked to the Bunburys for a response.

Lord Bunbury mumbled under his breath and tugged on his cuffs. He left it to Lady Bunbury to defend their honor. "We did purchase them from Lady Treloar, as it happens. She tricked us."

But Lady Treloar was having none of it. She would not be blamed for something she didn't do. She gave an unladylike snort. "I did nothing of the sort. You probably sold your real paintings and had that forger make replicas for you to hang in their place. Just like you've done with all of your jewelry. It's all fake," she spat.

Lady Bunbury clutched the necklace at her throat. It was probably paste. But she remained quiet. Beside her, her husband stiffened, but he too didn't respond to the accusation. They stood together like two statues weathering a storm. But this storm would not blow over soon.

With all eyes now on the Bunburys, and the whispers increasing to a crescendo, the detective made his exit behind the uniformed policemen and Lady Treloar. He winked at me before closing the door.

I glanced around, but no one saw, not even Miss Hessing. Her attention, like everyone else's, was on the Bunburys.

I watched on, unable to contain my smile. It wasn't that I particularly relished their social downfall. It was somewhat of an ugly spectacle. My smile was more for Harry. He'd orchestrated that arrest like the director of a play. He'd found the Quornes' painting in Lady Treloar's gallery, spoken to Mr. Underwood about his involvement, and filled in the remaining gaps in our knowledge. Along with his father, he'd apprised the detective of the evidence and told him what to say when taking Lady Treloar into custody, making sure that I wasn't involved. He'd even made sure the conversation circled back to the Bunburys and their fake paintings. Of course, that could have been entirely the arresting detective's doing.

I preferred my version, however, with Harry pulling the

strings. All his hard work had almost come undone when Lady Treloar tried to push me down the stairs, but thanks to Miss Hessing, and the detective's timely entrance, the finale had continued as Harry scripted.

I wouldn't tell Harry that Lady Treloar tried to kill me. Some things were better left unsaid.

Speaking of being saved from death or, at the very least, broken bones, Miss Hessing deserved more than mere thanks. "Would you like to join me for lunch this week?" I asked.

She took a moment to answer. Like everyone else, she was watching the Bunburys descend the stairs, their arms linked as if propping one another up, pretending to ignore the whispers.

"That would be lovely. I'll check with my mother to see if we're free."

"Your mother isn't invited."

She smiled. "It'll be just the two of us? Or will Miss Bainbridge join us?"

"I hope there'll be a third, but not Flossy."

She frowned. "Who?"

"A particular fellow whose name appears on your card an unseemly number of times."

She glanced at her dance card and flushed. "Oh," she murmured. "That would be... Uh, well, that would be nice. If he'll come, that is. Don't expect it, Miss Fox. Indeed, he probably won't. He's just being kind dancing with me three times. He feels sorry for me. But having lunch with me will be a step too far, I'm sure."

My smile widened, partly at her naiveté, and partly because Lady Bunbury suddenly looked directly at me. She knew I was to blame for her downfall, but she didn't quite know the role I'd played and so couldn't retaliate.

With a final flare of her nostrils, she snatched her capelet from the footman and strode out the door. Her husband hurried behind in her wake.

I patted Miss Hessing's arm. "Don't fret. Leave him to me. You just make sure your mother is occupied for the day."

She drew in a fortifying breath and gave a firm nod. "I will."

* * *

THE GUESTS DIDN'T WANT to stay much longer. A public arrest of one of their own and the humiliation of two others were sobering experiences and no one was in the mood for a party. They filed out in a steady stream as carriages pulled up at the front steps.

I smiled at Uncle Ronald as he assisted me into the cabin of our vehicle. "Thank you, Uncle."

He smiled back. "My pleasure, Cleopatra. It's what we uncles are for, after all."

I squeezed between my cousins, somewhat surprised that Floyd was coming home with us. I expected him and Jonathon to make their way to Dutch's gaming house. It would seem I was wrong.

But I doubted it.

Flossy hugged my arm. "I know it's cruel to say so, but I'll say it anyway. The look on her face was the best part of the entire evening."

I knew she was referring to Lady Bunbury, not Lady Treloar.

"Don't be smug," Aunt Lilian said, without any heat. "Smugness in a young lady is unbecoming."

"Whereas it's very becoming in an older one," Floyd quipped.

His mother pursed her lips.

"I'm glad we left when we did," he went on. "The evening was something of a bore."

"It had barely begun," Flossy said. "Honestly, that policeman could have waited until later in the night. I would have liked to dance at least once with that dashing Mr. Fredericks."

Floyd screwed up his face. "You're better off not."

"Why?" his father asked. "What have you heard about him?"

"He gambles." Floyd held up his hands. "So I hear on the grapevine. Could be mistaken, of course."

Back at the Mayfair, I suggested they go on ahead of me as I wanted to get a book from the hotel library. Once the lift doors closed on them, however, I doubled back to the foyer and sat in one of the armchairs while I waited.

I waited for over an hour before I was rewarded.

Floyd stopped in front of me. "Is this an ambush?"

I stood. "That depends entirely on your attitude."

"I don't have an attitude."

I laughed.

"What do you want, Cleo?"

"I want you to take me with you."

"Take you where?"

"Don't play the fool, Floyd. We both know you're not one."

"Thank you," he said, quite sincerely.

"Take me with you to Dutch's gaming house or I will find my own way there. I'm sure Phillip knows the location." I nodded at the night porter who'd kept me company for much of the last hour.

"You can't come," Floyd blurted out. "The only women who go to that place are whores."

I crossed my arms.

Floyd crossed his.

"Philip!" I called out.

Floyd swore under his breath. "If Father finds out, I won't take the blame."

"He won't find out."

I smiled at a rather confused looking Philip as he held the front door open for us.

We caught a cab to a very respectable looking townhouse with a very disreputable looking man guarding the door. He could best be described as a bull crossed with a rat, all thin lips and sharp nose with a bulging forehead and muscles where his neck should be. He greeted Floyd and didn't bat an eyelid at me. He probably assumed I was Floyd's mistress.

A footman took our coats in the vestibule and directed us to the drawing room. Even if he hadn't pointed the way, I would have found it by following the smoky haze.

The drawing room was the size of the Mayfair's smaller sitting room with three card tables set up in the middle. Mismatched sofas and armchairs were arranged around the perimeter. No two were alike. Some were upholstered in pastels and made in the delicate Queen Anne style, whereas others were modern and upholstered in dark fabrics. The curtains were dark too and the carpet thick, deadening our footfalls. No paintings hung on the walls, and the only items on the occasional tables were glasses and ash trays. Discreet footmen wove between the tables, refilling empty glasses.

Floyd gripped my elbow. "Don't make eye contact and don't speak. Understand? Not a word to anyone."

I had no intention of striking up a conversation. Most of the men were too interested in the card games to notice a newcomer anyway. Those seated on the sofas or armchairs had a woman on their lap or draped over their shoulder. Considering the bodice of my evening gown was considerably higher than theirs, I doubted I would garner much interest from that quarter.

Floyd swore under his breath. "What's he doing here again?"

I followed his gaze to Jonathon, standing behind a seated man at one of the tables. Then the seated man looked up and my stomach lurched.

I'd half expected Harry to be here, but even so, seeing him quickened my blood. I wasn't sure why. I knew a lecture would be forthcoming.

He finished his game and rose, scooping up several tokens and pocketing them. He and Jonathon strode towards us. Jonathon looked shocked to see me.

Harry looked as welcoming as an ice-cold bath. "Why did you bring her?" he growled at Floyd.

"Good evening to you too, Harry," I said. "Don't blame Floyd. I insisted, and you know how I am when I insist."

Harry's jaw firmed. "Whatever she threatened to do if you didn't bring her, she won't follow through with it. Trust me. Take her home now, or I will."

I expected Floyd to take offence at being ordered by a man he considered his inferior, but he simply sighed so heavily I thought he'd deflate altogether.

Jonathon conformed to type, however. "Don't tell him what to do, Armitage. You're only here because Floyd got you in. He can get you thrown out just as easily. As can I."

Harry ignored him, but I couldn't let such rudeness slide without comment. "He's only here to help Floyd."

"Some help he's been so far."

A slim man dressed in a dove-gray tailcoat over a crimson silk waistcoat clapped Floyd on the shoulder. A skull ring with rubies for eyes flashed in the low light. The man's eyes were the palest blue and focused on me. "She's a cut above your usual, Bainbridge."

"She's my cousin," Floyd said, defensively.

The man looked me up and down. "Introduce us."

"Cleopatra Fox, this is Dutch."

I suppressed my shiver as he took my hand and kissed it.

Despite his slight build and eccentric dress sense, there was something sinister about him. It could be that he had ice for eyes or it could be that his reputation preceded him. I couldn't withdraw my hand fast enough.

He smiled at that. It was slick and humorless.

"Come, gentlemen. Play!" He indicated empty seats at one of the tables with a flourish of his hand.

"I'll sit this one out," Floyd said.

Dutch clapped him on the shoulder again. "Probably wise, all things considered. Speaking of which, we need to have a conversation later. My man will come and get you before you leave." He indicated a figure in the shadows by the door who I hadn't noticed when we entered. He looked so much like the guard at the front entrance they could be brothers.

The thug eyed Floyd and cracked his knuckles.

Floyd swallowed hard. "Not yet, please, Dutch. I just need a little more time."

"Enough business," Dutch said. "We don't want to bore Miss Fox. It's time to play." He appealed to Harry and Harry nodded. Dutch clicked his fingers and a footman appeared carrying a tray with a glass of brandy on it. Dutch handed the glass to Harry and pulled out the chair for him.

Harry glared at me and mouthed, "Go."

I nodded then moved away, out of his line of sight, taking Floyd with me. I didn't want to distract Harry while he was playing, and letting him think I'd left was the best way to do that.

Jonathon joined us and we watched Harry play from a distance.

He won almost every round. At first I thought Dutch and the other players were letting him win somehow, but by the annoyed look on Dutch's face, I gathered it wasn't part of his plan.

Both Jonathon and Floyd confirmed it with their hopeful glances and almost smiles. Both were glued to the table where, one by one, the other players lost everything and had to bow out. It was just Dutch and Harry left, and it was clear that Dutch was growing more annoyed by the minute.

With Harry's pile of tokens rising and Dutch's pile shrinking, Dutch called for a pause in the game. "To stretch my legs and enjoy charming conversation with Miss Fox," he declared loudly.

Those who'd been watching the game now turned to me.

Dutch rose but didn't approach. He disappeared into an adjoining room and closed the door.

Harry joined us and accepted a hearty clap on the shoulder from Floyd. "Good show, Armitage. You're winning legitimately this time."

"Legitimately?" I asked.

"Last time, Dutch let him win. It's his tactic to get a player to return." Floyd's face fell. "Then he fleeces him."

Jonathon had told me as much, and claimed it was how Floyd got into so much debt to the gambler.

I clasped Floyd's arm. "I'm glad you haven't succumbed to the urge to join in."

"It's not easy, I admit, especially being here again. The thing is, I know I can't beat him. I can't prove he cheats, but he must."

"Do you think he cheats?" I asked Harry

Harry shook his head. "He's just very good."

I stood on my toes and he bent down so I could whisper in his ear. "Do you cheat?"

He straightened. "What do you think?"

I didn't know what to think. Harry was an honest man, but Dutch was not. He was capable of fighting fire with fire, but would he stoop to Dutch's level? Was there enough at stake for him to cheat? Harry wouldn't care about a mere dent to his pride, but I suspected he was working his way up to saving Floyd somehow. That would be something Harry would consider worth cheating for.

Otherwise why come here and play at all?

Dutch emerged from the other room and approached, all toothy smiles and flashing eyes. "What do you think of the games, Miss Fox? Are you amused?"

"Let's just say my eyes have been opened tonight."

His smile widened. "Is the little Fox feeling hunted by these brutish hounds?" He indicated the other gamblers, some quite drunk, others impatiently waiting for the tussle between Dutch and Harry to resume, while others were too absorbed in their women to notice anyone else.

"I'm quite all right with my cousin, thank you. Don't concern yourself with my welfare, sir."

"Please, call me Dutch." He took my hand again, but instead of kissing the back, he turned it over and kissed my wrist. Fortunately I was still wearing long evening gloves, not short day ones, and he kissed nothing but silk. Even so, I had to force myself not to recoil. "You bring class to my little establishment, Miss Fox. I am honored."

"You honor *me*, Dutch. But I think you ought to return to your table. The hounds are getting restless."

His eyes gleamed. "Let me know if they bother you and I'll send them away. *All* of them."

The three men with me bristled. Harry stepped towards Dutch, his fists clenched at his sides.

Dutch glanced from Harry to me to Jonathon and chuckled. "Bainbridge. A word, if you will." With an arm draped across Floyd's shoulders, he steered my cousin to the table. He whispered in Floyd's ear.

Floyd shoved Dutch's arm off. "Not a chance." His gaze flicked to me.

Dutch also looked at me. He crooked his finger, beckoning me.

Harry caught my arm. "Don't go."

"I have to see what he wants," I said.

"You know what he wants." Harry winced, as if it was painful just saying it.

I think I knew what Dutch wanted, but Harry's concern confirmed it. Dutch wanted me.

Jonathon agreed with Harry, for once. "I'm taking you home, Cleo. This is no place for you."

Harry's grip on my arm tightened. His gaze didn't waver from mine. Then he released me. "Take her," he said to Jonathon. "Take Bainbridge too."

Jonathon didn't even bristle at being ordered by Harry. He must be concerned indeed.

It was too late for concern, however. Perhaps they were right and I should never have come, but now that I was here and I saw what Dutch wanted, a plan formed. It wasn't even a risky plan, considering Harry was cheating to win.

"Do you want him to bellow it across the room?" I asked.

Before either one could stop me, I joined Dutch and Floyd at the table. Dutch smiled slyly. Floyd looked like he wanted to grab my hand and march me out. I made a point of staying further than arm's length from him.

As I suspected, Dutch suggested Floyd play against him, excluding Harry altogether. That alone convinced me my plan would work. Dutch didn't want Harry to play anymore because Harry was winning. Dutch knew Floyd would lose.

Dutch lifted a finger off the table and the dealer took it as a signal to pick up the deck of cards. Dutch then removed the tokens he'd won earlier and pocketed most of them. He suggested Harry loan ten to Floyd. "We have no need for more."

"I don't want to play," Floyd whined.

"You will when you hear the stakes."

Floyd rubbed the back of his neck and bit his lip, warring with himself. "Go on," he finally said.

"If you win, I'll wipe your debt."

The small crowd that had gathered around the table gasped, sensing a spectacle.

"All of it?" I asked, pleased that I didn't need to suggest the prize.

Dutch gave a shallow bow. "Of course. Now, if I win, the stakes must be equally appealing. What do you say to an evening with me, my dear little Fox?"

"No!" Floyd, Harry and Jonathon said in unison.

237

Dutch ignored them. He focused entirely on me. "Well?"

"I agree," I said.

Jonathon swore. Floyd protested at the top of his voice. Harry merely lowered his head.

"On one condition," I went on. "Mr. Armitage plays on Floyd's behalf."

Harry's head jerked up. Instead of looking hopeful, he looked like his ship had sunk and he was adrift on a life raft without an oar.

"I agree to your terms," Dutch said quickly. "Armitage, sit."

Harry didn't sit. He caught my arm and pulled me away. The crowd parted and closed behind us, obscuring the table from sight.

I jerked free and planted my feet on the floor. "Harry," I hissed. "You can do this. You can beat him. I know you can." I winked.

He stared at me, his mouth ajar. Then he dragged a hand down his face. When it came away, he was ashen. "I am not cheating," he whispered back.

I drew closer and lowered my voice. I didn't want anyone hearing this conversation. "It's all right. You don't have to pretend to be the upstanding gentleman with an iron-clad code of honor with me."

"I'm not pretending."

Oh God. I felt sick. "Then...how?"

"Mathematics, mostly, and a good memory for what's already been played. Also, my face is hard to read."

I groaned. "Probability."

He gripped my arms. "Will you please leave now before this gets out of hand?"

I glanced at the large guard blocking the door. Behind me, the crowd parted again to reveal Dutch seated at the table, smiling that slick smile of his. One word from him and both guards would make sure we didn't leave.

"I'll create a distraction," Harry whispered. "You get ready to run."

I drew in a deep breath to steady my nerves and my voice. "Dutch, do I have your word that you'll wipe Floyd's debt if Mr. Armitage wins?"

"You do."

"Cleo," Harry whispered. "What are you doing?"

"And if he loses, that an evening will suffice?" I went on.

Dutch smiled. "I am a gentleman, Miss Fox. My word is as good as a written contract. An evening with you is all that is at stake."

I turned to Harry. "There, see? If you don't win, I'll simply be obliged to spend some time with him. We'll attend the opera or theater. I'll be home by midnight."

"I didn't think you were that naïve," he growled.

He was right and I knew it. Dutch would insist on more than a theater show, and it wouldn't be in public place.

CHAPTER 19

$\mathcal{I}$ stood behind Dutch as some of the other women did with their favorite player. He politely asked me to move away then firmly suggested Floyd and Jonathon do so too. He didn't want us signaling his hand to Harry, now seated opposite.

It was just the two of them, for this game. They both placed ten tokens in front of them while the dealer dealt.

"The first player to run out of tokens is the loser," Jonathon explained. "After each round, the cards played are removed from the deck and out of play for the following rounds."

That was something in Harry's favor, at least. If he kept track of which cards had been played, he had a better chance of winning. He had a formidable memory and a quick mind. With his fondness for mathematics, he shouldn't have any difficulty determining which cards were still in play and his probability of winning.

Then it struck me that Dutch was using the same method. He wasn't cheating either, but using probability and a good memory to out-smart his opponent. Against different players, these two men would be near impossible to beat. Against one another, their equal skill canceled the other out. It was a fair contest.

I stayed well back, out of Harry's line of sight so as not to distract him. The game required his full concentration.

He won the first round, but lost the next five. His stack of tokens shrank to just two. On at least two occasions, his hand was weak but still better than Dutch's, yet he'd given in. He couldn't read Dutch's face and so couldn't guess what he held. He could remember every card played and calculate the probability, but without a clue from Dutch, he still needed to guess in these early rounds.

"Christ," Floyd muttered with a hand to his stomach. "I'm going to be sick."

He wasn't the only one.

The dealer dealt again. From where I stood, I could just make out Harry's hand. It wasn't very good. I smiled anyway and allowed my eyelids to flutter closed, as if relieved.

When I opened them, Dutch was watching me. He threw down his cards, giving in. As Harry threw down his, I winked at Dutch and licked my lips suggestively. I smiled.

He smiled back then looked down at the table and Harry's discarded hand.

But the dealer had already scooped the cards up and placed them face down on the pile that were out of play.

Dutch appealed to the dealer but the dealer refused to show them. It was against the rules. Dutch accepted the decision. He couldn't overrule the dealer in front of everyone. It would be a sign that the fellow was in his pocket, and no one would trust Dutch again. He would lose all his customers.

Harry won the round, and the next and the next. That one missed hand was enough to throw Dutch off course. He grew more frustrated with every loss and that frustration probably made him lose concentration even more. He couldn't claw his way back into the game.

He lost all of his tokens.

Harry stood amid a scattered round of applause. He held out his hand.

Dutch hesitated. Then he stood and shook it. "Good show, Old Man. You're a formidable opponent."

Harry asked one of the footmen for paper and ink. "It's not that I don't trust you, but it is a large sum."

Dutch smiled through clenched teeth. "Of course."

The footman brought writing implements and Dutch

wrote a note, signing it with a flourish. Harry handed it to Floyd.

Floyd clasped Harry's shoulder and blinked fiercely. "I know you didn't do it for me, but thank you anyway. You saved me."

Harry didn't speak. He didn't even flicker an eyelash in my direction.

Jonathon, however, watched me from beneath lowered lids.

"I need some air," I said.

I suspected I wasn't the only one. Harry looked like he could hardly breathe.

I was about to lead the way outside when Dutch suddenly appeared at my side. He caught my hand and pressed it to his lips. "I am devastated, my dear little Fox. I was looking forward to our night together."

"It was for an evening not a night," I said, trying to sound amused when I felt cold to my bones. "I had the theater in mind."

He chuckled. "I do enjoy play acting. Another time, perhaps. I would very much like to spend more time with you. Alone."

He went to kiss my hand again, but I found myself being pulled away by both my cousin and Jonathon.

Harry stepped into the breach, clenched his hand into a fist and punched Dutch in the stomach before he saw it coming. "You can't afford her."

Dutch doubled over, coughing.

The brutish doorman rushed towards us and it took both Jonathon and Floyd to persuade him not to hit Harry. Harry raised his hands in the air and agreed to leave. The doorman slammed the door behind us.

Outside on the pavement, Jonathon signaled to a waiting coachman.

Harry went to walk off, but I caught his hand, stopping him. "He can't afford me?"

To my surprise, he laughed softly. His simmering anger had disappeared, left behind in the gambling house. Punching Dutch must have been cathartic. Winning probably helped too.

"It's all I could think of at the time," he said. "Sorry. It sounds crass now that I hear it again."

I clasped his forearm and squeezed hard. I wanted to get my point across. I needed to make sure he knew how much I appreciated his actions. "You have nothing to be sorry for, Harry. I'm the one who is sorry. I put you in a predicament tonight, and it wasn't fair."

"It wasn't your fault."

"In my defense, I thought you were cheating."

He laughed again. "Ordinarily that would offend me, but right now, nothing can."

I skimmed my palm down his arm to hold his hand. His fingers curled around mine and his smile faded. His gaze turned soft.

"Are you all right?" he asked.

"I am." My grip tightened and his responded in kind. "I know words aren't enough, but thank you, Harry. What you did tonight…it means a lot to me."

His chest rose and fell with a sharp breath.

"Cleo!" Jonathon called out from where he stood beside the carriage. I hadn't noticed it pull up alongside us.

Harry released me. "Goodnight."

"Aren't you coming?" I said. "We'll take you home."

"I'd rather walk."

I glanced behind me at a scowling Jonathon. Floyd stood beside him, nibbling his lower lip, looking uncertain. "Don't mind them," I said to Harry. "Their bark is worse than their bite."

"Even so…" He nodded at Floyd and my cousin nodded back, then Harry walked away.

I watched him for a few moments to see if he turned around, but when he didn't, I joined the others. "Why didn't you offer him a ride home?" I asked my cousin.

It was Jonathon who answered. "We're not going his way."

"Do you even know where he lives?"

"No, but I'm quite sure it's not Mayfair." He held out his hand to assist me into the cabin.

I ignored him and climbed in unaided.

**

THREE DAYS LATER, as I was walking along the fourth floor corridor, I saw the most unexpected person leaving my uncle's office. I smiled at Jonathon, but he did not smile back. Indeed, he looked rather grave.

No, not grave. Guilty.

He dipped his head and hurried to the staircase ahead of me.

I took a step towards Uncle Ronald's office, but stopped. There were few reasons why Jonathon would speak to my uncle alone, none of them good. It was likely my uncle was now angry or upset, and I didn't want to encounter him when he was in either mood. No doubt he would seek me out when he was ready to lecture or punish me. Hopefully it wouldn't be soon. I needed time to prepare a defense for each of my transgressions Jonathon could possibly have mentioned to my uncle.

I headed down the stairs, relieved not to see Jonathon. The foyer was quiet, as was often the case around midday. Peter and Mr. Hobart stood together, talking quietly, while Goliath hovered near the front desk, chatting to the check-in clerk. Guests wandered through, nodding at Mr. Hobart, in no hurry to reach their destination. There was no sign of Miss Hessing, but I was a few minutes early.

Mr. Hobart joined me under the central chandelier. "Good morning, Miss Fox." He glanced at the clock. "Indeed, I should say good afternoon. I hear you're going shopping with Miss Hessing today."

"Mr. Hobart, I am surprised at you," I teased. "You're usually much better informed."

"You're not shopping with Miss Hessing? But her mother told me just an hour ago as she went out that you two were enjoying the day together."

"Mrs. Hessing isn't the best informant on this occasion. I must say, I am pleased to hear she has already left. I was worried she'd insist on coming with us." At his quizzical look, I leaned in. "Miss Hessing and I *are* going out together, but to lunch, not the shops."

"Ah. And you didn't want Mrs. Hessing joining you."

"No, we did not. She wouldn't approve of the third member of our party."

His eyebrows almost shot off his forehead.

"Although I think he's very nice," I went on. "Miss Hessing does too. Unfortunately, Mrs. Hessing wouldn't approve of him for her daughter as he lacks a title and fortune."

He shook his head sadly. "Are you sure it's a good idea for them to have lunch together if the relationship is doomed to fail?"

"Where is your sense of romance, Mr. Hobart? Lovers with the odds stacked against them is what great literary classics are made of."

"You're right. And if the couple are perfect for one another, then they ought to be together."

"Well, for more than a few minutes at a time, at least. We'll have a better idea after today whether theirs is a relationship worth fighting for." I smiled at him. "I must say, you seem very cheerful. Have you some good news to share of your own?"

"I'm just pleased for my brother. Harry is taking him out to lunch today, but it won't be just the two of them. Stephen doesn't know, but Harry has organized for his friends from Scotland Yard to be there. It will be a proper and fitting farewell from the police force."

"And nothing less than what he deserves. I'm so pleased for him. Have you heard how his former superiors reacted to the arrest of Lady Treloar and the subsequent downfall of the Bunburys?"

"Apparently it did not go down particularly well, but there was nothing they could do about it. Lady Treloar admitted guilt and the Bunburys were caught in the crossfire. I'm just glad Stephen had nothing to do with it."

I merely smiled and didn't set him straight. Although I hadn't spoken to Harry about it, I knew he was directly involved in the discovery of the painting in Lady Treloar's gallery and that his father either helped or took that information to his colleague at Scotland Yard. He was very much involved in her arrest, but he would never receive any accolades. Nor would Harry, which was a great shame. The publicity would have been good for his business.

The front door opened and Aunt Lilian and Flossy breezed into the hotel. They'd been to the dressmakers this morning to be measured for new outfits. I hadn't expected them back before I left for lunch so had declined to join them.

My aunt had never looked so happy. She was positively glowing. It wasn't until she drew closer that I saw the telltale shake of her hands and the tired eyes. She wasn't under the influence of her tonic, but something had cheered her.

Flossy couldn't contain herself any longer. She rushed up to me and grasped both my hands. "Cleo, guess what we've just heard! Oh, it's the most wonderful news! No, don't guess. I simply have to tell you immediately or I'll burst. Lord and Lady Bunbury are leaving London."

"But the social season has just begun. How long will they be gone?"

"Forever! They've sold their London house and are moving permanently back to the country."

"Hush, Child," Aunt Lilian scolded. "We are saddened by their departure. Remember?"

Flossy grinned. "Oh yes. Very sad indeed. They will be missed." She winked at me.

"Poor Lady Bunbury," Aunt Lilian said without a hint of sympathy in her tone. "She hates the country. I once heard her refer to it as 'that backwater where nothing happens and no one goes.' I shall think of her from time to time and wonder how she fares."

"Particularly after a ball or party," Flossy added.

The lift door opened and Aunt Lilian smiled as Miss Hessing stepped out. "Good afternoon, Miss Hessing. May I say how well you look. Lavender suits you."

They exchanged pleasantries then we set off for lunch in one of the hotel carriages. The teashop was an informal venue, suitable for ladies to dine in alone or with a gentleman friend.

I tried to be as invisible as possible throughout. Although the couple needed some help getting the conversation started, they were soon speaking without blushing and tripping over their words. By the time we finished eating, I sensed they wanted to be left alone. They asked me to join them for a walk in the park, but I made up an excuse and sent them on their way.

With a satisfied sigh, I walked in the opposite direction. I had no plans for the afternoon so wandered around, looking in shop windows and enjoying the spring sunshine. Unfortunately, my mind also wandered, back to seeing Jonathon leaving Uncle Ronald's office.

He could only be in there for one reason—to stir up trouble for me.

Clouds scudded in front of the sun for a brief moment, and when they moved away, I found myself squinting up at the tall figure of Harry Armitage standing on the pavement ahead. He looked very dashing in a charcoal gray suit with his hair neatly combed back.

I strode up to him, but he was looking the other way and didn't see me. "I thought you were at your father's farewell luncheon today."

He swung around, his lips parted with his silent gasp. "Cleo!" He quickly looked past me. "What are you doing here?"

"Nothing in particular. I've just had lunch with Miss Hessing and her friend and now I'm filling in time, avoiding returning to the hotel." I considered telling him about Jonathon and my uncle but decided against it. It was likely Jonathon's complaint involved Harry and I didn't want to burden him. "And you? Has your father's lunch finished?"

"Not yet. I left him there with his former colleagues, reminiscing over beers."

"I imagine they have some interesting stories to tell. It seems like the sort of thing you'd want to hear."

He gave me a flat smile.

An awkward silence followed. Why was it that whenever Harry and I worked together on an investigation, we got along as though we were old friends? Silences were usually thoughtful rather than tense, our conversations free-flowing and filled with banter. But when we met up outside of an investigation, we couldn't think of much to say.

I felt a compulsion to fill the silence. "Thank you again for helping Floyd out of his situation. He's the happiest he's been in weeks. I'm not sure he can ever repay you."

"He has already thanked me in the best way he knows how."

"How? He has no money."

"He sent clients my way. Cases involving lost dogs and missing jewels, mostly, but I've also had to discover the source of leaked gossip. Just this morning, I was hired by a gentleman to find out everything I can about his sister's potential suitors."

"And you think Floyd sent all those clients to you?"

"They're all friends and acquaintances of his, so I'm sure of it."

I was proud of Floyd. Not only did he seem to be honoring his vow of never gambling again, but he was repaying Harry in the best possible way. Harry didn't want money for what he'd done and saying thanks would only embarrass him. By funneling potential clients to his agency, Floyd was showing his appreciation and respect for Harry while avoiding awkward exchanges.

"Is that what you're doing now?" I asked. "Investigating the girl's suitor?" I looked around and noticed we stood outside a teashop.

"I, uh..."

"It's all right, Harry. I'm not muscling in on your investigation. In fact, I'll leave you to it."

His gaze shifted to someone he'd spotted behind me. "That's a good idea. Enjoy the rest of your afternoon."

"You too."

I walked off, but couldn't resist a glance back to see who he was spying on. There was a chance I might know them from all of the balls and parties I'd been attending lately.

I almost tripped over my own feet.

I'd been expecting a gentleman, not a woman, and especially not the beautiful Miss Morris. My insides plunged as the administrative assistant from Searcys smiled a dazzling smile at Harry.

He held the door to the teashop open for her and she entered ahead of him. Before he followed her, his gaze connected with mine.

I nodded and offered a smile, hoping it looked genuine and not as hollow as I felt. He didn't deserve to feel any guilt for being with her. He may have liked our kiss a few weeks ago, but I'd instigated it, not him. I'd also made my intentions, or lack of them, clear and had no right to feel jealous now.

He deserved the elegant, clever, tall and beautiful Miss Morris. I wanted him to enjoy his afternoon with her. I truly did.

I drew in a steadying breath and turned my face to the sunshine, determined to find some way to lighten the heaviness that had settled in my chest.

Available 6th June 2023 :
MURDER AT THE CROWN AND ANCHOR
The 6th Cleopatra Fox Mystery

A MESSAGE FROM THE AUTHOR

I hope you enjoyed reading MURDER AT THE DEBUTANTE BALL as much as I enjoyed writing it. As an independent author, getting the word out about my book is vital to its success, so if you liked this book please consider telling your friends and writing a review at the store where you purchased it. If you would like to be contacted when I release a new book, subscribe to my newsletter at http://cjarcher. com/contact-cj/newsletter/. You will only be contacted when I have a new book out.

ALSO BY C.J. ARCHER

SERIES WITH 2 OR MORE BOOKS

The Glass Library

Cleopatra Fox Mysteries

After The Rift

Glass and Steele

The Ministry of Curiosities Series

The Emily Chambers Spirit Medium Trilogy

The 1st Freak House Trilogy

The 2nd Freak House Trilogy

The 3rd Freak House Trilogy

The Assassins Guild Series

Lord Hawkesbury's Players Series

Witch Born

SINGLE TITLES NOT IN A SERIES

Courting His Countess

Surrender

Redemption

The Mercenary's Price

ABOUT THE AUTHOR

C.J. Archer has loved history and books for as long as she can remember and feels fortunate that she found a way to combine the two. She spent her early childhood in the dramatic beauty of outback Queensland, Australia, but now lives in suburban Melbourne with her husband, two children and a mischievous black & white cat named Coco.

Subscribe to C.J.'s newsletter through her website to be notified when she releases a new book, as well as get access to exclusive content and subscriber-only giveaways. Her website also contains up to date details on all her books: http://cjarcher.com She loves to hear from readers. You can contact her through email cj@cjarcher.com or follow her on social media to get the latest updates on her books:

facebook.com/CJArcherAuthorPage
twitter.com/cj_archer
instagram.com/authorcjarcher

Printed in the USA
CPSIA information can be obtained
at www.ICGtesting.com
LVHW031439270823
756442LV00010B/143